Chocolate Dove

Chocolate Dove

Cas Sigers

www.urbanbooks.net

Urban Books, LLC
78 East Industry Court
Deer Park, NY 11729

Chocolate Dove Copyright © 2012 Cas Sigers

ISBN 13: 978-1-60162-346-1
ISBN 10: 1-60162-346-1

First Trade Paperback Printing May 2012
Printed in the United States of America

10 9 8 7 6 5 4 3 2 1

Distributed by Kensington Publishing Corp.
Submit Wholesale Orders to:
Kensington Publishing Corp.
C/O Penguin Group (USA) Inc.
Attention: Order Processing
405 Murray Hill Parkway
East Rutherford, NJ 07073-2316
Phone: 1-800-526-0275
Fax: 1-800-227-9604

Chapter 1

Basra Sadiq intensely stared at her dark brown reflection in the mirror. Without a hint of makeup, her skin was flawless, and her complexion perfectly even. Even still, she never felt dressed without her face painted with creams, powders, and bright colors. She studied makeup as though it were her profession and experimented with colors most women her complexion would shy away from. But Basra was well aware of her beauty and could get away with more than the average woman, for her confidence could easily flip a sketchy look into an instant success.

Still analyzing her face, Basra took her pointer fingertips and stretched out the corners of her eyes.

"I sometimes wish my eyes weren't so round," she called out to her roommate, Lucia.

Basra loosened the tension on her eyes, finally stopped analyzing her face, and placed her focus on the color palette of shimmery hues of silver and blue. While applying her first layer of foundation, Lucia walked in and stood over her shoulder.

"What did you say?" Lucia asked.

"My eyes are too round. Do you think he wants to go out with me because I'm black?"

"That's not what he said, but probably. More so because you're Somali."

"Gee, that makes it better," Basra mumbled.

"It's no different than men wanting to go out with me because I'm Italian. Men have this half-baked fantasy about exotic women, like we do it better or different."

"He didn't know I was Somali."

"He knew you were exotic, and that's all that matters."

Basra shrugged her shoulders and continued to decorate her face.

Lucia, who was just as long and skinny as Basra, propped her scrawny body up on the counter, and pushed the makeup over with her bum.

"We need to talk," she said.

Basra kept her face toward the mirror, but cut her eyes toward Lucia while applying eye shadow.

"Are you sure he's going to want to have sex?" Basra asked.

"You work for an escort service."

"So . . ."

"This may be a new concept to you, but men who go out with escorts expect sex."

Basra placed her makeup on the counter and looked Lucia squarely in the face. "Then I might as well be on the street corner."

"Oh, hell no. Streetwalkers don't wear two-thousand-dollar shoes," Lucia said, handing over a brand new pair of Jimmy Choos. "I can't believe I'm letting you wear these."

Since the age of nineteen, Lucia Giovanni had been at Choice, one of the world's most elite private escort services, known for their international beauties. She was discovered on a photo shoot for a top Italian shoe designer. Lucia and Basra modeled under the same agency and Lucia knew she'd be a great candidate for Choice, but didn't know how to approach her. When Australian native Lawson Hughes, heir to one of the largest coal mining productions, approached Lucia about Basra, it was the perfect opportunity to bring her into this new world.

Basra rubbed her hands across the expensive pair of soles and her eyes sparkled as though they were diamonds and emeralds. "Thank you," she said.

"You are quite welcome. I want you to look and feel your best. How many hookers on the corner get one thousand an hour, and health insurance?"

"I'm not having sex. And I made that clear when we talked on the telephone."

"Well, things always change in person. You might change your mind. He is very sexy, very charming, and very, very rich."

"I am not like you. No offense, but I can't just sleep with a man and blank it out like it doesn't mean anything. I wish I could, but I can't. If I didn't need the money so bad, I wouldn't even do this."

"I think it's extremely noble that you're helping family back home, however . . ."

"Why are we still talking about this?"

"Fine!" Lucia yelled.

Basra started applying her eye shadow and Lucia was compelled to give a last tidbit. "I wasn't always like this, it's just that the money numbs you after a while." With a sullen expression, Lucia left the bathroom.

"I didn't mean anything by that," Basra called out to soothe her friend, but there was no reply. She peeped out of the bathroom but Lucia was gone, and so Basra quietly continued to prepare for her date. Thirty minutes later, she sauntered downstairs in her shimmery crimson mini-dress, curly hair, and five-inch designer heels. Basra looked like a supermodel.

Lucia looked at her roommate and smiled. "He's in so much trouble. How many marriage proposals have you had?"

"None that I would take seriously."

Lucia smirked and shook her head.

Basra nervously fumbled through her purse and grabbed her phone. "Okay, you're going to call me in an hour and check on me, right?"

Lucia nodded.

"If I don't answer, call right back. We're going to dinner at Masa and jazz at Smoke. Make sure you call me, and keep calling until I answer."

"You're going to be fine. This is your first time; I promise it will get so much better."

Basra took a deep breath and blinked her big doe eyes. "Do I look okay?"

"*Assolutamente bello.*"

"*Mahadsanid,*" Basra replied, giving thanks in her native tongue.

It was a humid summer evening in New York, and the thousands of bright taillights lit up the evening. Basra nervously sat in the back seat of a black sedan. She repeatedly rehearsed the evening's future events. She would greet her date; they would have succulent Japanese cuisine and great conversation, and then listen to jazz over cocktails. She expected to be home by one in the morning, two at the latest.

"Oh, God, what if he wants to have sex?" she whispered to herself amid the thoughts.

Basra's stomach was turning flips. The more she practiced her programmed responses to his possible advances, the more nervous she became.

"Why did I agree to do this?" she quickly pondered. "Oh yes, four thousand dollars," she quickly responded.

When she looked up, the car was pulling up to the restaurant, but Basra couldn't move.

"We are here, Ms. Sadiq," said the driver.

Basra looked out the window and for two seconds thought about telling him to keep driving. But she knew this money would help her family back in Somalia. She was hoping that her sister could use this money to go to school until she was able to come to the States. Many women in her family never got the opportunity to get an education, and this small sacrifice was worth it.

"Do I call you when I'm ready to be picked up?"

"Yes, ma'am," replied the driver before passing off his card.

Basra smirked and responded, "I could get used to this."

Immediately, she tried to eat her regretted words. *I am going to school to get my psych degree so that I can afford things like car service,* she thought. *This is only a means to an end for now.*

"I will call, thanks."

Basra stepped out of the car, inhaled the night air, and walked inside to the fourth floor of the Time Warner Center. She'd never been to Masa before but had heard the wonderful reputation of its fresh fish and delectable truffles. She'd eaten a small meal before leaving the house so as to not look like a greedy date, but still couldn't wait to taste what she'd heard was the best sushi in New York City. Basra, standing six foot two in her borrowed shoes, leaned over and gave her name to the petite receptionist, who seemed a bit of a snob.

"I don't see your name, who's the reservation under?"

Just then, Basra's date, Lawson Hughes, wrapped his arm around her waist.

"Ah, Mr. Hughes, good to see you again," expressed the hostess.

"You too, Minami," he replied.

"Right this way," she said.

Basra and Lawson followed the woman, who was suddenly less snooty, over to the bar made of exotic Japanese wood.

"You must come here often," Basra asked.

"The chef and I are old friends," he answered. "Now pronounce your name again?"

"Bahs-rah," she replied slowly and phonetically.

"Very pretty," expressed Lawson.

They only sat for one minute before the server came over carrying a beautiful bottle of Kimuri, Akita.

"Hope you like sake," said Lawson.

"I do," replied Basra, who'd only tasted sake once in her life. Partly, because she wasn't much of a drinker, and secondly, because being only twenty-three, she hadn't had much partying in her two legal years in the United States. However, when she did partake it was white wine. Yet after a few sips of the very expensive sake, she was hooked, and kept her little cup filled most of the night. Lawson took the liberty of ordering for them both.

"We'll start with crab salad with yuzu and shiso flowers, toro tartare with osetra, and truffled uni risotto."

Basra was very quiet as she drank her sake and looked around at the minimalist decor. It was apparent that she was still very uncomfortable.

"You can relax," said Lawson.

"I am," she replied with a nervous chuckle.

"You look extremely beautiful tonight," he said.

"Thanks," she responded without eye contact. "Your accent is different. It's proper but has a weird rhythm. You don't sound Australian."

"It's what you get when you're raised in Australia but lived Texas for thirty years."

"Oh," Basra replied softly.

Lawson let a few seconds of silence pass and then he opened the floodgates. "So, why is it you don't want to have sex with me?"

Basra nearly choked on her sake.

"Didn't mean to startle you, but you've been so quiet. I was hoping to get a good conversation started. You okay?"

She nodded her head while clearing her throat. "Your comment surprised me, that's all. It's not that I don't want to have sex with you in particular. I don't have sex."

"You're a virgin?"

Releasing a demur giggle, she answered, "No. But, I don't have sex for money."

"Sure you do. Everyone does. A man takes you out, you eat or go to the cinema, or the opera, or maybe he takes you shopping, eventually you and he have sex."

"But we have sex because I like him, not because he spends money on me."

Lawson gave a look of doubt.

"Are you saying you don't believe me?"

"I'm saying that whether or not you thought you were doing it for free you weren't. In his mind, he'd paid for it. Unless you meet a man off the streets, introduce yourself, and then immediately have sex with him, he's paid for it."

"Not true."

"Yes, true, even if he only paid with time, and attentiveness, he still paid."

"If that's the way you see it," she said.

"That's the way it is," he replied.

Basra said a silent prayer and took a bite from one of the appetizers. "This is very good."

"One of New York's finest."

"So I've heard."

Basra was used to men staring, but Lawson's eye games were making her increasingly anxious.

"Please stop staring at me."

"You seemed annoyed," Lawson said.

"A bit."

"Discuss."

"I don't agree with you and your opinions about sex, I don't like how you are staring at me—"

Interrupting, Lawson asked, "How am I staring?"

"Disrespectful."

"I don't mean it that way. I think you're beautiful."

Basra could no longer control the thoughts running through her mind. Lawson wanted to have sex and his looks confirmed it. Was this delectable meal the enticer? What had she gotten herself into?

"This is a very expensive restaurant, right?"

"Some would say that."

"So tonight, you might spend, what? Just on dinner and drinks?"

"I don't know, maybe $2,500."

Basra's eyes nearly popped from her skull as she dropped her food onto her plate.

"You paid at least four grand for an evening with me, two or three grand for dinner. So it's fair to say you may spend almost eight thousand dollars tonight."

Lawson nodded and commented, "More like ten," then gave a curious look to see where Basra was going with her statement.

"I'll be back."

Basra pushed back from the table, and rushed toward the restrooms. She immediately grabbed her phone from her tiny clutch and called Lucia, who answered on the first ring.

"Is everything okay?"

"I can't do this," Basra replied as she stepped in the bathroom.

"Do what? Aren't you at dinner?"

"This man is going to spend thousands of dollars tonight."

"So what? He's a billionaire. You have to stop thinking regular thoughts; you're in another league now. To you that's a lot of money; to him, it's pocket change."

"He wants to have sex," Basra whispered as another patron entered the restroom.

"He told you that?"

"No, but it's obvious. I just don't want to do this. I can't be myself, and I feel like a whore. This isn't normal."

"By whose standards? Again, stop thinking regular thoughts. Lawson is a good guy, not some weirdo who is into crazy sex fantasies. He thought you were beautiful and wanted to take you out."

"Then he should have just asked me out."

"But you were with me, and he thought you were an escort. You know all of this. You're the one who asked me to get you on with the agency. You're the one who gladly took four thousand from the agency fee. This is what you signed up for. If you don't want to sleep with him, fine. But you have to finish the date or else we both look bad."

Basra stopped pacing the bathroom and stared at herself in the mirror. "I'm just nervous."

"I understand, but just have dinner and hang out. Get to know him, pretend like it's a real date. It's acting. Tonight you are a character. Give your character a name, and that's who is entertaining, not you."

"Okay," Basra replied.

"You sure you're okay?" asked Lucia.

"I am. I will see you later tonight."

"Okay, call me if you need me."

Basra hung up and leaned over the counter so that her nose was almost touching the mirror. "You're a character," she said. "Get into character." She took several deep breaths and walked out.

When Basra returned to the table, it was covered in small bowls of colorful, wonderfully smelling dishes. Lawson was already eating.

"You didn't wait for me?"

"Was I supposed to?" he asked.

Basra didn't reply, she simply took her seat and placed her napkin in her lap.

"Try this," Lawson said, sliding a small plate across the table.

As Basra lifted a small piece of the white filet, she asked, "What is this?"

"Blowfish sashami with lemon vinaigrette," Lawson replied.

She tasted a small amount, smiled, and replied, "Interesting."

After the blowfish, she sampled each of the dishes spread across the table, which included lobster sashami, foie gras, Japanese gingko nuts, and several different truffles. As soon as a few bowls emptied, more were brought over. Finally, Basra was stuffed.

"I can't eat anymore, but it's so good I can't stop."

"I can imagine that's what the men say about you," Lawson replied with a contemptible grin.

"Get your mind from the gutter," Basra said.

Lawson's grin evolved into a full chuckle. "I can't help myself. But I promise I won't touch."

"Are we going to dinner?" Basra asked, only to receive a puzzled look from Lawson.

"Dinner? We just—"

"I mean dancing. Are we going dancing? I'm sorry, I'm just—"

"A little nervous. I can tell. You've had two hours to warm up. Am I making you that uncomfortable?"

"I have a confession," Basra expressed. "This is my first date like this."

"When you say like this, you mean as an escort."

Basra nodded her head.

"Good, I've always been fond of virgins."

This time, his look started to make her stomach rumble with rolls of nervous energy, but luckily the head chef came to the table and greeted them.

"Lawson, it's good to see you again, my friend," Chef said.

Lawson rose and gave the chef a hearty hug. They spoke in Japanese for a few seconds and then Lawson introduced Basra.

"I hope you have enjoyed your experience," said the chef.

"My taste buds thank you," Basra replied with a sweet smile.

"This one is beautiful," Chef said to Lawson.

"I'm sure they're all beautiful," Basra mumbled to herself. Lawson cut his eye in her direction but Basra pretended as though she'd said nothing. The chef walked away and Lawson placed his card on top of the ticket. Basra tried to sneak a peek at the bill but couldn't see the numbers and dared not to ask.

It's pocket change. It's pocket change, she continued to think.

"So you mentioned dancing?" Lawson asked.

"Only because you mentioned it earlier when we spoke on the phone. We don't have to go dancing. If you're ready to go home . . ."

"Home? I have you for the evening. And the evening has just begun," Lawson said while reaching across the table to hold Basra's hand. She lowered her head to gain her composure and then lifted it with a pleasant smile. She felt like rented property, and there was nothing she could do about it, and so they left dinner and headed to Smoke for cocktails and jazz. Smoke was much more casual and laid back. She immediately felt more at ease once they walked in the door. But Lawson once again took control of the situation as they approached a table near the back corner.

"I'm getting a bottle of champagne," he said before walking away from the table.

"I don't like champagne," she whispered into the atmosphere. "He doesn't care," she sighed. Basra looked around the room at the couples holding hands, flirting, and smiling. She honed in on an Italian-looking couple canoodling three tables over. Somehow, she became so lost in their world that she didn't realize Lawson had snuck up behind her.

"I bet they're having sex tonight," he whispered in her ear.

Basra, startled by his presence, let out a small yelp. "I'm sure they're having sex tonight, and I'm sure they're a real couple. Unlike us."

Lawson sat as the server placed the bottle of champagne and two glasses on the table.

"I don't like champagne," Basra said.

"That's because you've probably only had cheap champagne. You will like this, I promise." Lawson took the liberty to pour her a glass.

"I've been drinking sake all night. I don't think I should mix—"

"Shhhh," Lawson said, placing his finger to her lips. "Drink. It will make me happy."

Basra placed her lips on the edge of the glass, sipped, and pretended to enjoy.

"See, I told you. Once you've had the finer things in life, it changes your entire perspective."

They listened to the jazz band that covered at least nine Tony Bennett songs throughout the next hour. But Lawson was losing interest and Basra could tell.

"Are you ready to leave?" she asked, hoping he would say yes and they could part ways.

"Yes. I have an apartment not far from here, let's go."

"Wait a minute, I thought we were just doing dinner and jazz. I can't go to your place."

"What do you mean? The deal was we were going out for the evening, and it's still evening." Lawson reached in his pocket, pulled out his cell, and called the car.

"The key word being 'out.' Not in, or inside. I can't go to your place."

"I get it. No means no. I'm not a rapist. I'm not going to try to have sex with you. I'm a wealthy man. I can have sex with ninety percent of the women I meet, and that's because the other ten percent are underage. You intrigue me. I simply want to engage in more conversation with you. Let's go."

Lawson rose and held out his hand. Basra felt trapped. She knew if she didn't go, he would call and give an unpleasant report to the agency, and she didn't want that. But she knew if she went that it might lead to a situation beyond her control. Yet she continued to follow him toward the door. As she approached the exit her grip tightened and anxiety heightened. The car pulled up moments after exiting Smoke and Basra slowly got in. Lawson was very lucid considering the grand amount of sake and champagne he'd ingested. There was no way he was going to pass out, as she wished the entire ride over to East Seventy-seventh Street. They walked hand in hand into The Pavilion and went up to the thirty-first floor, two floors shy of the penthouse. It was nice, but not as extravagant as she'd imagined. As she walked in the apartment, Basra immediately took her shoes off, a habit she'd grown accustomed to as a child in an African household.

"Your feet are very nice, as I assumed they would be."

Basra looked around and took a seat on one of the black leather couches. "How often are you here?" she asked, looking over at the seemingly untouched kitchen.

"About once a week. I normally stay at my home on Long Island."

"Oh."

Lawson grabbed an ice-cold Voss from the refrigerator and took a sip. From the kitchen, he looked at Basra, who was now reading a magazine. Both were quiet.

"I guess we discussed everything we had to say over dinner and music," Lawson joked.

Basra looked up and replied, "I guess so."

"Time for bed, I guess."

Basra's body stiffened. "But . . ."

"I'm kidding," Lawson said, removing his buttoned top shirt, exposing a heather grey shirt underneath. He sat close to Basra on the couch, placed her feet in his lap, and began rubbing her arches. Although she welcomed the foot massage, she was too nervous to enjoy it.

"So, we didn't talk too much about Somalia. What do you miss most about home?" Lawson asked.

"My family. We have a big family. I have six uncles and too many cousins to count, and we all lived close to one another. I miss the dinners and laughter. I had a great childhood. I miss my best friend too, a lot. It was so much fun, I never realized how poor we were until I came here."

"I can't imagine what that would be like."

"Why would you want to imagine being poor?"

"I meant having family. My dad worked all of the time, my mother drank all of the time, and I have no siblings. I spent my entire childhood in boarding schools."

"That sounds horrible."

"Like you said, as a child you don't know any different. I didn't really know we were rich until I was in high school."

Basra gave a big smile at the first sign of similarity. Lawson saw this as his opening and leaned over and kissed Basra. She pulled away and jumped up from the couch. Lawson quickly rose as well and pulled her body close.

"Just one kiss," he said.

"No. I have to go."

"Kissing is not sex!" he yelled, following her to the door.

Basra grabbed her shoes and tried to exit, but Lawson placed his hands on the door.

"I'm sorry, please stay," he said gently as though he were suddenly another person.

"No. I am not comfortable."

"But we were having such a good time. I'll pay you extra, under the table. What do you want, another couple grand?" Lawson said. "Wait right here."

Lawson disappeared into the back room, and when he was out of sight, Basra quietly but quickly exited. She hurried down the hall with her shoes in hand and jumped inside the elevator. She heard Lawson calling her name as the doors closed. The temptation of the extra cash didn't even hit her until she was rushing through the lobby and nearly tripped over her long feet, trying to place on her high-heels.

"An extra two thousand," she whispered before shaking the thought from her mind. Outside, she hailed down a taxi. But, immediately after sliding in, the tears started to stream as she rested her head on the back of the torn leather seat.

"Where you headed?"

"To hell, probably."

"Excuse me, ma'am?"

"Thirty-seven West Twenty-first Street."

After five minutes in traffic, the tears subsided and Basra started to think of the money she'd just made. For the five hours she'd hung out, she would get $4,000. As uncomfortable as it was, she couldn't deny the easy money.

"This is how people get caught up," she whispered. "I can't get caught up." Basra took a deep breath, rolled down the window, and loudly yelled, " I won't get caught up!" into the late-night air. The release sent surges of energy through her body, and its power brought another flow of tears to her eyes. She rolled up the window, leaving a small crack for fresh air. Then, with a tiny smile on her face, she closed her eyes the remainder of the ride home.

Chapter 2

The following morning at nine, Basra was buzzed upstairs to the penthouse suite of 155 Riverside Drive. She was immediately greeted by Hollis Perrigo, owner of Choice.

"Basra, my love. How are you doing this Thursday morning?" Hollis greeted Basra with a tight embrace. "A glass of wine?" she offered.

Basra shook her head with confusion. "It's early for wine, right?"

"Jesus served wine at every meal, and if it's good enough for His people, it's good enough for you," Hollis said with a giggle. "Have a seat and tell me how the date went."

Basra walked over the plush white leather couches and sat. She looked out of the ceiling-to-floor windows and gazed at the smog whisking across the Hudson. She daydreamed about the thousands of cubicle sitters who worked eight to ten-hour days just to bring home a fraction of what she'd made last night. Was she wrong to complain?

"My date went well," she mentioned.

"Lawson is a pussycat. He's been with us for a while, has a thing for brown skin. God bless him with his pale self."

Basra burst into loud laughter.

"I know I have no right to talk about him. I'm as pale as snow myself but at least I get a good tan once a year. Those red-headed Aussies repel sun rays."

Basra continued to laugh at Hollis, who often said just what was on her mind whether it was appropriate or not.

"You know we don't have many ladies of color; in fact, there are only two: you and Jasmin. She's American. So you are going to be one hot commodity as the only African. Many of my clients will pay top dollar to have an African princess."

"You're not telling them I'm a princess, are you?"

"I'm in the business of selling fantasies."

"Yeah, but what if they look it up? There are real princesses in my country and I am not one of them. I don't think lying is good."

"You could be an indentured servant, they wouldn't care. In their minds you are a queen, and who doesn't want to make love to a queen?"

"Yeah, about that part. I'm not going to be able to have sex with these men."

Hollis paused and peered straight into the eyes of Basra. Her eyes held such a serious look of disdain that Basra quickly feared for her life. She didn't know Hollis that well, but had heard from Lucia that she had the temper of a scorned Greek goddess. Basra looked away for fear she was being cursed.

"I mean no disrespect to you or your company, I just don't feel comfortable sleeping with these strangers for money."

"But you feel comfortable enough to take their money, correct?"

Basra's mouth moved but no words formed. She was speechless, but Hollis filled in the blanks.

"If you want these men to pay thousands of dollars for your time and conversation, you must have one hell of a vocabulary. The audacity . . ."

"Really, I thought that I could but I can't."

"There are no rules saying you must do this or that. I'm not your pimp and I'm not making you open your legs for any of these men. However, there is an unspoken code. Our clients spend millions to have a good time, and that good time includes whatever they request."

"Maybe there are men who would pay less just for my company?"

"You overestimate your beauty."

Basra lowered her head.

"So, hold up. Did you have sex with Lawson last night?" asked Hollis.

"No, ma'am, I couldn't."

"Dammit! Lucia said you weren't going to be a problem. If you cost me a good client, you will not get a penny of your money."

Hollis walked into the kitchen and snatched her cell from the counter. She rushed over to her desk, pulled up her contacts, and dialed Lawson's number. She got no answer.

"I'm holding your check until I speak with him."

"I'm sorry," apologized Basra.

"I have a few clients who are into bondage, S&M, things of that nature. But, normally, they require you to do things far more out of sorts than sex. I just don't understand how you think your company alone warrants that type of money. Sex should at least be on the menu."

"It's just not an option for me."

"Then guess what, pretty eyes, I'm afraid you're not an option for me." Hollis rose and motioned Basra toward the door. "We'll talk after I speak to Lawson."

Basra took the cold ride back down twenty-seven floors and exited the building.

Normally, she loved to stroll along on the Upper West Side and glide in and out of the shops, but Hollis had taken the wind from her sail. She had plans for that $4,000 and the thought of not receiving it was making her ill. Thus, with her head hanging low, Basra left the building, turned right down Eighty-eighth Street, and walked aimlessly until she reached Broadway. She continued down Broadway until she came upon Columbus Circle. She paused and glanced at the Time Warner building, where she'd met Lawson.

"Why couldn't I just sleep with him?" she murmured. "I at least thought I'd get my money."

Frustrated, Basra kept walking down Broadway with no destination in mind. She crossed over to Seventh Avenue and, before she realized it, she was passing through the Garment District. Though she had several errands to run, Basra continued down Seventh until she reached Twenty-third Street, took a left, and walked two blocks down to Twenty-first Street, where she and Lucia lived.

Standing right outside of the Echelon, Basra looked behind her and took a long sigh and whispered, "I can't believe I walked from Riverside to Chelsea." She shook her head and went inside the luxury apartment building.

"Good afternoon, Ms. Sadiq," said the concierge.

Basra smiled politely and waved as she continued toward the elevator. Once in her place, she removed her shoes, walked into the kitchen, and grabbed a cup of yogurt. She strolled onto the terrace and sat down. From her view on the tenth floor, she could see a small corner of the Fashion Institute, the school her younger sister, Amina, desperately wanted to attend. Though the morning had been unpleasant, Basra began to smile thinking about her baby sister who started putting on fashion shows for the family at the age of ten. She would find anything that she could cut and stitch and turn into a work of art. Amina had dreamed of becoming a designer for as long as she could remember and Basra was determined to turn that notion into a reality. Right now, it was important for Amina to simply go to school, but she desperately wanted to help with her dream. As the oldest, she felt it was her responsibility. This is why she began modeling in the first place.

Growing up, she despised her long, lanky figured that was often the cause of ridicule and neighborhood fights, but as she became a teenager, she realized it would be her ticket to freedom. Therefore, she studied models and read every article on modeling that she could find. She had a friend back home help her with a portfolio. He wasn't much of a professional photographer, but he was handy with a camera. Basra's family had a few friends from home already living in New York, and they helped finance her first visits to Manhattan. Basra was very fortunate; it only took two visits and five interviews to procure an agent and get steady work. Her first year was very consistent with catalogue ads and some high-end fashion magazines, but though she made decent money modeling, New York was more costly than she'd assumed. She knew going to school and modeling wouldn't allow her to save enough for Amina. Just when she was considering taking an extra job, Lucia mentioned Choice. At first, she thought it was crazy that someone would pay that kind of money for a date, but after Lucia showed her a bank statement, and told her about Choice's clientele, she figured one or two dates couldn't hurt. It wasn't ideal but definitely an option. Basra's plan was to work at Choice for a few months and save enough to bring Amina to the States and pay for her degree at FIT. Basra knew all along she had no intention of sleeping with the dates but didn't say anything. She figured she could stall the men and the agency long enough to get a few thousand saved and then quit. But Basra had no idea of the underworld territory she'd crossed into.

She gazed back toward the corner of Seventh Avenue, and then reminisced about her family back home until Lucia walked up and interrupted her daydream.

"What's up, chica? I see you survived."

"Ha ha," Basra replied while slowly turning to acknowledge Lucia's presence.

"I was hoping to be here last night when you got back. How was 'Awesome' Lawson?"

"He's an interesting man," Basra replied.

With anxious eyes, Lucia took a seat beside Basra to get more details. "So, tell me how it went."

"I didn't sleep with him, if that's what you're asking. But we went to dinner, had a few drinks, and went back to his place."

"His place? You went to his place? What did you do?"

"Nothing. We talked."

Lucia leaned back in her seat and took a long look at Basra.

"Stop looking at me. We didn't have sex. I promise."

"Was he mad?"

"He wasn't happy," Basra said with a very jaded expression. Lucia was silent. Basra turned her focus back toward the skyline and continued to talk. "I went to see Hollis and she's holding my money until she speaks with him."

"You what?" Lucia yelled. "You shouldn't have gone to see her without me. I swear you better not mess things up." Lucia hastened off the terrace while whipping out her cell phone.

Basra followed while quickly spilling out an explanation. "She knows you have nothing to do with my decision not to have sex."

Lucia held up her hand to silence Basra when Hollis answered the cell phone line. "Hi, Hollis, this Lucia. Let me first apologize for Basra's behavior."

"You shouldn't be apologizing for me!" Basra chimed in.

Lucia quickly walked into her bedroom and shut the door in Basra's face. Basra propped her back against the door and waited. Less than a minute later, Lucia opened her bedroom door, nearly causing Basra to fall on the floor.

"She wants to speak with you," Lucia said while handing Basra the phone.

Basra took the phone and walked back onto the terrace. Lucia followed with anxiety.

Hollis had a peculiar excitement in her voice when she began and Basra didn't know how to anticipate the pending conversation. "So, I spoke with Lawson," she started. The five-second pause before the next sentence seemed to last five minutes. The rhythms of Basra's heartbeat grew. "He absolutely adores you. Said you were his innocent, doe-eyed angel. He loved the fact that you made him chase you, and said it felt like a real date. So you can have your money. However, I'm very leery about sending you back out. Other clients will not have this same reaction. I need some time to think about this. I'll be in touch."

"Okay," Basra simply replied and then hung up.

Lucia was aflutter as she stood over Basra with intense eyes. Basra looked at her but kept quiet for longer than Lucia could stand.

"What did she say!"

"I can have my money. Lawson loved me."

Lucia stood in disbelief as Basra exhaled and released a small snicker. Lucia began her nervous sidestep shuffle that she often did when she was perplexed about a situation. It was a peculiar idiosyncrasy that resembled the beginning of a Broadway dance move.

"How did she sound, excited or crabbed?"

"She sounded normal like she always talks, very business, straightforward."

"Well . . ."

"Well, what? Aren't you happy?" asked Basra.

Lucia gave a slight shoulder shrug, and walked back into the condo. Basra could see the obvious traces of jealousy and she refused to let it ride. She knew this was a victory and demanded that Lucia admit it.

"Think about it," she yelled, walking into the living room, closely following Lucia. "This could set a new precedent. She said he liked the chase, and wants to go out again."

Lucia walked to the freezer and removed an ice cream sandwich. She said nothing as Basra went on her anti-sexual tirade.

"If more women held out then I can see there being an entire group of escorts like me. There will be those who do and those who don't. And the ones who don't have sex can be called—"

"Broke," Lucia finally interrupted by placing her frozen treat close in front of Basra's face. "You are delusional. This is a very old profession and there are rules whether you like them or not. You want to play like you're innocent, but you're no better than the rest of us."

Lucia took a large bite of her ice cream, stared into Basra's eyes for a few seconds, then marched around her and went into the bedroom, where she remained for the rest of the afternoon.

Chapter 3

Basra saved $1,000 of the $4,000 from her first date with Lawson. She sent the other $3,000 home to her mom and dad in Somalia. However, on her second date with Lawson, she pocketed $5,000 and kept all of it except one grand. In two weeks, her bank account went from $400 to $5,000. The lifestyle was quickly becoming addictive. However, Hollis wasn't calling her for any other men, and Lawson was headed back to Texas. She desperately wanted to convince Hollis that her "no sex" theory was worth exploring, but Hollis wasn't willing to take a chance, and Lucia wasn't helping. In fact, Lucia was barely talking to her. Basra didn't know if Lucia was more upset about the fact that Hollis hadn't insisted she leave the agency, or the fact that she was receiving thousands of dollars to keep her legs closed. However, in Basra's mind, she didn't need to convince Lucia. Hollis was her target, and since she wasn't returning her calls, Basra knew she had to plan to "accidentally but conveniently" run into Hollis on the street.

Basra put on her plaid Tom Ford shirt dress, with a pair of Converse, and took a cab to the Upper West Side. She breezed in and out of a few boutiques before she wandered over to Ninety-third Street and took a seat by the Joan of Arc statue. She had passed the statue several times but never really paid attention to it until that day. As far as she knew, it was just a random woman on a horse. She thought it was an interesting sculpture, and had heard the name of the woman on the horse, but didn't know much about Joan of Arc's story, nor cared. However, that day, she had close to an hour to spare before Hollis returned from her daily yoga class and so she decided to look up Joan of Arc on her iPad. As Basra read, she became more engrossed in her story.

"I had no idea," she found herself saying aloud. "Wow, how crazy," she continued to speak while gazing back and forth between the computer and the statue. Hollis read six stories on Joan of Arc in those few minutes. She put away her iPad and stared at the sculpture that she now knew was created by Anne Hyatt Huntington. She smiled proudly as though it were 1429 and she were riding in the French Army brigade next to Joan, the unconventional leader. Basra continued to think to herself. *I can be a leader.* Somehow, Basra had connected with this young girl and likened her mission to create a new escort service to that of Joan's to conquer the English. Though the missions were polar opposites, Joan's story gave her a spark of confidence, which was all she needed to talk Hollis. Basra quickly rose and walked over to Caffe Mocias, which was across the street from the yoga class. As soon as she ordered her latte and paid, Hollis walked through the door. Her coincidental meeting happened perfectly.

"Hollis, how are you?"

"Great, just finished yoga. What are you doing on this side?"

Basra expressed a silly grin and took a sip of her latte. She had placed so much focus on running into Hollis that she didn't think beyond the meeting for an excuse as to why she would be on the Upper West Side at ten in the morning.

"They have the best lattes," she replied with a quick chuckle.

Hollis motioned with a slight nod to the cashier, slid two dollars on the counter, and moved to the side to wait for her cup.

"You must come here a lot."

"Why would you say that?

"Because she knew what you wanted without you speaking."

Hollis grabbed her cup and took a sip. "The Ethiopian Ardi blend is delish. But, you probably wouldn't like that, right?"

"Why?"

"I mean Ethiopia and Somalia have been at odds for years."

Confused, Basra squinted and replied. "What does that have to do—"

"It was a joke," Hollis interrupted. "Why are you on this side again?"

Basra spit out an excuse. "I have a friend who lives over here. I spent the night. Oh, and they have the best lattes." She smiled bashfully.

Hollis smirked. "How sweet. Friends don't last long in this business," Hollis said, walking out of the door. Basra followed as she saw this as her segue.

"Well, I think they can. It's about honesty."

Hollis stopped walking and took another sip of her African morning brew. "What is it with you? You can't have it both ways. Either you play the money game and do what you have to and become rich, or play nice, work hard, and retire at sixty. The choice is yours and you can't feel guilty about the lifestyle you want to have. How many people from your country would kill to live like us?" Hollis continued walking.

"Actually, there are lots of rich people in Somalia. Wealth beyond your comprehension."

"I've partied with royalty; I doubt it."

Basra ignored Hollis's crass remarks and kept focus on her mission. "Where are you headed? May I walk with you for a minute?"

"Walk," Hollis coldly remarked.

Basra continued up Amsterdam, walking just half a step behind her boss. This was her closing argument and she knew she only had minutes before her verdict, therefore her points had to be strong and effective. "There are other men out there like Lawson. Men love the chase; it actually makes men feel like the woman really likes them. I'm sure you know that when a woman likes a man, she doesn't give it up so quickly. Me not doing it is another type of mind game. I'm the girl you want but can't have. The majority of your clients may not want to go out with me, but a few will love me. You pride yourself in offering a variety. I'm another choice for Choice." Basra stopped walking as added punctuation to her statement. This decision forced Hollis to also halt. She turned and gave Basra a once-over.

"I'll put some feelers out there and get back with you. Is that all?"

Basra knew she'd said enough and so she nodded quietly and smiled. Hollis lowered her shades and gave Basra another glance. She placed them back over her eyes and turned away.

"I'll call you," she said after taking two steps.

Basra watched Hollis walk down the block and turn the corner. Whether Hollis called or not, Basra felt victorious. Joy began growing from within her belly. When she thought about the recent deposits into her bank account, the joy grew and her nervous energy grew to an emerging smile. Basra quickly turned and tossed her coffee cup, which she had been carrying empty for two blocks, into the green trash bin on the corner. Ironically at that moment, her cup collided with an empty fast food bag also being tossed in, and the bump knocked her empty latte container onto the dirty pavement.

"Sorry," said the gentleman as he knelt to pick up her cup.

Basra spotted his nice physique and perfectly shaped chin that held a small cleft. Their eyes connected and there was a silent moment as they both took notice of each other's beauty.

"You're, um . . . you're quite beautiful," he said.

"Thanks," Basra said with a giggle. "Well, um . . . I'm going to go."

"Hold up, I'm Grayson."

"Basra."

There was another pause just before he extended his hand to shake hers. She knew he wanted more conversation, and though he was absolutely adorable, she didn't want to add a man to her complicated life.

He nervously adjusted his black-framed glasses and asked, "You live over here?"

"No."

Grayson sensed that she wasn't giving up any information, but he wasn't ready to give up. "I'm an artist. I don't live over here either. I'm hanging some of my work in that gallery right there."

Basra glanced to her left and saw the gallery space. She smiled politely, and commented.

"It was nice meeting you, Grayson. I have to go." She gently brushed her hand against his arm as she turned and walked away.

Grayson stood by the trash and watched her stroll down the sidewalk. The moment was like a daydream, as he was literally captivated by the jolt of energy she'd just placed within him. It was so jarring that as soon as she disappeared, an idea for a painting came to mind. He rushed inside the gallery to write down his concept.

Basra hopped on the train and headed back home. She liked the train but had become accustomed to taking taxis because of Lucia, who only took taxicabs or private cars everywhere. Basra enjoyed the lavish lifestyle, but didn't want to become a slave to it. She knew Lucia wasted mounds of money and Basra's plan was to save not spend. Thus, she was thrifty whenever possible. By the time she hopped off the number one and stepped out on to Twenty-third, Basra no longer wanted to go home. She wanted to go shopping. Other than a few pair of jeans, she hadn't purchased any new clothing in months. Lucia shopped daily and didn't wear half of her things, so when Basra had the craving to wear a new dress, she shopped in Lucia's closet where half of the items were still adorned with high priced tags. But Lucia had been acting more like a "frenemy" lately, and since Basra didn't know where their relationship stood, she didn't want to ask any favors. In truth, Basra wanted to start saving for her own place, and so as quick as the shopping thoughts appeared, she put them out of her mind and went to the fresh market for items to make a fruit salad. Proud that she'd only spent fifteen dollars, Basara quickly went home to dig into her healthy lunch.

A few feet from the elevator, Basra was approached by Lance, one of the tenants in the Echelon.

"Basra, right?" he said as he rushed to catch up with her.

"Hiiiiiiii," she replied, stretching out the word in hopes his name would pop into her head before it became obvious she'd forgotten it.

Lance said, "I live above you and Lucia, I'm Lance."

"Yes, I know. How are you?" Basra continued to walk.

"I'm good. So, I've been trying to catch up with you to talk."

"About what?"

"Can you stop walking for a second?" Lance asked.

Basra halted and turned to face him.

"We should go out."

"Are you asking me out?

"I am. Tonight. Come with me to a party."

Basra paused and contemplated his request. Lance was definitely a great catch, on paper at least. He was an architect for a large firm, single, and very handsome. She'd heard his name mentioned within the circles of women in the building but he didn't seem to date that much.

"It's taking you a long time to respond," he expressed.

Basra wasn't sure how long she had been standing there, but it was apparent she was not jumping at the idea of going out with him.

"It's just a party, we'll have fun. If not, we'll leave and I will bring you back home."

"What time should I be ready?"

"By eight. I'll meet you in the lobby."

That was quick and painless. Basra knew she over-thought most situations and sometimes it was just best to do, but spontaneity wasn't in her character. But this worked in her favor, for she simply needed the excuse to do something she already desired, which was shop. Hence, Basra went upstairs, quickly made her fruit salad, and then headed back through the Flatiron

District to a few of her favorite boutiques and searched for an outfit for her evening with Lance.

That evening at 7:50, Basra applied her final layer of gloss across her scarlet-red lips and walked downstairs to the lobby. Lucia was out of town, which was perfect. She didn't care to explain the details of how Lance approached her, how she responded, and how the date went. Lucia was extremely nosy, and often asked details that were a bit out of order and sometimes rude. Basra didn't mind so much, but lately Lucia was getting on her nerves and her bothersome little characteristics were becoming increasingly annoying. She was definitely glad to not be agitated by her that evening. Basra stepped into the lobby wearing her white Stella McCartney ruffled blouse and tan tuxedo-striped shorts. Lance was waiting by the front door when she walked up behind him.

"You look hot!"

"Thanks, so do you," Basra said, making note of his brown Gucci suit.

Basra liked the fact that he was six feet five, which meant she could wear her heels and still look up to her date. Most times when she wore heels, she was eye level with most of her male companions.

"You ready?"

Basra nodded and they headed into Manhattan.

The party was a red-carpet opening for one of the buildings Lance's company had designed. In short, it was a glamorous corporate party. She and Lance mingled but he held her hand throughout the night and made all aware that she was his date for the evening. They received awkward stares upon entering because although it was 2012, people were still curious and sometimes thrown by interracial couples. Ironically, Lance was of African American and Jewish descent, but he had assimilated 100 percent into the Jewish community. His skin was light, his hair was straight, and from afar he looked Caucasian, with very few black traits. He never hid the fact that his mother was black, but it rarely came up. Basra had only learned the fact because of nosy Lucia, who got everyone's background within the first hour of meeting. But despite the occasional glances, Basra enjoyed her night out with Lance; it was quaint, and required little conversation, just nods and smiles. He networked most of the evening so after he made introductions, she stood by his side and looked beautiful. After two hours, he was ready to go.

"I know you don't want the evening to be over just yet," he said as they stepped into the cab.

Basra surprised herself when she replied, "I would like to hang out a little longer."

Lance leaned up and gave the cab driver an address. Traffic was thick but close to thirty minutes later they were pulling up at a brownstone in Brooklyn.

"One of my friends is having a house party. We'll hang out here for a little while before going back in."

"Sounds good," Basra replied.

This crowd was much more laid back and trendy, and Lance's posture changed drastically upon crossing the threshold. Suddenly, he had swag. He immediately dapped up the guy who opened the door and began swaying to the hip-hop music that was blaring through the speakers. He could tell from Basra's expression that she was shocked.

"I know how to have fun, too. It's not always about work."

"I see."

"This is my boy Victor," he said, introducing Basra to the host.

"Nice to meet you."

"Make yourself at home," Victor said as they walked in.

The party was a mixture of all ethnicities and cultures, but the one obvious common denominator was wealth. But it wasn't that nouveau riche crowd. This was old money. Kids whose ancestors had buildings named after them in downtown Manhattan. Lucia said you can always tell old money from new because most of them were not ostentatious or braggadocios. The casual manner in which they left their four-thousand-dollar purses unattended instantly told Basra that money was not a big deal and that they never had to work hard for it. Yet, except for an occasional stock tip, there wasn't much conversation about money, it was a just a party with plenty of liquor and loud music. Lance didn't stay as close once they got inside Victor's four-level townhome, and Basra spent most of the first hour going room to room looking for him. Finally, she gave up and decided to enjoy herself. She mingled with some of the girls, one in particular who had recognized her from a recent spread in *Grazia,* an Italian fashion magazine. The girl mostly wanted to know what designers Basra had worked with and how many exotic places she'd traveled to. The woman was obsessed with modeling and finally Basra had to ditch her by escaping to another part of the house. Oddly, no matter what room she wandered in, she noticed this guy always checking her out from across the room. She'd seen him in the building a few times with Lance, but was never introduced. He finally decided to approach after he spotted her looking at him.

"I'm Campbell; my friends call me Camp."

"Hi, Campbell, I'm Basra."

"You can call me Camp."

"But I'm not a friend," Basra commented.

"We can work on that," he said. "You live in Lance's building. I've spoken to you."

"Yeah, I remember," said Basra.

"You play poker?" he asked.

"Believe it or not, I do."

"Let's go."

Basra followed Campbell into another part of the party, which was now packed with at least a hundred people. They went to the fourth floor where three other men had a poker game just starting.

"We want in," Campbell said as they entered.

"It's five to get in," said one of the guys.

"I'll cover us both," replied Campbell as he pulled a roll of money from his front and back pockets. He glanced over at Basra and motioned for her to sit.

"I didn't realize you were playing for real money."

"How else would you play?" another male responded. "Texas hold 'em, beautiful; you sure you want to get in debt with us?"

"It's cool, I got you," said Campbell while throwing $1,000 on the dealer's table.

"But what if I lose?" she asked.

He shook his head and motioned once again for her to sit.

The men introduced themselves and asked a few questions about her while they played the first hand. Yet, when questions were addressed about Basra the guys deferred to Campbell. The men were basically talking around her.

"She came with Lance, one of his models," he remarked with a wink.

While they were talking across her, Basra stayed focused on the game and soon it was down to her and Nick. The first pot was already at $500 and Basra was sure she was going to win as she held four of a kind. However, she was cautious and didn't want to raise the pot. She and Nick stared at each other across the table and he confidently threw two more chips in the pot.

"I raise you a hundred," he said.

Basra didn't hesitate, wanting to look very comfortable in the poker environment. She immediately tossed in her chips. "I call," she replied with assurance.

Nick gave her one more glance and then placed his five cards on the table.

"Four of a kind." He grinned, displaying his set of tens.

The other three folded players released anxious sighs and remarks. Basra then laid her hand down.

"Four of a kind, all ladies." She smiled, displaying not only her pearly whites but her four queens.

"I'll be damned," Nick murmured as the dealer announced, "The pot of seven hundred goes to our lovely lady."

"I win!" Basra yelped and she grappled through the mound of chips.

After a few more re-ups, and three more hands, all players cashed out. Basra had won $1,400, but Campbell was the big winner with three grand. Nick unfortunately left the game with two hundred bucks.

"I don't know where you came from, but you're bad luck. Don't come back to any more of my games."

"Excuse me," she said.

Campbell pushed him aside. "Go sober up. You'll play better."

Nick pushed back but then quickly turned and went out of the door when he didn't see Campbell backing down. Basra handed Campbell his $500, took her remainder, stashed it in her purse, and then looked at the time.

"Have you seen Lance?" she asked Campbell.

He shook his head.

"I'm ready to go." Basra removed her cell phone to call him but quickly realized she didn't have his number.

"Do you have Lance's number?" she asked Campbell.

"You don't?"

Basra nodded. "No, we live in the same building and this is the first time we've been out. We've been together all night so there was no need for his number."

"I can't help you with that."

"You don't have his number, but that's your friend," Basra said with confusion.

"I can't believe you're ready to leave."

"Yeah, I'm tired, but I had fun, thanks."

"Hold up," he said forcefully, grabbing her hand.

Basra tried to pull away but his grip was too strong. "You're hurting my arm. Let go."

He did but remained close. "I can take you home," he said.

"No, I'm going to find Lance."

"I'm not good enough to take you home?" said Campbell, raising his voice.

Basra made her move toward the door but Campbell blocked it with his arm.

"I just want to spend some time with you. What's the rush?"

"We just spent an hour together playing poker," she said.

"Alone time," he said, trying to kiss her. Basra dodged to avoid his lips but he quickly grabbed her around the waist and pulled her into his body. She squirmed to shake loose but couldn't.

"Stop acting like you don't want this."

"Stop it!" she yelled. "Let me go."

He pushed Basra down on the floor and held her down with his weight. He held her hands above her head and used his feet to block the door. Basra yelled, but no one could hear her over the music.

"It will be easier if you stop moving so much." Campbell licked her face with his hot, sticky tongue. "You taste good," he growled. Tears slowly rolled down Basra's face. "What's the matter? Oh I'm sorry, I didn't pay you. Here!" Still smothering her body, Campbell took the money from his pocket and tossed it in her face.

"There's three thousand and some change, that should cover it."

"Please stop," Basra whimpered.

"You're too good for my money!"

"No, it's not like that. I don't have sex like that. Please let me up."

"I don't know a whore worth more than three grand."

Campbell placed his left forearm over her chest to hold down her upper body as he attempted to remove her shorts with his right hand. His upper body weight kept her pinned to the floor.

"Okay okay!" she yelled. "I will sleep with you, but you have to be gentle. This is not how it's done." While Basra was attempting to bargain with Campbell, she managed to bend her leg and remove her shoe. Campbell lifted up slightly but still used his forearm to keep her pinned.

"How can I trust you?" he asked.

Basra paused, and then spoke, "You can't." She drove her five-inch stiletto directly into his temple. Stunned, he reared back and she clocked him again with the heel in his neck and a punch in the face. She quickly hopped up and kicked him in the stomach. Basra looked down and saw blood trickling near his ear. Frightened, she rushed from the room.

"Lance! Lance! Lance!" she yelled throughout the stairs, hallways, and into the main room. There was no sign of him. Still, Basra didn't stop until she was out of the front door. She finally paused to take a deep breath once she was outside on the steps. There were people mingling but no one seemed to notice her turmoil. She wanted to yell out, "I was almost raped!" but she wasn't sure anyone would hear or care. As she bent to place on her shoe, tears streamed with more force. "I was almost raped," she whispered. Her body shook as she held on to the banister and walked down the remaining five steps. Basra looked back at the home in disbelief. She could have been raped that evening and no one would have known. It was obvious Lance knew what she did for a living and he must have informed Campbell. So she couldn't help but wonder that if Campbell told everyone about her occupation, possibly know one would even care that she was attacked. Basra walked down the street a few feet and hailed a taxi. She hopped in while wiping her face, even though the tears continued.

"Where to?" asked the driver.

"Chelsea, thirty-seven West Twenty-first," she spoke, nearly out of breath.

Basra placed her head against the window and let the tears continue to stream. Her legs and arms were still shaking as she heard Campbell's words in her head. *I don't know a whore worth more than three grand.* The tears welled more and rolled faster as she played the word "whore" repeatedly in her head.

"I'm so stupid," she whispered.

Basra closed her eyes and tried to relax but her tears didn't dry until well after the morning sun had blanketed the sky.

Chapter 4

Basra spent the next day in bed. Though her mind flurried nonstop with thoughts, she couldn't muster the energy to get dressed. She only rose from bed to relieve her bladder, but had no appetite for food. Around ten that night, her self-loathing emotions turned to anger. She began thinking about Lance and wondered what he had said to Campbell about her. Could the whole thing have been a setup? She wondered. Basra contemplated the situation for close to another hour and hopped from bed a little after eleven. She tossed on jeans and a T-shirt, and brushed her teeth. Moments later she was on her way up to the penthouse to pay Lance a visit. Basra had lived in the building for close to a year but had never been up to the top floor, which only held two apartments. Yet she knew where Lance lived, because he held parties every other month at his place and there was always morning-after buzz about the events in 15B.

However, the elevator wouldn't allow her to go past floor fourteen. Frustrated, she went back down to the lobby to speak with Abdul, the concierge with the huge crush.

"Hi, Abdul, you look nice this evening," she flirted. "I was hoping you could help me out." He obliged with a smile. "I'm looking for Lance, have you seen him?"

"Not tonight," he replied.

"I need to get up to the penthouse."

"Call him," Abdul suggested.

"See that's it, I think he has my cell phone. We hung out and I asked him to hold my things . . . You know what, never mind, I don't want to bother you," Basra said, batting her big, sad eyes.

"Let me see if I can help," said Abdul.

He whispered to the other concierge and came from around the desk. As the two of them were stepping into elevator, Lance was exiting.

"You!" Basra yelled before turning to Abdul to say thanks.

"What happened to you last night?" he asked.

Basra pushed him back into the elevator and when the door closed she commenced to yell.

"I was attacked because of you!"

"What?"

"Your friend Campbell tried to rape me! What did you tell him about me?"

"I didn't say anything to Campbell. He's asked about you a few times and I told him you and Lucia were roommates. Hold up, he attacked you?" By now they were back to the top floor and Lance invited Basra in. "Start over, what happened?"

Basra explained the entire ordeal, but to her surprise Lance wasn't completely shocked.

"So he didn't rape you?"

"No! But he tried. This is serious. Why aren't you angry?"

"Campbell gets out of control when he drinks and . . ." Lance paused.

"What?"

"He's gone out with Lucia before and so he assumed it was okay."

For the first five seconds Basra bought the reply, but then she became more enraged. So much so that she punched Lance on the arm. "No! He tried to rape me! I was saying 'no, please stop, don't do this,' and he just kept going."

"Did he try to pay you?"

"That doesn't matter."

"Sure it does."

"No, it doesn't. I told him no."

"He probably thought it was part of the chase. Some men like that. Unfortunately, you are judged by the company you keep. Your girl Lucia is a wild woman."

As she processed the conversation, Basra rose, walked over to his enormous terrace and gazed out into the night sky. "Why did you ask me out?"

"Wanted a no-pressure date. I'm at the settling down age, and I can't go on a date without a woman asking me if I plan on having kids and settling down. You're easy on the eyes and I didn't think you'd be trying to marry me within the first ten minutes of the date. Come sit down," he requested.

Basra slowly sat on the couch beside Lance.

"When I asked Lucia about you, she said you were one of the girls. You didn't seem like one of them, but then again, I don't know you. I have to admit, though, I was curious about you. You never come to my parties. You don't spend hours in the fitness club like everyone else in this building and you're very beautiful."

"So, basically, you wanted my services for free."

"No. I could have easily paid you for the evening but I didn't want to have sex, or have you feel the pressure. I just wanted to go out with someone I was interested in. It was just a date, plain and simple."

"But you left me. I couldn't find you."

"I'm sorry, I looked all over for you. I thought you'd left me, and so I came home. I didn't have your number."

Basra saw the sincerity in his face. "I really did have fun at the party for your job," she said, walking toward the door.

"What are you going to do about Campbell?" he asked.

"I'm not sure. If I go to the police, it's going to be an even bigger issue. He'll tell them I'm a call girl, and I can't get into that. I don't know."

"I'll talk to him." Basra nodded as Lance came to the door to walk her out, and got on the elevator with her. It was silent on the five-floor ride down to Basra's place, but when she stepped out Lance asked, "Can I get your number?"

Basra simply smiled as the doors were closing but never gave a reply. Close to five minutes later, Basra was undressed and back in her bed where she remained until morning.

Feeling a bit more rejuvenated, Basra walked to the Union Square Greenmarket first thing Sunday morning. She loved to juice and owned a very expensive high-powered juicer that hadn't been getting enough use. She returned home with bags of organic carrots, celery, tomatoes, and an assortment of fruits. As she juiced, Basra looked online for apartments. She knew she couldn't afford anything as luxurious as her current domicile, but that didn't matter. She knew that she had to slowly dissociate herself from Lucia, get back in school, and find a job.

"There's nothing wrong with living a normal life," she stated to herself.

Problem was, Basra had sampled an appetizer of the good and lavish life. Working a nine-to-five making meager means would prove to be difficult, and deep inside she knew this. Via e-mail, she reached out to her agency and let them know she was available for any and all international work.

"I need new pictures," she mumbled while sipping on her carrot and celery blend.

Basra needed new pictures for her book: photos with straight hair. She'd booked 90 percent of her jobs as a Somali model with thick, curly hair. But when she straightened her hair, she looked more American. To procure more work, she needed to diversify her image. Hence, she set a salon appointment that Thursday.

"Today is going to be very productive. I can feel it," she said with a smile.

Basra got dressed, and headed to check out the neighborhoods of the few places she'd found online.

Throughout the day, she thought of her incident the night before with Campbell, but she refused to let it get her down. Her ability to overcome distress and traumatic situations developed when she was a young girl. In Somalia she was exposed to so much, so early in life, that there was nothing that Basra knew she couldn't endure. Her community back home had been pillaged several times. At twelve, she witnessed her aunt being beaten to death for having an affair. She had young cousins recruited as warlords and knew of many killings and murders. Basra knew how great her opportunities were in New York, and again it was her responsibility to aid her family. She wasn't going to let Campbell or Lucia cause a diversion in her mission.

That evening around seven, Lucia strolled in, and plopped down next to Basra on the couch. She wrapped her arms around her roomie and placed her head on Basra's shoulder.

"I missed you," she said.

"Are you schizophrenic?" asked Basra.

"Bipolar maybe, but not schizoid," Lucia answered.

Basra wasn't sure if she was joking and so she didn't give her reply any attention.

"I had the best weekend," Lucia said. "I was in Miami at this party, where the cocaine flowed like snow."

"You shouldn't do that."

"I don't. Not all the time. Just an occasional party now and then."

Basra slid her shoulder from underneath Lucia's head and continued to watch television as she scooted a few inches away.

"What did you do this weekend?" Lucia asked.

Basra, with the task in mind to slowly detach from Lucia, decided to keep mum about her eventful weekend. The less Lucia knew the better. Basra replied, "Nothing," and continued staring at the boob tube.

"Well, listen to this. Next week there is a party in Isla de sa Ferradura, Island of the Horseshoe," Lucia said with excitement in her voice. Basra cut her eyes toward Lucia but refused to give her full attention. "You can make some real good money."

"I'm not going."

"You're going to hate you didn't go. Have you ever been to a private island? It's near Ibiza. I know you've never been there."

"I don't care. I have two interviews this week," Basra lied.

"Doing what? Waitressing? You'd rather bring home fifty dollars in tips when you could make five thousand?"

Campbell's words were still haunting her. "I'd rather not be thought of as a whore," Basra said as she rose and walked into the kitchen. Naturally, Lucia followed.

"I'm trying to help you. You said you wanted to save money. You said you wanted to help your family. It's not about what others think of you, but what you think about yourself. I don't care if people call me a whore, because I will be a whore who's retiring as a millionaire before the age of thirty. I can invest, become a multimillionaire by thirty-five, and no one will care how I earned my first million."

Lucia's words now had Basra's full attention. "I hear what you're saying, I just wasn't raised that way."

"You think I was? You think my mother sat me down when I was little and told me I had gold between my legs and that I should exploit my body for a better life? My mother, God rest her soul, wanted me to be a pastry chef like her and the other women in my family. But my mother died with two hundred euros to her name, which is about three hundred dollars. I'm not living like that. I have been given a great opportunity that most would kill for, and so have you. Squander it if you want, but I'm not, and there's nothing you can say to change my mind." Lucia grabbed the big bottle of homemade carrot juice and motioned. "May I?"

Basra nodded. She finally got to see a side of Lucia that wasn't the money-loving party girl she so casually displayed. Even though they'd been roommates for seven months, Lucia never talked about her family, and since Basra wasn't one to pry, fashion, modeling, and men were the bases of their conversation.

"I don't judge you," Basra said.

"Even if you did, I wouldn't care. The juice is good," Lucia commented as she walked toward the back.

Basra realized that her and Lucia's missions were very similar, and until that conversation, she saw Lucia as being the weaker female in the apartment. But now she pondered the strength and determination of Lucia's mind, to go daily without caring about what people thought.

"I could never do that," Basra whispered as she watched Lucia stroll toward the back.

It didn't change her mind about sleeping with men for sex, but she understood Lucia's desire to create a new generation of wealth, and there was a piece of her that admired that.

School was starting in a month and Basra knew she didn't want to wait another semester before enrolling full time. She had a few classes under her belt, but was anxious to delve into her major at Saint John's University. Although she had a little money saved, she went to the school that week and applied for financial aid. While there, Basra also got information on a few grants. She went by the Fashion Institute and even got some information for her baby sister. She didn't have enough money in the bank to do half of the things she wanted, but with a few thousand saved, she felt empowered. Her dream was becoming a blueprint. But, unfortunately, the plans she made that week only increased her desire to get more money. Basra applied for three jobs, all at high-end restaurants, one referred by a friend in the building, who bragged about making over one hundred dollars in tips every night. Sure that sounded like a lot of money, but it was nothing in comparison to what Basra knew she could make. Yet she felt she was on the right path, one her family would be proud of and that mattered. Thursday evening when her sister called, Basra couldn't wait to talk to her about her new American look and the FIT visit. But Amina was not in the mood for lighthearted gab.

Her first words were, "They're bulldozing the home next week."

"What do you mean?" Basra questioned with panic.

"The land is being used to build a plant. Everyone complained but there is nothing that can be done. Remember Mr. Gaalid? They burned his house."

"Where are you going to go?"

"Me and Khalid are going to Mogadishu to stay with Abukar until we get another place. Dad got a job in Ethiopia for the next three months and Mom . . ."

"Mom what? What's wrong?"

"She just cries all of the time, Basra. She doesn't want to leave the neighborhood and she doesn't want the family to become broken. I don't know where she's going to go. She won't come with us to Abukar's house. She said there's not enough room and she doesn't want to be a bigger burden than necessary."

Amina began to cry and Basra spent the next hour trying to figure out a plan of action.

"It's going to be okay, I promise," Basra expressed.

"No, I don't want to go there. Can't I come there with you? I can stay with you and apply for my visa."

"You can't leave Khalid right now."

"I can bring him," Amina suggested.

"I can't take care of you both. Khalid is only twelve. And if you left right now, think about what that would do to Mom."

"I know. I just hate this."

"I'll do what I can, I promise," swore Basra.

The sisters spoke a few more minutes and then disconnected. Basra's stomach was churning and her eyes were red from crying. She stretched her long body across the bed for a few minutes while tossing and turning. Eventually, she rose and knocked on Lucia's door. Basra knew what she had to do, and for the first time, no longer cared what anyone thought.

"What's wrong?" Lucia asked.

"I really hope it's not too late for the horseshoe party."

Chapter 5

Lucia, Basra, and three other ladies arrived by boat on Isla de sa Ferradura on that Saturday morning. Basra was overwhelmed by the beauty of the island.

"It looks like a painting," she kept commenting to Lucia, who was also in awe.

As Basra walked on to the property, she was overcome with joy, feeling so blessed for the opportunity. Yet, in that same breath of gratification, she wondered about the consequence and questioned whether this good fortune was indeed good. Her mom used to say a great fortune can be a great slavery. Was she tangled in a weave that would be impossible to escape?

Basra glanced at Lucia, who was chatting with the other girls about the beauty of the mountainous cliffs. They seemed totally blissful with no worries or cares. But was it all an act? Were they any different from people who worked a nine-to-five and hated their jobs, but had to come into work each day with a smile so they could make ends meet? Everyone had to pretend at some point and time just to get by, and this was her moment on stage. Basra wandered a few feet away, gazed into the waters, and said a quiet prayer.

"God, let your will be done, protect and watch over me," she whispered.

Over her shoulders she heard more voices on the pontoon. The staff was coming to escort them into the hacienda.

"Come on, Basra," called Lucia.

"Welcome to paradise," said one of the ladies.

The private island, which was situated just off Ibiza in the beautiful bay of San Miguel, had a beautiful hacienda, accommodated fourteen people, and was equipped with a spa, fitness center, elegant dining quarters, and a beauty salon.

Each of the ladies placed their bags in their rooms and walked on to the north terrace.

"My name is Yasmina, and I will be your maidservant this weekend. These are my assistants, Annisia and Sofia. If you need anything, feel free to call upon one of us. We have made appointments in the beauty center for each of you, so please enjoy, and welcome to paradise."

The ladies followed the staff to the salon where Basra was treated to a facial, manicure, and pedicure. Lucia opted for the spa and relaxed with a warm basalt stone massage. In a few hours the ladies were primped and prepped to meet their hosts, a group of international steel magnates who rented the island that weekend. The women were asked to meet the men in the laguna garden and so they changed into swimsuits and lounge attire.

"This looks like the Garden of Eden," said Lucia to Basra as they gazed at the cascading waterfall that emptied into the huge lagoon-shaped pool.

"And those must be the serpents," Basra whispered while pointing to the steel moguls sitting around the pool.

"Stop it. Be pleasant," Lucia said.

The women were introduced to the five men and for the first hour they all had fun mingling and dipping into the cool waters. Basra didn't want to dip in the pool because she wanted her straight hair to last as long as possible. However, the Mediterranean mist was already curling her edges. She continued to look at the beautiful waterfall and finally couldn't resist any longer. She untied her sarong and splashed into the blue waters. For a second, she almost forgot about the purpose of her trip. However, as she was swimming from underneath the cave and through the cascading waters of the waterfall, she saw the men gathering at the far left side of the laguna. With lustful, leering looks, they pointed like overzealous ranchers eyeing their new herd of cattle. Basra quickly swam over to Lucia, who was lounging by the side.

"Hey, look over there," she said, pointing to the men.

Lucia looked up, glanced at the men, and then stretched back across her chair.

"They're talking about us."

"I'm sure they are. I hope I get the young one with the mustache."

Basra looked at the men again. The short one caught her looking and smiled. Basra quickly looked away. Lucia could feel her anxiousness.

"Basra, don't flake on me. You asked to come here, and you need the eight grand."

"I'm not flaking, I just feel like property."

"At two thousand a night, you are property. Rental property. After Wednesday, you never have to see them again."

Basra frowned and plopped deep down into the water. Lucia sat up to see that her friend had disappeared completely into the pool. Lucia bent over and looked into the crystal blue water.

"You better not be trying to kill yourself," she called out while smacking the water with her hand. "Basra, come up here! Basra!" she called again.

Within a few seconds, Basra bobbled up and exhaled deeply. She pulled her body from the water and propped it up on the sandy edge.

"Listen—" Lucia started, only to be halted by Basra.

"I don't need a lecture or a speech. I'm fine."

"Good, 'cause they are calling us over."

Basra and the girls walked over to the deck. Yasmina and the staff handed the women towels and ushered them into the salon room, which was beautifully decorated with pristine white furnishings. The men soon followed. The youngest man, Fahad, spoke first.

"Once again, we want to thank you beautiful ladies for joining us this week. We work very hard and it's nice to be able to come here, relax for a few days, and forget all of our worries. Helen, would you join me for drinks." He held out his hand and he and the tall, blonde Swiss escort walked off.

Basra quickly whispered into Lucia's ear. "Do we stay with one man for the week or do they switch? How does this work?"

Lucia ignored Basra and smiled at her next man of choice. Since she didn't get the young one, she was hoping for the tall, thin guy who appeared to be in his forties. Seconds later, he walked over and picked her. One by one, the women were carried off like abandoned pets at a rescue shelter. Basra was last. She tried to smile as she stood with sad puppy-dog eyes when her date approached. Earlier by the pool, he'd explained that his birth name was Daiwik, which means by the grace of God, but he changed it to Derrick for ease of doing business in America.

"Would you like some food?" he asked. Basra quietly nodded. Derrick motioned for Annisia to bring them a menu. "Why don't you look at the menu, order, and then go change."

"Okay," Basra said softly.

Rummaging through her suitcase, Basra found a long salmon-colored halter sundress. She returned to the dining area and joined Derrick. Upon her presence, he stood and was the perfect gentleman, even pulling out her chair and waiting before he sat. He avoided direct eye contact, as did she, and Basra could tell he was just as nervous. Their meal was served within minutes of her return and Basra felt it would ease her nerves if she simply broke the ice.

"Am I your girl for the entire week, or will you trade me off after a few hours?" she delivered with a quirky smile and a slight chuckle so as to not come across too brash.

"Well," he slowly responded. "I do believe that you will stay with me this week. I do hope so," Derrick said with a pleasant smile.

I can do this, I can do this. Basra continued to burrow this phrase in the base of mind. Derrick placed his hand on top of hers and rubbed it gently.

"Are you all right?" he questioned.

Basra nodded and continued to eat.

"You should think about changing your name. Are you Muslim?"

"I was raised Muslim," she replied. "I no longer practice the religion."

"Interesting. Why is that?"

"I just don't. No reason. By the time I became a teenager, we stopped going to the mosque and when I moved to the U.S., I went to a Presbyterian church with a friend. Islam can be very confining." Derrick stared pensively. "I don't mean to offend you. But it's not for me. I loved how we grew up and I believe it was what I needed as a child."

"None taken. Islam has its place in society, but it is not for everyone," Derrick commented.

"Why should I change my name?"

"You should choose something easier, sexier. Basra is very traditional for such a nontraditional girl."

"I'm traditional. I mean, my lifestyle doesn't necessarily reflect that, but I still have a lot of traditional ways."

"I'm sure," he replied.

They ate for a few more minutes in silence, but Basra couldn't resist revisiting the name conversation once more. "So what would you name me?"

Derrick paused and stared quietly at Basra. "I don't know, Rebecca maybe?"

"Uhghh. I look like a Rebecca to you? I'm certainly not a Rebecca. I need something more exotic, and unique."

"Okay, how about Sandy?"

"I said exotic." She chuckled as the tension began to dissipate.

"I'm from India, they are all exotic names to me." He laughed.

The two chatted over a few more names, finished lunch, and went into the parlor room to listen to music. As the hours progressed, Basra only saw one other couple. As the sun set, her nerves grew.

"Where is everyone?" she asked Derrick.

"In their separate quarters, I would imagine."

Basra grew very quiet, for she knew that they soon would be heading to their private suite, and that she'd start the performance of a lifetime.

They made it to the Bamboo Suite close to eight that evening, and Basra was surprisingly calm. Derrick didn't seem to be a pervert or a crazed sex maniac, and she had psyched herself into the idea that this would be similar to having sex on the first date with a man she genuinely liked. Truthfully, she'd had a good time with Derrick and if it weren't for the looming sexual proposition hanging over her head, it would have been a great time.

"Is there music in here?" she asked, sitting on the foot of the bed.

"I'm sure," Derrick replied, looking around the room. He discovered a remote to a satellite radio and found a station playing ambient tunes. Derrick removed his shoes and lounged on the chaise. Both he and Basra were like quiet school kids, each waiting for the other to make a move.

"This is weird. Is this weird?" she asked. Derrick grinned and shrugged his shoulders. "I'll be back," she expressed.

Basra walked into the restroom and quickly removed her dress. "I'm going to just get it over with, and then fall asleep." She took a deep breath and exited, wearing matching dark blue undergarments. Basra posed against the bamboo posts of the canopy bed. Her body looked absolutely perfect, like an airbrushed lingerie ad. Derrick stayed seated and stared. Basra thought he'd make a move, but since he didn't, she strutted across the floor and draped her body across his. He continued to stay still and so she leaned up and kissed him. He indulged in the lip lock for a few seconds and then pulled away.

"I'm sorry," he said.

"What's the matter?" she asked, lifting off his body.

"Could you just have a seat? I just want to look at you."

"Oh," Basra responded softly and walked back to the foot of the bed.

Derrick rose and poured a glass of wine from the chilled bottle on the table. "Would you like some?" he asked.

"I'm good."

Derrick walked back to the chaise and took a seat. An uneasy feeling came over Basra as he continued to stare. She was now more nervous than before when she thought they were just going to have sex. *What is he going to ask me to do?* she wondered.

In the Laguna Suite, Lucia certainly was not wondering what was on the mind of her date, as he was very verbal and demanding.

"Dance, strip, and then come over here and please me orally," he insisted.

He also asked that she continue to shower him with compliments while demoralizing herself with distasteful, derogatory comments. This display of gratuitous behavior had been going on for two hours, and even Lucia was growing tired of his antics and questioning the value of the gig.

"Dance harder!" Ahsan called out.

Lucia jutted her hips to the right and slightly rolled her eyes.

"You make faces at me?" he asked in anger. Lucia didn't respond and continued to dance.

"Turn around, you slut, and swing your hair." Lucia made another small gesture of dislike. This time Ahsan clearly saw the disgust. He hastened to her side while yelling.

"You will love this! You will do it with pleasing eyes. You are filthy and you have no say!" Ahsan wrapped his long, skinny fingers around Lucia's neck and began to choke her. At first she went along with his force, for she was familiar with men who used force as foreplay. However, when she began feeling lightheaded, she struggled to break loose. He continued to choke her until her body went limp. Lucia collapsed on the floor. Ahsan stood over her body and grinned.

Basra's evening was moving in the complete opposite direction as Lucia's. Although Derrick asked that she not place her clothing back on, he only wanted to sit and talk. Basra was relieved but still wondered if he was setting her up for a surprise act of debauchery. If so, she would have to wait until the morning, because the two of them talked throughout the night until Basra finally fell asleep on the edge of the bed.

The following morning the group of women met on the roof terrace for breakfast. The men ate on a separate side. The girls were full of chatter just like any girl would be after a first date. Basra was amazed at how conditioned the women had become. She didn't say much, which was normal, but she was shocked at the quiet, still manner of Lucia, which was the antithesis of her personality. As Lucia devoured her French toast, Basra stirred up conversation.

"You okay? You don't look so well."

Lucia didn't say anything, only smiled with a mouthful of breakfast, and nodded her head. Lucia was always the loquacious ringleader but this morning as she sat quiet as a church mouse, Basra knew something was awry. Yet she knew not to pry while others were around. Immediately after breakfast, the girls were asked to join the men on the luxurious fifty-foot yacht. Once again, Basra was enraptured by the opulence of the twenty-four-karat gold trimmings and marble accents. She'd seen wealth like this from afar but never experienced it firsthand. *Who wouldn't want to live like this?* she asked herself. The group began branching off into couples but before Basra left Lucia's side, she pulled her aside for quick line of questioning.

"Are you okay? Did something happen to you last night? Why are you so quiet?"

"Par for the course," Lucia replied before looking to her right and left.

Basra moved closer and stared into Lucia's eyes. "Something happened?"

Lucia leaned in to whisper. "It's Ahsan, he—"

From around the corner, Ahsan appeared. "There you are. Let's go to the top, the view is wonderful."

Lucia placed on her pageant smile and held out her hand. "Let's go," she replied. The two walked down the corridor hand in hand. Basra went to the restroom and then met Derrick in the sky lounge of the upper deck. They sat and had drinks as the yacht sailed slowly into the Mediterranean.

"Whose boat is this?" Basra asked.

"It belongs to Ahsan's family. They usually keep it in Ibiza at their home."

"Ibiza's that way? Right?" Basra said, pointing west.

"Yes," Derrick commented, scooting a bit closer to his date. He smiled at her and then softly grazed her leg. This intimate gesture didn't make Basra cringe or pull away. It was as though she almost welcomed it.

"You're not attracted to me, are you?" she asked.

"You are very beautiful," he replied.

"But you didn't answer my question."

"You look like the women from home. I find you very attractive."

Basra thought about his response for a second before responding. "How come you haven't tried to sleep with me?"

"Because I am happily married."

Basra was shocked. "We've been talking all this time and you never said you were married."

Derrick laughed quietly and cast his focus into the waters.

"So . . . why did you come here?"

"These are my business partners and I was invited. It would have been rude to decline."

"But you knew there would be women on the boat, right? Escorts?"

"Of course. They have these sorts of excursions often. I normally do not participate; however, my stake in the company is greater now, and I'm expected to entertain with them. All of us are married. I simply choose to be faithful to my wife."

"So you don't want to sleep with me?"

"It isn't a matter of desire, it is a matter of discipline."

Basra gave a half-grinning, half-unsettling expression and quickly turned away to avoid Derrick from seeing the tears well. However, he rose and walked to her other side, forcing her to face him.

"I didn't mean to upset you."

"I'm not upset," she uttered.

She placed her head on his shoulder and sobbed while speaking. "This is not what I want to do. I do it because I have to right now. I don't . . ." Basra lifted her head. "I will still get paid, won't I?"

"Of course. In fact, I'm willing to pay you a little more for your discretion." Basra's tears filled again. She knew without a doubt that in spite of her actions, God was still watching over her, and so she whispered a quiet thank you, and continued to look out into the sparkling blue waters of the Mediterranean.

On the roof deck, Ahsan seemed to be a little gentler than the night before. Lucia was enjoying her coffee as he smoked a His Majesty's Reserve Ghurka. He turned toward Lucia and blew a puff of the cognac-infused cigar smoke in her face.

Ahsan looked at Lucia and released a devious grin. "I could toss you over this deck right now and no one would know."

Lucia smiled through the cloud of tobacco haze and replied. "Then I guess I should thank you for sparing my life."

"You should. I should also get a reward."

Lucia leaned over and gave him a kiss on the cheek. Ahsan took her hand and forced her to grab his crotch and squeeze. Lucia's hand tensed up as he pulled her upper body close to the railing. Lucia immediately went into character.

"I'm just a worthless slut. Why would you risk your soul with Allah on someone like me?"

Ahsan peered into Lucia's eyes and then burst into a strong, lusty laugh. "I like you!" he jeered and continued to chortle while releasing her hand.

Lucia, who had been holding her breath for the last thirty seconds, finally exhaled and laughed along with him.

"Excuse me," he said and walked away to the restroom.

Once he got out of eyesight, Lucia furiously ran downstairs to find Basra.

"Dove!" Derrick called out. "Your name should be Dove."

"Dove? I like that."

"Yes, it's exotic, it's simple. And it's a symbol of peace. Your spirit is very peaceful. They are thoroughbreds of the sky, you know. Wherever they are released, they typically find their way back home."

"The only thing I know about doves is that they are pigeons. I don't know if I want to be a pigeon," chuckled Basra.

"Doves are very smart. In the Bible a dove was released to help Noah find land."

"You're Muslim; what do you know about the Bible?"

"It is wise to be knowledgeable in all aspects of theology. From now on you are Dove: innocent, peaceful, and intelligent."

Basra continued to giggle. Suddenly, Lucia rushed up behind her.

"I need to talk with you."

"Is everything okay?" asked Derrick.

"Yes, I just need to talk to my friend. Female stuff."

Lucia pulled Basra from her date and pushed her around the corner.

"What is it?" Basra asked.

"Ahsan is going to kill me. We have to go!"

"What!" yelped Basra. "He is not!"

"Last night he choked me until I passed out and when I became conscious, he had bound my feet and arms together. I can't even get into the rest."

"Oh my God."

"But that's not the worst of it. I've had some very kinky encounters with men, and I normally don't judge, but just now he said he could throw me off the boat and kill me and no one would know or care because I'm just a dirty slut."

Basra's eyes bulged. "That's not good."

"We have to go," persisted Lucia.

"Go where? We can't go. We're on an island."

"We have to go somewhere. He is horrible. He smells like stinky cigars, his feet are like claws. His penis is the size of my middle finger and did I mention that he's going to kill me."

Basra's big eyes grew larger.

"You okay?" asked Lucia.

"Uh huh," she answered while furiously blinking and nodding.

Her odd, rapid actions made Lucia turn around. Standing over her shoulder was Ahsan, who appeared from nowhere with a raging expression indicating that he was not pleased with Lucia's attempt to escape.

Chapter 6

Lucia clung tight to Basra's arm.

"Now he's going to kill us both," Basra whispered with a tinge of fright.

"You disrespect me?" Ahsan said.

"She didn't mean it!" Basra called out. "We weren't talking about you. She was repeating what I said about Derrick."

Ahsan looked at both girls and approached slowly. Their bodies tensed.

"What are you doing down here?" he asked Lucia.

"I was checking on my friend. She's new to this business and—"

"Shut up!"

Just then Derrick came around the corner.

"Is everything all right?" he asked.

Basra nodded but kept quiet.

"Dove, I would like to show you something," commented Derrick, and he extended his hand to her.

"Maybe we could all go," she suggested, holding on to Lucia's hand.

"It's okay, Basra. I'm fine," said Lucia, whose palm had become clammy from fear.

Like a Western showdown, all four individuals stood still and waited for someone to make his or her move. Everyone's eyes shifted from right to left, but no one made a step.

Finally, Ahsan flipped his demeanor. "Let's have a drink," he said to Lucia. "Come on." He took Lucia's arm and she finally disconnected from Basra. As Ahsan ushered Lucia away, she looked desperately over her shoulder until they disappeared into another part of the boat.

"She's very scared of him," Basra immediately said to Derrick in an unsettling tone.

"Why?"

Basra wasn't sure how close the two men were, and she didn't want to make his friend sound completely insane, but she felt someone should know the truth. "He said he could throw her overboard, and no one would care."

Derrick chuckled a bit. "He was joking. I'm sure."

"I don't know."

"She'll be fine. Let's have some lunch," he responded.

It was apparent he didn't want to mess in Ahsan's affairs and so she left it alone. Besides, Lucia was normally overdramatic, and Ahsan wouldn't do anything crazy in front of his business partners. Furthermore, the last thing she wanted to do was jeopardize her money and so she continued to keep quiet.

They ate a pleasant dinner and stayed on the yacht until the evening. This was the easiest money Basra had ever made, but she was still concerned about Lucia and couldn't fully relax. Although Derrick tried to assure her that everything was well, she wasn't buying it. Neither Ahsan nor Lucia was at dinner and she didn't see them the remainder of the night.

By morning, Basra was completely on edge. She woke early Monday, got dressed, and rushed to the roof terrace to meet the girls. They trickled in one by one, but there was no sign of Lucia. No one had seen her since last evening. Basra became panicked, thinking

Lucia was truly in danger. She went back to the suite to inform Derrick.

"Maybe she decided to sleep in," he replied.

"No! She knows I'd be concerned. Plus, she loves food, and would never miss breakfast."

"You're upset over nothing," he said calmly.

Basra went back to the roof, asking about Lucia's whereabouts along the way. No one had seen her. An hour later, the men gathered. Without hesitation, Basra approached Ahsan.

"Where's Lucia?" she questioned.

Ahsan, bothered by Basra's tone, glanced at Derrick and then replied. "I have no idea where your friend is."

"You're lying," she exclaimed.

Derrick quickly walked over and attempted to pull her to the side. Basra refused to go quietly.

"You know where she is! What did you do to her?"

"You cannot speak to him like that." whispered Derrick.

"I can speak to him anyway I want, especially if he did something to Lucia," she countered.

By now, Ahsan had walked away and the commotion calmed. "I will help you find her," said Derrick.

The two walked off and frantically inspected every nook and cranny of the home for Lucia. None of the staff admitted to seeing her, but Basra insisted that someone had to know something.

"She couldn't have just disappeared," she said. "What would he do with her body?"

"Well, this is an island, and we are surrounded by the Mediterranean Sea." He chuckled.

Basra slapped him on the shoulder. "It's not funny."

"Nothing has happened to her. I promise. Maybe she's on the yacht."

"Good idea."

Basra and Derrick looked in every crevice and cubby. But they couldn't find her. On the roof-top deck, Basra walked to the edge and looked out over the water. She started to cry, but quickly wiped her tears as she heard Derrick's footsteps.

"I will speak with Ahsan," he insisted.

Basra buried her body within his chest and took comfort in his sincere embrace. Once they got off the boat, Basra spent the rest of the day at the hacienda looking for Lucia, but no one seemed to either know or care about her whereabouts. The men paid her no attention, and the women didn't want to get involved.

"I can't believe people," she continually said to Derrick throughout the evening. "I appreciate you for helping."

The evening hours passed slowly and by now Basra was convinced something had truly happened to Lucia. She had no appetite and spent the night sulking.

Tuesday, the men had several meetings and so the ladies spent most of the day lounging by pool. Around three that afternoon, one of the cooks saw Basra sitting alone on the deck. He rushed up to her and spoke his best English.

"Your friend, I see her," he whispered.

"You see her where?"

"At night."

"Was she alone?" Basra asked.

"I saw the man, he look too."

"What man? Ahsan?"

"No name," said the cook. "She was upset. I show her the way."

"Why didn't you take her there? What if he got to her?"

"I see things here, no trouble this way."

"I understand, *gracias*."

"*De nada*." The cook looked around and rushed away.

Basra's mind reeled with horrible possibilities. "What really goes on here? And why is he so scared?" she asked herself.

This once Fantasy Island had become the land of terror. Basra was ready to leave. She went to the dining area where the men were gathering for another meeting. She quickly got Derrick's attention. He asked her to wait momentarily. Basra paced outside of the glass door until he was able to come out.

"I can't get any cell phone service on the island. How do I get some transportation over to Ibiza?"

"Are you leaving?"

"I just want to be able to call Lucia or see if she left me a message."

"And what if you cannot find her? Then what? Do you return?"

"I don't know. But . . ."

"But what?" he asked.

"I need the money. I will be back. I don't want to cause any trouble, I just want to find my friend."

"You have to take the ferry over."

"I will be back."

Basra inquired about the ferry but realized the last ferry had already left. Outside of a private boat, which she had no access to, there was no way she was going to get off the island. Basra was forced to spend another night not knowing if Lucia was dead or alive.

Wednesday morning Basra woke early and made her way to the pontoon to inquire about a ferry ride. Luckily, there were two hacienda staff workers going over to Ibiza to get supplies. Basra kindly asked to ride the private boat with them and they obliged. As soon as she got on the mainland, she tried her cell, which was supposed to get international service. She was unable to get through. The ordeal was making her stomach tremor into knots. She tried a few more times and then waited at the dock where the men said they would return. There were a few stragglers at the dock and so Basra pulled up a picture of her and Lucia and showed it to a few men in hopes that someone would have some information, but she had no luck. However, when the men returned with the supplies, she saw one of them on the phone.

"Can you call America?" she asked.

"America? Yes, I do believe," he replied.

"May I?"

He handed Basra his cell phone and she eagerly dialed Lucia's number. It didn't go through until the other gentleman took the phone and dialed a code.

"What is the number?" he asked.

Basra gave him the number and seconds later she was connected. She nervously listened to each ring. But after six, Lucia's voice mail blared through the receiver.

"Lucia, I'm so concerned about you. Please e-mail me when you get this. Let me know if you are okay. Please don't forget. Please!"

Basra handed the man his phone and then boarded the boat. Bara couldn't eat or sleep. Derrick did his best to comfort her but there was no use.

That evening before the group loaded on the ferry, Derrick requested Basra's information.

"I have deeply enjoyed your company. Please record your information in my phone so that I may send you a gift."

Basra left her information with Derrick and started her journey back home.

Due to sheer exhaustion, Basra slept most of the plane ride back to the States. She couldn't wait to get back into her place and sleep in her bed, and as soon as the plane landed, she called Lucia. Still, there was no answer. She called her again in the cab, but no answer. Basra rushed into the condo, yelling her name.

"Lucia! Lucia! You better be asleep," yelled Basra.

She looked throughout the place, but Lucia wasn't there and it looked the same as it did when they left: clean. Lucia's bed was untouched. There were no wet towels in the bathroom and no old coffee in the maker. Lucia always left traces of old coffee. She always made enough for two cups, but only drank a cup and a half.

"Where is your other half a cup!" she screamed. "Hell, where are you?" Basra called Lucia's cell phone once more. There was no answer and now the voice mail came on immediately.

"Oh, God, what if they killed her for real?" Basra whispered. *Her body would never be found and how could I explain any of this to her family?* "I don't even know her family," Basra said to the empty seat next to her. "Shit!" she yelled. "I have to call Hollis."

Basra left a message on Hollis's phone but didn't allude to any trouble. She poured herself a glass of wine and sat on the terrace. By her third glass, she was crying. She couldn't stop the continuum of heinous thoughts. She picked up the phone to dial Hollis again, but before she could dial, her phone rang.

"Hollis. Have you talked with Lucia?"

"I thought she was with you. Didn't you return this morning?"

"She left early."

"Was there a problem?"

Basra didn't want to alarm Hollis without solid proof, but the sudden burst of tears gave her away.

"I don't know where she is. The guy was very mean and she thought he was going to kill her, and then she just disappeared."

"Disappeared? What man?"

"Ahsan. One of the guys from the island."

"Hold up, what island?"

"Isla de sa Ferradura. The steel guys," Basra said.

"I don't know what you are talking about. I had a party in Washington that I needed three girls for. Lucia said you wouldn't be available because you two were going on a vacation and would be back Wednesday."

"So the island trip wasn't your job?" "No, and it is against our policy to take private gigs or ones with other agencies. You signed an exclusive deal with Choice."

"I thought this was a Choice job."

"Did you receive any documentation or information on the gentleman?"

"No. Lucia gave me my ticket and I just followed her."

"So where is Lucia now?"

"I don't know. She was at the hacienda and then the next morning she was gone."

"Have you called the police?"

"No. I just got back this morning and I thought she might have left the island early. But she's not here and she hasn't been here. Should I call the police?"

"I can't get involved. I didn't have anything to do with your trip."

"What? But you know Lucia. How can you not be involved?"

"Lucia is an adult. She chose to go to this function. I don't have any information and so I can't be of help." Hollis's tone was callous, borderline cruel. She quickly got back to business. "Lawson will be here this Friday, are you available?"

"Yes, and I'll have to call you back."

Basra hung up and sat dumbfounded. "No one cares!" she screamed.

"No one cares about what?" said the hoarse voice behind her.

Basra turned and saw Lucia strolling through the living room toward the open terrace door. She leapt from the chair and hurled her body in Lucia's direction.

"Where in the hell have you been? I thought you were dead!" Basra beat Lucia in the chest.

"Oouch!" Lucia screamed. "My chest is burned."

"Where did you go! Why haven't you answered your phone? You heifer, I cried over you!"

"I left you a message, a note in your bag." Lucia walked over to Basra's bag and dug in the front pocket. She pulled out her makeup bag and gave her a small folded letter. Basra took it and read it silently.

"Why would you leave me a note in my makeup bag?"

"'Cause you open this bag every day. I knew you would see this. I had to get out of there. Ahsan was crazy. After we left each other, he kept saying he was going to suffocate me and watch me struggle. I paid one of the spa ladies to find me someone to take me back to Ibiza. I told Ahsan I was taking a shower and when he went up to the deck, I left and hid on the yacht until that morning."

Basra slapped Lucia on the shoulder. "I am so mad with you. I was going to call the police. I really thought he had killed you. And, this wasn't a Choice job!"

"I know. I never said it was."

"We aren't supposed to take private jobs," said Basra.

"Everyone does. It's our bodies. Hollis can't tell us what to do with our bodies."

"I called Hollis because I thought this was Choice!" Basra smacked Lucia's arm again. "I am so mad with you. We could have both been killed. Did you do a background check or anything?"

"It was one of Sloan's people."

"Then why didn't Sloan go?"

"That time of the month."

Basra gave Lucia one long stare. If looks were actions, she would have been punching Lucia square in the face.

"I've been calling you and calling you."

"I left my phone somewhere at the hacienda. I got a new one in Miami, but it has no numbers."

"Miami?"

"Oh yeah, when I got back, I ran into Petra at the airport. She was on her way to a party in Miami. I grabbed my bags and got on her flight."

"Unbelievable." Basra turned and walked to her room. Lucia followed, apologizing. Basra was now more sure than ever that she had to distance herself from Lucia, for she was too much of a wild card. "I want my money. Where do I get my money?"

"I have to call Sloan, she did the deal. I think she's starting up her own thing."

"Call her," said Basra.

"I need her number. I haven't put my old info into my phone yet."

"Get out of my room."

"Don't be mad. I left you a note."

"I am mad that I wasted energy on thinking something had happened to you. I am mad that after a man threatened to end your life, you hop off to another party like it was nothing. I'm mad that I was the only one who even cared. None of the men, the other girls, not even Hollis thought twice about your supposed murder. I am mad that this industry numbs your sensitivities. Now let me be mad!"

"Okaaay, be mad then." Lucia walked out of the door.

Basra pulled out her iPad, went through her bookmarks, and looked over the apartments she'd considered renting.

"I'm moving out!" she yelled through her closed door. Lucia didn't respond. Basra didn't know if she heard or if she even cared. Nevertheless, at this point, Basra no longer cared. Lucia was like a bad drug, and it was time to be weaned.

Chapter 7

Sloan upheld her end of the deal and delivered money to Lucia and Basra that Friday morning. Basra sent six of the eight thousand home to her family. This would be enough money to move her sister, brother, and mom into a small place in their hometown. The joy in her mom's voice traveled across the world and through her doors and Basra could literally feel the exuberance in her room. At that moment, the precarious situation she'd just experienced vanished. All that mattered was that she was able to save her family, and Basra beamed nearly out of her skin and bawled as her mom cried tears of joy.

"Your modeling must be going very well. I'm so proud of you," her mom commented.

The statement hit Basra's heart like a thud. She knew her family would be extremely upset if they knew how she was making a living. Respect and pride was the basis on which they lived. Her mom would rather live impoverished before taking money that compromised her family's integrity. But Basra knew she was doing the right thing. Once she was able to bring her family to the States she would put this secret past behind her.

"There's nothing I wouldn't do for you, Mommy," Basra replied with tears from a conflict of emotions. "I will do more when I can," she said, wrapping up her call.

After Basra disconnected from her mother, she cried for another hour. She was filled with emotional turmoil. She disliked the agency, but knew she could do so much good with the money she made, and she was moving out and, for the first time, had to live alone in New York. Basra buried her head within her pillow and thought about Derrick, Ahsan, and the men on the island. *They make enough money to save everyone in my village, probably my whole country.*

Basra clutched the pillow tight and screamed. "It's not fair!"

Like a fish out of water, she flipped and flopped across her bed until she had released most of her frustration. Afterward, she retreated to the kitchen to juice a combination of carrots, apple, and ginger to release the remaining irritation. As she stood in the kitchen and drank her healthy delight, she once again took pleasure in knowing that she was making a better life for her family. Instantly, that overwhelming feeling chased away any testiness she had about the world's unjust disbursement of wealth.

"I'm very blessed." She sighed.

Basra squinted her eyes tight as the juice went down. She had used too much ginger and it was stronger than she'd have liked. As she reached for a pinch of sugar to cut the taste, the buzzer rang.

"You have a package here at the desk," said the concierge.

"Okay, thanks," Basra responded.

She slipped on her sandals and walked down to get her mail. It was two dozen tulips courtesy of Lawson, with a card that read: "See ya tonight, darling."

"It's Friday already?" Basra said to herself while walking back to the elevator. While in the hunt for an apartment, she'd forgotten about her date with Lawson that evening. She rushed upstairs and gave him a call, but she had to leave a message.

"Hello, dear, what time are we meeting? What do you have planned?"

She glanced at herself in the mirror, peered at her eyebrows, and contemplated if she had enough time to go get them done. She quickly decided and rushed from her apartment to her spa for a manicure and pedicure. Two hours later, when she returned, she still hadn't heard from Lawson. Normally, he called three to four times when he reached town just to double and triple confirm their date. Basra's stomach began fluttering from anxiety. She felt as though this was a real date that he could possibly be standing her up. This was when she realized that she hadn't gotten gussied up for Lawson because of the money, but she truly wanted to look good for him.

"What am I doing?" she asked herself while flopping down on the living room sofa. Just then her phone rang, and she nearly tripped over her feet to find her cell. She followed the ringing through the living room and the tune finally lead her to her bathroom.

"Hello."

"Hiya, my darling."

"Laaaawsoooon," she sang. "I thought you forgot about me."

"Never in a million years," he said. "I'm on my way to pick you up."

"I can meet you," she quickly replied.

"You still think I might be a stalker, huh?"

"Of course not."

He laughed and gave her the address of a gallery. "I've been in meetings all day, and I'm in the mood for a good laugh. We're going to one of those contemporary exhibitions with overpriced pieces of crap and people who take themselves way too serious."

"That sounds interesting. I will meet you there in an hour."

When they hung up, Basra caught herself smiling but then forced the grin away. "This is business," she said. But she couldn't deny the fact that she enjoyed his company. It no longer felt like work when they went out. She and Lawson had many common likes. He was kind and made her laugh. She didn't want to feel guilty about enjoying his company, but in that same idea, she knew he still looked at her as an escort, and it was this thought that erased her smile. Basra got dressed, and went to work.

Basra arrived at the Midtown space within the hour and walked in. She stood at the door and read the mission of the Fountain Gallery. While reading, Lawson crept up beside her.

"Do you know about his place?" she asked.

"I know there's some crazy looking art in here. I'm just a plain ol' still life kinda guy."

"Well, this gallery supports artists with mental illness. This is beautiful. No one cares about people with mental disease and I'm just . . ." Basra stopped talking and looked around at the art. Her eyes began to well. Basra thought about her baby brother back home, who suffered from autism. It wasn't something she spoke often about, although he was always on her mind. There wasn't much medical treatment for autism in her town and so creative therapy was a way the elders helped those with mental deficiencies. She vividly imagined her brother back home painting and making art.

"He would love to do this," she spoke.

"He who?" said Lawson.

"Just thinking out loud. Let's mingle."

Lawson and Basra walked through the space, admiring the avant-garde pieces that adorned the walls. He didn't know anyone, but Lawson was never a stranger; he talked to almost everyone there. While Basra was near the back admiring a huge green dot framed on a canvas, she happened to take a whiff of one of her favorite scents, Eternity by Calvin Klein. When she turned to see who was tingling her nose, she recognized another face. They caught a glance of each other at the same time and both smiled. He approached quickly.

"You're the girl," he said.

"And you're the boy," she responded.

"Yes, I'm the boy. You've been thinking about me a lot I see."

Basra giggled nervously. The instant attraction that she'd felt when they first met on the Upper West Side was stronger this time.

"Don't tell me; your name is Bas . . . Basor, Bastal . . ."

"Basra," she told him.

"I said not to tell me."

"I couldn't continue to stand here and let you butcher my name. I'm sorry, I don't remember yours."

"I'm Grayson."

Basra extended her hand. "Nice to meet you again," she said.

Grayson wasted no time in showing his interest. "I want to take you out sometime. Coffee, dessert, whatever."

"Uhhm. That would be . . . uhmm . . ." Basra contemplated his offer. But as she peered through his old-school Buddy Holly frames, she couldn't help but to say, "Yes, okay, we can go out."

However, just as the words were leaving her lips, Lawson appeared around the corner.

"Grayson, my man. I see you've met the lovely Basra," he said.

Basra suddenly tensed up. *Did they just meet or do they know each other?* she wondered. More importantly, did Grayson know about the relationship between her and Lawson?

"So you two know each other?" said Grayson.

"Yes, I'm one lucky man," said Lawson as he cupped his hand within hers. Basra left her fingers straight and didn't grasp on to his hand. She was hoping Grayson would catch this as a sign that they weren't a couple.

Grayson noticed her taut body language and nervous eye flutters. "Lucky indeed. I guess my luck ain't so great," he said.

"Gotta pay to play," Lawson responded.

Basra flicked her head in Lawson's direction. "I'm ready to go."

"Of course, dear. Grayson, it was a pleasure meeting you. I have your card. I will come check out your work."

"I'll come check it out too. Next week, as a matter of fact," said Basra.

"Great. I'll be at the gallery every day."

Basra and Lawson walked away. Basra desperately wanted to glance over her shoulder to see if Grayson was watching, but thought it to be rude, so she just followed Lawson out the door. Once they got in the cab, Basra's tone changed.

"You gotta pay to play!" she yelled. "Must you announce that I'm your escort to everyone? Whom else did you tell?" she asked.

"I didn't tell anyone. I don't want people to know that. I want them to think that I'm cool enough to be with someone like you."

"Huh? But you said 'you gotta pay.'"

"I meant that it takes money to date high-end women. Look at you. You're exquisite. You have expensive taste. He's a struggling artist. You would never date a man like him."

"You keep using the word 'date' like that's what we're doing."

"When we are out together that's how I see it."

"But you pay. It's different," Basra commented.

"You know I'm a wealthy man. When I go out with women, I pay one way or another. At least with you, I don't have to worry about you asking me to pay your tuition, or buy you diamonds—"

Basra interrupted, "Women ask you to buy them diamonds while you're on a date?"

"Women have asked me to buy them cars on a first date. It's easier this way, that's all. And on top of it all, I like you." Lawson kissed Basra's forehead and leaned back in the seat. "That was some weird artwork," he said.

"Don't say that. It was expressive, not weird."

"Oh, darling, I do love your outlook on life."

The cab whizzed through traffic and was on the Upper East Side in no time. "You didn't even ask if I wanted to come over," Basra said.

Lawson ignored her and stepped out. Basra followed and walked inside the lobby of The Pavilion. Inside his place, she and Lawson drank wine and watched *9 to 5,* which happened to be on one of his hundreds of channels. They laughed and drank and the more wine that flowed the sillier the conversation became. This night, it wasn't Lawson making moves, but Basra was strongly coming on to him. She was tipsy but very aware of her actions. Part of her wanted Lawson to see her as a woman, not an escort, and for a second she'd convinced herself that he would. She leaned in and kissed him as the credits rolled and Dolly Parton sang the theme. It didn't matter that Lawson was humming the tune in between the locked lips. Basra wasn't at all distracted. He didn't question her behavior, but quickly conceded and led her to the bedroom. Basra quickly stripped and Lawson followed. She glanced as his pale physique covered in light auburn freckles. It wasn't drawing her in, but oddly enough it didn't repulse her either, as she once thought it would upon their first meeting. Basra had only slept with a few men, all of African descent. She couldn't help but to continue looking at his skin as he softly caressed hers.

"It's like cocoa," he said.

Lawson kissed her shoulder, arms, and hand. Then he quickly lifted his body and leapt from the bed. As she was about to ask his whereabouts, he called from the bathroom.

"Gotta wrap up the dragon," he called out.

Basra laughed hysterically. When he returned she was still giggling. Lawson didn't bother to ask why. He plopped back in bed and loved on his African beauty. Basra tried to get into the act, but her mind kept asking her questions. *Why are you doing this? How is this going to change things? Is this a mistake?* She was so boggled with questions that she couldn't enjoy the moment. After it was over, she still held no answers. In fact, her brain spilled out more uncertainties. Basra tightly closed her eyes and tried to stop the outpouring of doubts.

"Boy, that was some good ol' loving right there," he said, kissing her shoulder once more.

Basra turned and smiled at him. "I enjoy you, Lawson," she replied.

"I enjoy you too, darling," he said with a grin. "I sure am going to miss you."

Instantly, all thoughts honed in on his statement. "Where are you going?" she asked, lifting from the pillow.

"I'm finally hitching my wagon to a trailer."

"You're what?" she asked.

"I'm getting married," he said.

"But, you . . . Why didn't you say you had a girlfriend?"

"We never get too personal, and you never asked."

"I just assumed."

"She's an old love. Known her for years. I didn't think I'd ever try marriage again, but this old body is going to need someone to take care of it one day. And she cooks up a fancy pot roast."

Basra's face wrinkled with confusion. "But we just . . ."

"And it was lovely. I couldn't part from you with a better gift."

"Gift?"

"And I thank you. I still may call you when I come to the city, but I don't want to be too tempted, especially now that I've tasted the forbidden." Lawson pretended to take a bite from Basra's arm. He laughed but she still held a muddled look. As though she were his jilted lover, she insisted on knowing about the other woman.

"Is she Australian, American? Where did you meet her?"

"She's American, but our families are in the same business."

"So she's rich too?"

Lawson didn't respond; instead he gave an inquisitive stare.

"Now you sound like a jealous lover."

"I'm not jealous, just curious. You're marrying this woman and I don't know anything about her. I feel like you kept her from me on purpose."

Lawson sat up and smirked. "Well, there's not much to tell you. She's from Texas, born and raised. Was a Dallas Cowboys cheerleader in the '80s, and she's just as sweet as cherry cobbler. She doesn't work in the family business but she has dance studios all over the state. She has two kids, grown of course, and we met about fifteen years ago, right after my divorce. She puts you in the mind of a Jayne Mansfield."

"Who?"

"American actress. Blond bombshell."

"I don't know her."

"Well nevermind," replied Lawson

How old is your fiancee?"

"She's fifty."

"How old are you?"

"Fifty-eight," he answered.

Basra compiled all of the information and was finally satisfied. She asked no more questions and simply said, "Good luck."

Basra rose from his bed, grabbed her clothing, and went into his bathroom. She quickly washed off, placed her clothing back on, and prepared to leave.

"I don't want you to leave. Stay until morning."

"Nah, I need to get home."

"Well, at least let me call you a car."

Basra smiled, walked back to the bed, and kissed Lawson's forehead. She began walking from the bedroom, but turned to ask one more question.

"Do you like the name Dove?"

"Dove? It sounds a tad bit cryptic."

Basra smirked, gave a flirtatious wink, and strutted away.

Chapter 8

Basra spent the next two weeks focusing on her search for a new apartment. She finally settled on a small one bedroom on the seventeenth floor of The Brooklyner. She was skeptical about leaving Manhattan but she figured this would provide a more low-key lifestyle and she could use the break in rent. It was still luxurious with twenty-four-hour concierge, a fitness center, and a private balcony. Most importantly, it was hers. As she settled in, she wondered why she hadn't done this earlier. The first two nights were a little lonely without Lucia popping in and out of her room, but by the third night, Basra was thoroughly enjoying the silence. She'd become so used to the constant noise of the city, she'd forgotten that quietness could bring clarity. She hadn't spoken to Hollis or Lucia since the move and with the exception of her agent and her family, Basra's phone hadn't rung. She was enjoying her time away from it all; however, into the third week, she realized that she had to get a plan of action together because the money she'd saved was quickly dwindling. The sexual encounter with Lawson calloused a section of Basra's heart, mostly the moral part. She was rethinking her opinion about the exchange of money for sex. Basra had developed feelings for Lawson, more than she'd expected. And since they weren't having regular sex, the relationship held more of an emotional value. They talked, laughed, and found ways to enjoy each other. If she'd just had sex with him, she would have been doing exactly what was expected, nothing more. Perhaps, trying to be "the date" was the wrong idea. Basra thought she'd feel cheap the morning after sex with Lawson, but she didn't. She felt empowered, like a woman pulling strings on puppets that were silly and insecure.

The mind games were mounting and Basra was more than happy to let them take over. She pulled out her cell and called Hollis.

However, before she could finish dialing, Lucia was calling on the other line. She'd thrown the idea into the universe and just that quick, it was acknowledging. Basra clicked over.

"I've given you time, are you still mad at me?" was Lucia's first comment.

"I'm not mad at you. I just needed a break from everything. But I'm actually ready to go back to work."

"Good. You have a package here."

"What kind of package?"

"I don't know. It's FedEx and I can't make out the name. What do you want me to do with it?"

"I can meet you in the city. Let's have lunch at the Eatery."

"Oooh, I haven't been there in a while. I love their Mac and Jack," said Lucia.

"Good, but give me an hour. I'm still figuring out the trains."

"Take a cab," Lucia said.

"Too expensive. I live in Brooklyn now."

"Oh God, why?"

"I like it. See you in an hour."

Basra got dressed and arrived quicker than she'd expected and had soup while she waited for Lucia, who walked in carrying a big brown box with a white bow.

"Here's my peace offering," were her first words before extending a hug.

Basra took the box and sat down.

"Open it," Lucia said. Basra pulled out a beautiful Louis Vuitton handbag. "It's the Sofia Coppola collection," Lucia said with excitement. "I know you don't really care about designer pieces but this is classic and very understated."

Basra held the bag up and grazed her hand against the soft leather. "It's very nice."

"And no one will even know it's LV unless they get really close and see the logo right here," Lucia stated, pointing to the tiny signature engraved near the handles.

"Thank you. I needed a chocolate purse."

The two women ate lunch and chatted about Lucia's drama over the last few weeks. Her life was anything but dull and she seemed to love every bit of the chaos.

"Sloan's agency is picking up, she's been giving me regular work, and her guys pay just as much as Choice."

"Sloan sent you on a date with a man who was going to kill you. Did you forget that?"

"She's doing better at the background checks now. Besides, he didn't kill me and that could have happened at Choice."

"Are you not at Choice anymore?"

"When she calls. But Hollis got in some new girls and I think it's time for me to change up."

"I'm going to stick with Hollis for now."

"That's too bad, I had some easy money for you tomorrow night. It wasn't a lot, just $1,500, but he doesn't want sex, only dinner."

"Who is it?"

"Some boring guy from New Jersey."

"Okay, I'm in, what time?" said Basra with a slight sparkle in her eye. "I need to get at least ten thousand in my savings."

"You can make that in two weeks, maybe less. Oh, here before I forget," said Lucia, handing Basra the FedEx envelope from her purse. Basra took it, tried to read the scribble, and then opened it. She pulled out a stack of American Express Travelers Cheques along with a note.

My lovely Dove,

I truly enjoyed your company, and I appreciate your integrity.

Always, Derrick

Lucia grabbed the stack of Cheques and flipped through them.

"Damn, girl, there's twenty-five of these. That's $2,500." Basra snatched her money back. "Somebody obviously forgot about her no-sex policy."

"I didn't have sex with him," Basra expressed.

"You don't have to lie to me."

"I'm not lying. I didn't have sex with him. However, I'm considering sex if the situation is right."

"I see you're finally understanding how this game works."

"Just finish your lunch," griped Basra.

After lunch, Basra called Hollis. The talk was brief but she promised to keep Basra in mind when booking new clients. With a pocket filled with money, Basra hopped over to a few shops near Riverside, and while in that neck of the woods, she made her way over to the gallery to pay Grayson a visit. The small studio space had every inch of its white walls covered in art. Basra didn't see anyone when she first walked in and so she hung out near the front while checking out the work. Within minutes, a young woman, borrowing her look straight out of Woodstock, came from the back and asked if she needed help.

"I'm looking for an artist named Grayson."

"Grayson!" the tall, lanky hippie called out.

"You rang?" he said, making his way from the back.

Basra stood at the front, waving and smiling like a little girl. Grayson rushed over to her.

"I don't believe it."

"I told you I was going to stop by," said Basra.

"That was weeks ago."

"I've been busy moving."

"Give me a hug," he said as though they were old acquaintances.

"I like your space. Show me around."

"This is Guppie, this is Basra," said Grayson.

"You remembered this time," Basra commented with a big grin. "Guppie, nice to meet you." Guppie was not as pleasant, only giving a slight nod and walking out.

"Is that your girlfriend?"

"No, she doesn't shave her legs."

"I don't always shave my legs," Basra added.

"Yeah, right," Grayson said, taking his hand and rubbing it down the front of her shin.

Basra pulled her leg away but only after he'd caressed for a few seconds.

"Stop being fresh," she said. "Show me around."

Grayson placed his hands on Basra's shoulders and physically turned her body around. "This is it. One giant box."

"Show me your paintings."

"Later. We have to go."

"Go where?" she asked.

"Out. Hold on." Grayson rushed to the back and one minute later returned with a satchel draped across his body.

"Where are we going?" Basra asked again.

Without answering, Grayson grabbed her hand and led her from the gallery.

"You can't kidnap me like this," Basra said as she was being whisked on to the street.

The two of them walked down Riverside Drive to the shop that Basra intended on visiting before she went to the gallery.

"This is the only store I want to go in, I promise. If I don't see what I'm looking for in here, then we can go wherever you like."

Grayson happily agreed and waited while Basra tried on three dresses. She settled on one, paid for it, and they left only spending a total of thirty-five minutes in the store.

"I like the way you shop. My sister used to have me in the mall all day."

"I really don't like to shop that much. But when I do get something new, I go get exactly what I want and then I'm done."

"I think I'm in love," Grayson said jokingly.

Grayson held out his hand and Basra quickly latched on like a girlfriend of many years. It wasn't until they'd walked a few blocks until she even realized.

"Why are we holding hands?"

"Why not?" Grayson asked, but then suddenly released his grip. "What's the deal with you and the rich guy?"

"His name is Lawson, and why do you assume he's rich?"

"I know one of the owners at the Fountain and right after the visit he made a generous donation."

"Oh. Well, I can assure you, I have nothing going on with Lawson."

"He seemed very comfortable with you."

"He's just that way. We're friends, business acquaintances really."

"And what do you do again?"

"I model."

"Of course you do."

Basra gave him a peculiar look. She wasn't sure if he meant that sarcastically and she felt the need to reiterate and defend.

"No, really I'm a model. I actually book work in magazines, and get paid for it."

"Of course you do."

"Why are you saying that in that way?" Basra asked.

"What way? I'm saying of course because you are almost six feet and absolutely gorgeous. What else would you do?"

"I could be a doctor or an attorney."

"You could, but the natural choice would be for you to model. You look glamorous, that's all I'm saying."

Basra tightly puckered her lips and squinted her eyes just before extending her hand again. Grayson grabbed a hold of hers and they continued down the street. They took in a movie and then made plans to meet later for dinner. Basra beamed all the way back to Brooklyn. It was so refreshing to spend time with a man in whom she could have a genuine interest. She felt all girly inside and this gave her an extra pep in her runway strut.

That evening, the process of dressing took an extra hour because Basra tried on at least four different outfits. She settled on a short and flirty champagne-colored knit dress. She paired it with brown wedges and her new Louis Vuitton purse. Grayson lived in a loft in the East Village but offered to come to Brooklyn and meet her for dinner. They decided on The Pearl

Room. Over dinner, the energy between Basra and Grayson sparked to greater heights.

"I feel like we've been going out for months," Basra said. "I know I'm not supposed to say things like that on a first date, but it's weird."

"There's definitely a connection. Maybe we knew each other in another lifetime. What's your sign?"

"I don't follow astrology but I'm a Virgo. September twenty-fourth."

"I'm a Capricorn, January tenth."

"How old are you?" she asked.

"I'm thirty," he responded. "And you?"

"Twenty-three."

"A baby." Grayson laughed.

"I'm grown," Basra playfully bantered.

They giggled and joked over their appetizer and began making plans for later that week. The butterflies in Basra's stomach were doing somersaults. She couldn't contain her incessant chuckles.

"I know you think I'm totally silly, but I promise I don't normally laugh this much."

"It's cool, I think you're adorable."

As soon as they finished the appetizer of fried calamari, Basra's phone rang. She let the first set of rings go to voice mail, but when it rang a second time, she grabbed it from her purse, looked at the number, and then excused herself. Basra stepped into the restroom and spoke.

"Hi, Hollis, what's up?"

"I need you tonight. Where are you?"

"I'm at dinner with a friend."

"Well, wrap your plate up and take down this address. His name is Adam Sizemore."

"But I can't go right now, can't you—"

"You called me today and said, 'please consider me for new jobs.' You said you were willing and available."

"I didn't say tonight," Basra specified.

"You're not sick and this guy specifically wants a woman of color. If you're not dependable, then I need to know that right now."

"I am. I will be there in an hour. Thanks." Basra clicked off. "Shit!" she yelled. She paused and looked in the mirror. "God, I really don't want to do this. I like hiiiiiiim," she whined.

Basra walked out and delivered the bad news.

"I have an emergency," she moped.

"Is there something I can do?"

"No, but I have to go."

Grayson began chuckling. "You have to go pick up your friend who was in an accident?" he asked in between the laughs.

"This is serious. I have to go." Basra placed her purse on her shoulder.

"I'm sorry. Seriously, what do you need me to do?"

"Ask me out again."

"Will you go out with me again, Friday night?"

"I was hoping you'd say tomorrow."

"I wanted to, but I wasn't sure if you'd be okay with that. Are you sure everything is all right?"

"I'm fine. I just have to go take care of something. I'd love to see you tomorrow. Call me."

The waitress came to the table with two plates. Basra looked at her food and frowned.

"Can you wrap up her plate?" Grayson asked. "You have to eat," he said to Basra.

She sighed but then sat back and waited for the server to return.

"I'm sorry. I promised I'd help a friend prep for his photo shoot," Basra commented while rummaging through her purse. She couldn't face him and it was killing her that she couldn't be truthful.

"I can come help."

"No," she replied quickly.

"Oh, I see."

"See what?" she asked.

"This photographer is someone who'd rather you not show up with male company. Ex-boyfriend perhaps."

"No. He's just funny about people in his space. I'm so sorry."

"It's cool."

The server returned with her to-go plate. Basra kissed Grayson on the cheek. "Are you going to stay here and eat?" she asked.

"I sure am. Who knows, I might find me another date. Lonely, cute guy in a nice restaurant, all by himself, eating all alone . . ."

"Stop making me feel bad."

"I'm joking. Call me tonight when you get in."

"I will."

Basra hailed a cab and scarfed down her food on the way to Brooklyn. She needed to stop by the house and grab a few overnight essentials. She was hoping she wouldn't have to spend the evening with this Adam person, but she wanted to be prepared. With a slight scowl stretched across her face, she walked back through her lobby to grab another cab. Meeting someone new normally unnerved her, but she was so annoyed that Hollis had ruined her evening, her nervousness had been replaced by irritation. She gave the cabbie the Upper East Side address, and twenty minutes later, Basra was walking through another lobby with an even bigger grimace.

"Is there a restroom down here?" she asked the concierge.

"Are you here to see one of our residents?"

"Yes, I'm going to 1004. My name is . . . Dove," she answered.

The concierge picked up the phone to call.

"Is there a restroom down here?" Basra repeated with frustration.

He pointed by the elevators, and she turned to walk.

"Could you wait one minute?" said the concierge, halting her movement. Basra was angered by his rude temperament. She rolled her eyes, turned back, and waited until he'd confirmed her visit.

"He's expecting a Basra—"

"That's me."

The concierge asked for identification and finally released her to pass through. By the time Basra had made it to the restroom, her anger had boiled to rage. She had to pace the black-and-white tile floors to calm down. She called Hollis, who surprisingly answered.

"I'm here. Who is this guy again?"

"His name is Adam. He's a financial bigwig. Does business here but lives out west. He was referred by one of my oldest."

"Fine, how much am I making? I need five grand."

"Well, well. Someone has gotten quite demanding."

"I know Lucia gets that a night, and I'm more exotic than she is. That's what I really need to make."

"You got it," Hollis said.

Basra paused, surprised at how easy that was. *I should have asked for more,* she thought. Hollis had a strict policy and the girls weren't allowed to discuss money with the clients. They weren't even allowed to ask how much the agency retained from each date. But Basra had decided that if she was going to be used, she would get as much out of it as possible. The business was numbing her, and she could feel it. But she no longer cared. She wanted her money and she wanted to get back to Grayson, and at the time, that was all that mattered.

The door was partially cracked and so Basra walked into the one-bedroom, simply decorated apartment. It looked like a picture in a catalogue complete with fake fruit on the coffee table. Adam came from the bedroom wearing jeans and a T-shirt. He was in his late forties and slightly resembled Brett Favre, without the handsome ruggedness. His eyes were small and shifty and as Basra made eye contact, her nervousness set in.

"I'm Dove," she said, extending her hand.

"Adam. Have a seat."

She sat in the chair farthest away from the bedroom door, and gazed out of the window.

"Where are you from?" he asked.

"Somalia."

"I've had some business dealings in several parts of Africa. Never been to Somalia, though. How long have you been here?"

"About a year and a half." Basra appreciated him trying to make small talk, but she didn't want to chat. She wanted to know what he was expecting, so that she could deliver and then leave. It'd have been great if he only wanted company, but she assumed that wasn't the case since they met at his place and he wasn't dressed for a night out.

"So, how long have you worked with the agency?"

"Six months. I was introduced through my roommate, well, my ex-roommate."

"You in school?"

"I was, now I'm just saving money. I will go back in the fall."

"Would you like a drink?" Adam asked.

"Wine would be nice, red."

Adam poured her a glass of merlot and flipped on the television. Basra continued to sit and sip her wine, and as the minutes passed, the awkwardness grew. Finally, Adam made his move.

"Why don't we go into the bedroom?"

Finally, Basra thought. But then, suddenly, she felt sick. Her breath shortened, and her stomach cramped. She forced herself to think pleasant thoughts: images of her meeting Grayson for the first time, the way he constantly pushed his black-framed glasses into place. Then she thought of her sister and how happy she'd be at FIT. The thoughts led her to a happy place, and before she realized it, she was lying in bed with Adam.

"I just need another glass of wine," she said, lifting up.

He jumped from the bed and returned with her glass and the bottle. Basra quickly drank, removed her shirt, and turned to him.

"I promise this won't be as weird once we get to know each other," he commented.

She smiled and replied, "I'm sure,"

Adam wrapped his hand around her neck and kissed her. The lip lock took her by surprise. She didn't think he'd want to do something as passionate and intimate. Her body stiffened.

"It's going to be okay," he whispered while laying her body down. Her body refused to cooperate, but Adam didn't care about her unwillingness. He vigorously mashed his hips into hers. He tossed her lean body back and forth and his actions grew in intensity. Basra played along. She was no longer able to produce happy thoughts. All of her concentration was spent on holding back the tears. Eventually, she gave in to the natural emotion and buried her head in the down pillow and let the cotton soak up the moisture on her face. The tears fell, but Adam had no idea. He was too busy asking a barrage of stupid questions.

"Am I the best? Is this what you want?" kept ringing in her ear but before she could reply, he spouted more questions. "You want to tease me. Can I punish you?" Basra snickered slightly and tried hard to remove all emotional connection from the act. When she concentrated on other places and events, her mind physically left the shell of her body, that was being strewn about the bed. Although, his questioning continued, she remained silent. It wasn't until he grabbed her shoulders and slapped her across the face did her mind fall back into room 1004. The stinging on her skin caused a brash reaction.

"What the hell is wrong with you!" she yelled, lifting her body.

Immediately Adam caved. He pulled away from her and whimpered. "I'm so sorry. I don't deserve you. Please punish me."

Basra sat up and looked at him as he knelt by the edge of the bed.

"Punish me," he reiterated.

With confusion, Basra nervously looked around the room.

"Would you like to slap me back?" he asked.

Basra nodded slowly, feeling as though she were being pranked.

Adam, still on his knees, turned his face to the side and waited. Basra slowly moved toward the edge of the bed and softly slapped Adam.

"Don't you ever hit me again," she said softly with caution.

He bowed his head and apologized. Basra sat on the bed and looked at him. She didn't know what to do. Was it over? Could she leave?

Finally, Adam spoke again. "May I please kiss you?" he asked.

"No," Basra said loudly. She had no idea she was playing along with his fantasy. She simply abhorred the thought of kissing him again.

"If I let you beat me, may I kiss you then?"

Again, Basra looked around the room. This was very weird and she had no idea how to respond. But she figured she'd go for it. If he wanted to be beaten, she was more than happy. She took the liberty to slap him again, this time with more momentum. He seemed to enjoy it. Basra grabbed her shirt from the bed and stood over him. She covered the front of her body with her shirt and placed her foot against his chest.

"Look at me," she demanded.

He looked up.

"You don't deserve to kiss me. I should just beat you for asking."

"I'm sorry. Please don't hurt me," he said.

Basra held back the chuckles, and got more into character.

"Who do you think I am? I'm not playing with you." She took her foot and pushed him onto the floor. She got on top of his chest and dug her somewhat pointy knees into his ribcage.

"I will cut off your air."

"Are you going to choke me?" he asked.

Basra's eyes lit up. She was about to release all of her frustration and was more than glad to choke the shit out of him. She wrapped her hands around his throat and clinched tight.

"Is this what you want? I will punish you until you stop breathing,"

He seemed to enjoy it. The tighter she gripped, the more he smiled. She took her right hand and lapped it over her left and began to wring his neck back and forth. He coughed violently and turned red. Basra jumped up.

"I'm sorry, I'm sorry. Are you okay?" she said with fear.

Adam regained his breath and rolled over into the fetal position. Basra stood back and hoped she hadn't taken the act too far. He got enough wind to speak.

"I'm fine."

He rolled back over and stared at her. He grinned like a devious cat burglar with stolen treasure. "You're going to be perfect."

Adam rose and sat on the bed. He pointed for Basra to join him.

"I like Dove," he said before leaning over for another kiss.

This time, she covered his mouth to prevent their lips from touching. He grinned, pushed her down, and politely asked for another round of intercourse. Basra desperately wanted to deny him, but she knew this was part of the deal. She obliged; however, this time she was just as rough as he. She called him vile names and took pleasure in slapping his face and digging her teeth into his skin as often as possible. Two hours later she was heading back to Brooklyn. Her emotions were rapidly jumping between degradation and exhilaration. As soon as she stepped in her place, she pulled out her phone to call Lucia. But she saw the missed call from Grayson. Though she wanted nothing more than to talk to him, she knew the first part of the conversation would be an absolute lie. He was going to ask about the fake photo shoot and her imaginary photographer friend. Everything about Grayson made her feel warm and mushy. Yet, as much as she liked him, she knew she needed to end things. She wasn't in a place to start a relationship and she knew it was where they were heading. Their connection was an undeniable force that grew with every minute they shared.

"I have to end it," she said aloud. "But first, I have to call Lucia."

Basra was able to reach Lucia and she couldn't wait to spill the beans about Adam.

Lucia laughed fiercely as Basra told her about the night. "Don't you love it!" she yelped. "I have three or four guys like that, and I work out all of my frustration on them."

"Isn't it weird though?" Basra asked.

"I don't judge. It's the way they cope. He probably has a high-stress job, something with a lot of power."

"He does something in finances."

"Well, if you see him again, get in some licks for me. I'm for real, beat his ass."

Basra burst into laughter.

"So are you still going to see the guy who comes into town once a week from Philly? He's one of Sloan's clients. She had another girl on him, but now she needs someone else. You want to do it?"

"All he wants is dinner?" she asked.

"Yep. Sloan said he's a little weird, one of those loners with no friends."

"How did he get his money?"

"Inheritance, I think," replied Lucia.

"Why don't you do it?" questioned Basra.

"I'm not giving up my Friday nights for fifteen hundred."

"It's not all night, right? It's just dinner."

"No, but I travel on the weekends. I think this would be perfect for you."

"Yeah, it could be. It's six grand a month. He comes every Friday?"

"So far. And Sloan pays out on the next day. She just needs your account information."

"Okay, cool. I'll do it this Friday and see how I feel."

"Great. She'll call you."

"All right. Gotta go. I'll call you later." They disconnected.

Basra stripped and poured her bathwater. She filled the tub with fragrant bubbles and stepped in. Before sitting down, she stepped out, tiptoed to her room, and retrieved the Quran from her bottom drawer. She rushed back into the water and let it cover her skin, which suddenly felt filthy. It had been a while since Basra had opened her Quran. When she wanted to reference any religious material, she'd look through her Bible, but for some reason this night she wanted to read the Quran. She flipped through the pages looking for a section her mother used to read to her and her sister. Upon finding "Al Nisa," she read softly.

"But those who disobey Allah and His Messenger and transgress His limits will be admitted to a fire, to abide therein: and they shall have a humiliating punishment. If any of your women are guilty of lewdness, take the evidence of four (reliable) witnesses from amongst you against them; and if they testify, confine them to houses until death do claim them, or Allah ordain for them some (other) way."

Basra closed the book, placed it to the side, closed her eyes, and exhaled. The remorse sank deep into her skin and she immediately took her loofah and began scrubbing her arms. She moved down her arms to her stomach, and legs. She rubbed so hard that her skin turned a soft red. Basra began to sob.

"I'm not a bad person," she whimpered. "I'm not a bad person." Basra closed her eyes and rested her head on the edge of the tub. All the years of discipline and studying vengefully returned. She remembered at age twelve getting lashed for coming home stating that she had a boyfriend. Virginity was strongly preached in her home, and growing up, she knew nothing else. She and her sister were encouraged not to look men in the eyes and definitely not be flirtatious in anyway. It wasn't until she was twenty that she realized how attractive her neighbor, Dalmar, was. They were close friends but she spent years not looking him directly in the eyes. Once she did, the attraction was instant and at twenty, he took her virginity. At the time, she was enamored with him and they spoke about becoming married. She couldn't imagine being with any other man, and she wasn't until she came to America. Even then, it felt odd. But Americans were so comfortable with their sexuality that it seemed wrong for holding it to such sacred standards. So when she began dating a guy introduced by her cousin, it was assumed they'd have a sexual relationship. They dated for a few months and then things fell apart. She didn't remember who stopped calling whom, but one day they just stopped communication. After that, she had a quick fling with a waiter who was a dead ringer for Lenny Kravitz. That ended after a month, because Basra decided to buckle down and concentrate on school, and he was too much of a party animal. There were no more men until Lawson. Somehow she'd managed to go from chaste to wanton in a couple of years. Basra pondered her libidinous journey and it literally upset her stomach. She stepped from the tub, dried off, and took her

Quran into the bedroom. She tossed on a long T-shirt and crawled into bed. She opened the book once again and continued to read.

"Allah accepts the repentance of those who do evil in ignorance and repent soon afterwards; to them will Allah turn in mercy; for Allah is full of knowledge and wisdom."

She slid underneath the covers and whispered to the Most High. "You know my heart. Do my intentions make up for my actions?" Basra was very still as she waited for an answer. Her tranquility gave way to sleepiness and Basra drifted off.

Chapter 9

Basra didn't get going until ten the next morning. However, when she woke she felt more peace than she did the night before. Her first clear thought was Grayson. She could see his quirky smile and eagerly wanted to talk with him. Therefore, she ignored every impulse that said to just leave him alone, and instead grabbed her cell. Lucky for her, he didn't answer, and she hung up as the voice mail connected. However, while grabbing some veggies to juice, she decided to call again and leave a message. This time she didn't have the chance, for he answered on the second ring.

"Did you get my message?" he asked immediately.

"No, I didn't check. What did you say?"

"It's not important now. How was last night?" he asked.

"It was okay. I did what I was supposed to do and then came home."

Fortunately, he moved from that conversation on to their pending date. "So tonight, before I start, do you have any last-minute forgotten-about plans that might surface?"

"If so I won't remember them until tonight," kidded Basra.

"Okay, well I'm working right now."

"Working? Where?"

"I prep food for this restaurant. My hours are six to eleven A.M."

"Okay, well, call me when you get off."

"I will," he replied.

Basra spent most of her day housekeeping and washing clothes. That afternoon, she remembered that she still had those Traveler's Cheques, and so she went to the bank to get some savings or investment options. Currently, she only had a checking, a basic savings, and the money market Hollis set up. But Basra wanted to be smart about her money and wanted to learn as much as possible about investing. She spent a few hours in the city and though the time quickly passed, Basra caught herself constantly checking the time and waiting for Grayson's call. She returned home, worked, and just when she was about to call him, his number popped onto her phone.

"It's about time," she answered.

"I was giving you time to get all of your plans out of the way, because I'm not letting you out of my sight tonight."

"Where are you?" she asked.

"On my way to Brooklyn."

"But I'm not ready," she said.

"I'll wait."

"Okay, see you soon."

Basra hung up, jumped in the shower, and quickly got dressed. She threw on a pair of skinny black jeans and a lacy peach blouse. As she was changing purses, the doorman buzzed. When Grayson walked in, she jumped into his arms and wrapped her legs around him. He twirled her around, walked with her to the living room, and sat her down on the sofa.

"I missed you too," he said, kissing her forehead.

"I feel like a goofy teenager around you."

Grayson reached inside of his pocket and pulled out a bag of Jelly Bellies. He plopped a handful in his mouth. "Want some?" he offered.

"What is that?"

"Jelly Bellies."

"What?"

"They're flavored jelly beans. Guppie's a vegan but she loves these and now I'm addicted to them."

Basra grabbed one and chewed on it slowly. "I don't like it." She frowned.

"Open your mouth."

Basra opened up and let him see the half-chewed jelly bean.

"You got a bad one." He sifted through the bag and pulled out two pink ones. "Try these," he said.

She tasted the candy and smiled. "These are good."

"Yeah, they have crazy flavors like popcorn and root beer. If you get one like that, then you have to chase it with strawberry, or watermelon."

Basra dug her hand back in the bag and pulled out a pink one with green dots. She inspected it, and then popped into her mouth. "This tastes like watermelon, much better."

"You ready?" Grayson asked.

"Where are we going? Can I wear jeans?"

"Of course, I wear jeans everywhere. I don't go if I can't wear jeans."

"Then I'm ready."

Basra and Grayson attended *Tricks the Devil Taught Me* at one of New York's many Off Broadway theaters. Afterward, they met his two friends who were in the play for dinner, which was at a casual bar downtown. Basra sat and had drinks with the artistic three. There was nothing glamorous or luxuriant about the evening and it was the most fun she'd had in New York. They joked, drank beer, and laughed until two in the morning. Basra was normally a cab girl, and Grayson was a train guy, but he agreed to take a cab back to Brooklyn that evening.

"You can save a lot more money if you stop taking cabs."

"I tried, but the trains take too long."

"They don't if you know what you're doing," he countered.

"How much money do you think I'd save?"

"Probably five hundred a month."

"Nah, not that much. I ride the train sometimes, just not at night."

"Let's say you take a cab twice a day for seven days and the average fare is twenty bucks. That's . . ."

"$280."

"Exactly. You added that quick."

"I'm really good with numbers."

"What's 1190 times 258?"

Basra closed her eyes for exactly ten seconds, opened them, and then replied, "307,020."

"Shit, I was being funny, but that's impressive."

"I thought about teaching math at one time."

"But you are majoring in psychology, to become a therapist, right?"

"That's right."

"Well, it's still impressive."

The cab pulled over and Grayson looked at the fare. "Twenty-eight dollars. See? That's an outfit," he said.

"In what store? I can't buy a scarf for that."

He shook his head, paid the driver, and they went in. Grayson immediately removed his shoes, stretched across the couch, and got comfortable.

Basra sat close and placed her legs across his lap. Grayson gently began to massage her feet. She wiggled her toes as he dug his thumb down the center of her arches. "That feels so good."

"I'm sure; you've been in five-inch heels all night," he replied.

"They were only four inch."

"Why do women wear heels anyway? Especially you? You don't need them to make you taller."

"I wear flats sometimes, but I love heels. They're sexy."

"Do you know when you're the sexiest?" Basra shook her head. "It's when you're like this, relaxed. I'm sure you're even more beautiful without makeup."

Basra gasped as though he said she'd look better without a head. "I know you're not saying I shouldn't wear makeup."

"No, do whatever you like. I'm just saying you don't need makeup, and that I'm sure you're beautiful without it."

Basra, suddenly embarrassed, lowered her head and began blushing. She was used to men calling her beautiful, but there was something about Grayson's tone and expression when he looked at her. He slowly lifted her chin, gave her kiss, and her body tingled from head to toe. Though there was a strong attraction, much of their chemistry was platonic. But the energy in the kiss was definitely one that would skyrocket their relationship to another level. It was all happening too fast, Basra thought. She pulled back.

"This is a lot," she said.

"Did you feel that?" he said.

"I did, and . . ." Basra said, rising from the couch.

"What?"

"It's going really fast. It's like we've known each other for years. I'm extremely comfortable around you. I'm not normally like that. I don't even have that many friends."

"I don't want to scare you off, but this is crazy for me too. I'll be honest; I was dating a couple of people and I feel like calling and telling them to lose my number."

"See that's what I mean, it's too much."

"I'm being real with you. I want to see where this could go."

Basra stopped pacing and looked into Grayson's eyes. He removed his glasses, and reached for her. She grabbed his hand and allowed him to pull her over to the couch. She sat in his lap and kissed him once more. The tingling intensified, and felt like small electric shocks hitting each pore. Basra had never felt anything like that before. The jolt made her leap from his lap.

"I'm sorry, this is just taking me by surprise. I wasn't expecting to like anyone like you."

"I get it. We can take our time. I will be here."

"For real? I'm not seeing anyone or anything but if I want to wait, is that cool?"

"It depends on how long, but yeah, it's cool."

Basra sighed. "Good."

"Will you sit down now?"

"I'm actually tired, I'm going to hop in the shower. You can stay, though."

"The thought of you dripping wet, naked in the next room is a bit much for me tonight. I think I'm going to go."

"Oh nooooo. I wanted you to stay."

"They'll be other nights. I have an early morning anyway," he said.

Basra lifted him from the seat and smothered him with a loving embrace. He stared into her eyes and spoke. "I was serious about what I said. I want us to see where this can go."

"Okay," she softly replied.

Grayson gave her a soft, quick kiss and left.

"Call me when you get home," she said as he closed the door.

He nodded and disappeared down the hallway.

Basra, lost in Grayson's lingering effect, twirled through her living room, danced into the bathroom, and prepped for bed. She still held a glowing smile on her face as she closed her eyes and fell asleep.

Friday afternoon, she received a call from Richard Thorne, Sloan's Philadelphia client. They spoke briefly before agreeing to meet in the city for dinner. Basra was beginning to feel the effect of having a love interest. She didn't want to talk to anyone but him and she surely didn't want to sit and entertain another man over dinner. But these few hours a week would mean she could stash away $6,000 a month, and that was money she couldn't pass up. Therefore, Basra made sure she arrived at the Central Park Boathouse a few minutes before Richard, just so she could study his actions as he got out of the car and walked in.

He pulled up in a cab, got out, and straightened his clothing and nervously looked around.

"Very insecure," she whispered just before he walked in. He was wearing a moss-colored button-up and khakis just like he said, and he was carrying two roses.

"How corny." She giggled just before walking to the front door to greet him.

"Hi, Richard," she said with a wide smile.

Richard lit up like a firecracker. "You are stunning. I mean absolutely astonishing."

"Thank you, Richard, you're quite a looker yourself," Basra replied with a wide faux but very realistic-looking smile. She was quickly becoming an award-winning actress.

"Oh, I do all right," he replied, nervously pulling on his collar.

Basra ordered a glass of wine as soon as they sat at the table. Richard continued to peruse the wine list.

"I've never been here before," Basra commented.

"Neither have I," he said as he continued to stare at the menu.

"Do you prefer red or white?"

"I like white, but it's not masculine for a man to drink white wine, so I mostly drink red."

"I've never heard of that. Red is better for the heart. Either way, it's unnecessary calories, so I monitor my intake."

"I can't imagine you having to worry about calories."

"I model and the camera adds weight. I don't diet or anything, but I watch what I eat."

"I'm going to have the Shiraz," Richard said to Basra.

She nodded and within a few minutes, quaint dinner conversation began.

"So, I hear you are from Somalia?"

"I am."

"I spent quite a bit of time in Ethiopia and while I was there visited Mogadishu."

"I have family in Mogadishu, but I'm from *Kismaayo*."

"In the Jubaland."

"That's right," Basra said with a smile.

"Beautiful place, Somalia."

"What were you doing there?" asked Basra.

"Work. I was part of an investment group that built a few hotels there."

"Oh," replied Basra just before ordering.

Richard continued to talk but he couldn't hold Basra's attention as she occasionally stole glances at the lake. Finally, amid his boring talk about business and hotels, she spoke.

"I miss the beach," she said.

"New York has a beach."

"Not like home. We lived so close to the water I used to go every other day. I miss it."

"Have you been to Coney Island?"

Basra shook her head.

"You should go." Richard paused, reached across the table, and placed his hand on top of hers. "Am I boring you?"

Basra looked at his well-groomed nails. They were nothing like Grayson's. His were different lengths, and his nail beds were slightly dirty with oil paint stains. Grayson's hands had character. Richard's were very boring.

"I guess that's my answer," he replied after she never responded to his question.

"I'm sorry, I was thinking. What did you say?" Basra asked.

"I asked if I was boring you."

"Of course not. I was just lost in thought. I zoned out. I'm sorry."

"What were you thinking about?" asked Richard.

"Grayson," Basra called out accidentally.

"Excuse me?" he asked.

Basra's unintended exclamation was brought on as she noticed the server three tables over was none other than Grayson. She quickly snapped her head away from his direction and stared out of the window.

"Are you all right?" Richard asked.

Basra nervously and rapidly shook her head up and down. She peered to her left but was careful to keep her head turned away from the center of the restaurant.

"I promise you are not boring me," she responded much later than Richard would have liked.

"If you don't want to be here, now would be a good time to say so."

Basra scooted her chair at an angle so as to keep her back toward the other tables and replied kindly. "Richard, I'm just a little nervous when I meet new people. I want to make a good impression, that's all. Are you enjoying your fish? It looks delicious."

Basra just rambled off words as she continued to wonder how come Grayson had never mentioned working at that restaurant. "I'm sure everything on the menu is good. Are you enjoying your meal?"

Richard paused and slightly opened the left corner of his lips. With his teeth clinched together, he looked like he was showing off a cavity. Basra wasn't sure if it was a smile or a gas bubble.

"It's okay. I mean it's good," he mumbled. "I want you to have a good time."

Basra released a tiny exhale and scooted her chair around a little more.

"The bread is good, right?" she said, grabbing the last roll from the basket.

"Excuse me." Richard motioned for a server.

Basra's heart plummeted like an elevator with no cables. She knew what was about to happen. Her neck muscle tightened as she turned to see the male figure walking to their table.

"Yes, may help you?"

As she turned to face him, she respired heavily, causing a loud cough. The man was not Grayson. Thus, she caught her breath and tried and smiled.

"Can we get some more bread, or can you get our server?" asked Richard.

"Of course," he replied.

As she looked up to acknowledge him with a nod, she caught Grayson's view in her peripheral. She quickly turned, but this time the movement drew more attention and it was too late. She was spotted, and he wasted no time making his way to the table.

"How is everything for you two tonight?" he said upon approach.

"We'd like more bread, but other than that, we're good."

"And you, ma'am, are you good?" he asked.

Basra turned and smiled. "Grayson, this is Richard; Richard, Grayson."

The men acknowledged with small nods.

"So you work here?" she asked.

"Part, time, yeah."

"You never mentioned it."

"Yeah, and—"

"So how about that bread?" interrupted Richard.

"I'm not your server, but I will check on it for you." Grayson walked away.

"That was rude," Basra said.

"How? He's at work at a restaurant."

Basra didn't comment. Within a few seconds, their original server, Ginny, came out with hot rolls. Grayson didn't come back to the table until their meal was complete. But he made sure he kept Basra in his sight so that she wouldn't get away before he said his goodbyes.

"I hope you enjoyed everything," he said.

"It was good," Basra replied.

"Great," he said. "So, you two have a big night planned?"

Basra looked at Richard, who remained silent. Finally, she answered. "Not sure. But I'll hit you up tomorrow."

"Tomorrow, huh?" he said with a look that required no explanation. "Nice to meet you, Richard," he said and walked away.

Luckily Richard didn't ask any additional questions about Grayson and he didn't desire dessert. They left the restaurant ten minutes later.

"It's still early, you want to do something else?" he asked while waiting for a cab.

"What did you have in mind?" she asked, hoping he would say nothing.

He pondered a few minutes and replied, "Let's see if we can take in a play, it's still early."

"Great," Basra mumbled under her breath. She then plastered on her smile and dug deep for her finale performance.

She left Richard close to ten that night after going to see *The Road to Mecca*. Basra purposely left her phone in her purse the entire evening. She wasn't sure if Grayson would text, and she knew if he did, she couldn't resist responding. Richard didn't try anything at the end of the date. He only gave her a hug and asked if she'd be available next Friday.

Basra responded with "call me," and walked away. She was home before eleven, and at 11:14, a text from Grayson came through. Basra didn't text back, but opted to call.

"Hello, Ms. Sadiq," he answered.

"Don't be formal with me," she commented.

"How was your evening?"

"It was okay. Just so you know, I'm not dating Richard or anything like that."

"Hey, it's cool. We just met. I'm sure you have suitors of all types."

"You met me with Lawson and now Richard. I just don't want you to get the wrong idea."

"You're young, you should be dating. It's okay."

"But—"

"Basra, it's cool. I don't mind competition. Glad to know you made it home safe."

"Yeah, so we'll talk soon?"

"I'll call you this weekend."

They hung up, but Grayson didn't call that Saturday or Sunday. Basra gave in and called him on Sunday night, but he didn't answer. Either he was playing games, or she was the one in competition. Either way, she would pay him a visit the next day to get the truth.

Chapter 10

The next afternoon, Basra visited Grayson at his studio. She walked in and stood in the center of his place, but no one came from the back to greet her.

"Grayson, are you in here?" she called out.

"Hold up," he answered.

Basra took a seat on the bench near the front. She waited for close to a minute and then Grayson waltzed from the back. He gave Basra a warm embrace but she instantly felt the difference. There were hints of skepticism circling his aura.

"You're different," she responded. "Let's talk about it."

"Why do women always want to talk?"

"We don't always want to talk, but when there is something wrong, it's good to get it out."

"There's nothing wrong with me. What's up?"

"What are you doing today?"

"I'm working, I don't have the luxury of playing around all day."

"What are you talking about? I don't play around all day. Just the other day, you stopped everything without thought and hung out with me."

"Today I have to finish something for a client. Plus, I'm working on a show."

"Fine," Basra said with an attitude.

"I'll call you later," he said.

Basra stood still for a few seconds trying to figure out his energy. In her frustration, she turned around and walked out. Two steps away from the front door, she turned again and walked back inside the studio.

"Grayson," she said, walking toward his studio in the back. She managed to make her way to the back before he could come out. "I don't know exactly what's wrong with you, but you are not the same guy I was hanging out with last week. If you're mad because I was out with another man, then say it. I told you it was nothing. I have commitments already in action, and there are some things in my life that are going to take awhile to sort out. But I like you and I want to keep seeing you. If you don't feel the same way, then let me know." With her arms folded, she stood in the center of his room, anxiously tapping her foot.

"I see the type of guys you hang out with and I think I know what you're about."

"What—" she interrupted.

"Let me finish. I like you and I think we have something special, and I believed you when you said you weren't seeing anyone."

"I'm not," she expressed.

"But you're dating and having fun. I think we might be in two different places."

"You're the one who said we could take our time."

"But I don't want to waste my time playing games with you and I can't give you trips around the world, and expensive dinners. Not yet anyway."

"I don't need all that stuff."

Grayson doubted her answer.

"I know what you see, but my profession puts me around people with money and I can't help that. And I'm not going to lie and say I don't like nice things. I came from nothing! I mean nothing! I don't want to be broke, but I would never judge you for what you have. If I like you, I like you." Basra's tone softened as she took Grayson's hand. "And, I like you. I just don't want things between us to fall apart because we don't communicate."

Grayson kissed the top of Basra's hand, and replied. "Okay. I understand. I have a lot of work to do. I'll call you later." Grayson went back to his seat, grabbed a paintbrush, and went back to work.

Basra, totally irritated, snapped around and left. She got outside of his place, turned back, and released an indescribable sound of frustration.

"Uurrghuishooo! Uggh, I hate men," she screamed.

"Amen, sister," said a bitter passerby.

Basra positioned herself to the left of Grayson's studio and contemplated going back in, but she quickly realized there was no need. After her anger calmed, the tears began to form. She hurried down the street, desperate to avoid any contact with him. *It's not like he'd realize his mistake and come running after me.*

"This isn't a movie, Basra," she said to herself. "Life is not a movie."

Hollis's words were circling through her mind. "Friends don't last long in this business," she whispered, wiping the last few tears. Basra stopped and looked around to gather her bearings. She was close to her Joan of Arc statue and so she took a seat and had a quiet conversation with her heroine. Basra knew she was living a lie and so she couldn't be upset with Grayson's leeriness. He'd seen her out and very chummy with two men within a couple of weeks. She looked like a party-girl socialite, and as much as she could argue against that point, it was the life she was living. So the question became, did her heart or actions determine her character? This led her back to her thoughts from the other night. Did God judge by intentions or actions?

"Maybe I should just be honest with him," she murmured. Basra quickly recanted her statement, knowing he would never understand. "I have to let go and whatever happens, happens," she whispered. Twenty minutes passed while Basra was lost in thought. However, her trance was interrupted by a call. She looked down and saw Grayson's name. She started not to answer but knew those were the exact games she didn't want to play.

"Hi, Grayson."

"You got a second to talk?" he said.

"Yeah, but let me say I know that we don't really know each other and we're still figuring things out."

"Where are you?"

"I'm at the park down the street. You know where the Joan of Arc statue is? I'm there," she explained.

"I'll be there shortly."

Basra hung up, and pulled out her makeup case to freshen up a bit. While reapplying her lipstick, she spotted a smoothie shop across the street. Basra rushed over and ordered two smoothies, a strawberry mango for her and banana and peanut butter for Grayson. She recalled him sipping on that odd flavor the other day when they were hanging out. She was hoping this would be a peace offering to brighten his mood. As she was walking out, she spotted him walking down the street. She hurried back to the park and called his name. Grayson noticed her and sped up his walk. He approached with open arms. Basra could immediately see the difference even before they embraced.

"I'm sorry," Grayson expressed. "I had a bad morning. I was supposed to have an art show next weekend but my sponsor cancelled on me. I've got a good following, but he looked at my books and insisted that I needed to have more people buying to justify a show. But if I don't have a show, I can't get people interested in buying."

"Why don't you invite people to your space?" asked Basra.

"The location is good, but my space is too small and not commercial enough. If I'm asking for thousands of dollars, I have to look like I have money."

"But I thought Americans love the starving artist story. You guys do movies on that all of the time."

"In real life, it doesn't work like that. They want you to look like you're worth spending money on. Or you have to get someone like Donald Trump to discover you and say you're the best thing since sliced bread."

"Oh is that all; let me call him." Basra pulled out her phone and laughed.

Grayson gave a curious look. "Hey, for all I know, you may know him. I've seen the company you keep." They both giggled.

"Oh, my friend is back," she said, embracing Grayson again.

"And I have to admit I was a little jealous when I saw you with the stiff shirt guy. He doesn't seem like your type."

"Yeah, well, I'm working on a few things and I have to associate with people who aren't necessarily my type."

"I feel you. Well, do you. But, notice, I said do you, not do them."

Basra gave a nervous chuckle and looked away. Grayson finally took a sip of his smoothie. He gave Basra a peck on the cheek.

"Banana and peanut butter is the best," Grayson said.

"You're so weird."

"I have to go. What are you doing tonight?"

Basra shrugged her shoulders and made a quirky face.

"Want me to come over?"

"That would be cool."

Grayson smiled wide and walked away. Displaying a silly grin, Basra watched her crush walk out of sight. She continued to stand there, goofy expression and all, for another two minutes. Finally, she trotted away.

Basra wanted to help Grayson and she knew how to do it, but wasn't sure if that was the best idea. She placed a call to Lawson, who happened to be in town.

"Lawson, it's Basra."

"Hiya, darling," he answered. "Didn't think I'd be hearing from you anytime soon. I'm in town, why don't you meet me?"

"Perfect, I need to speak with you about something."

Basra met Lawson for lunch and told him her plan.

"So, basically, you need me to invest in this artist."

"Not just this artist but this really talented artist. Have your friends come to his show and when they buy some of his work, you can get your investment back."

Lawson wrinkled his brow. "I don't know."

"Why not? If you go out with me three times, you spend that amount and then some."

"Maybe, but that only involves me and you. This requires a bigger commitment. What if people don't like his stuff?"

"Then I'll pay you back. Not at one time, but I will pay you back. All I need is twenty thousand dollars. I will do the rest. But having a few of your billionaire buddies there would be nice."

"Billionaires don't grow on trees."

"In your backyard they do, and I'm sure some of your friends love art. All you have to do is endorse him."

Lawson reared back in his chair and took a look at Basra's expression.

"You like this fella. Why didn't you just say so?"

"I like him, but . . ."

"No, there's more to it. You're a lost ball in high weeds. I can see it in your eyes."

"You don't see anything," Basra said, glancing down at the table. "He's just very talented and I just want to help him."

"Where and when do you want to have the event?"

Basra looked up and her smile lit up the café. "This is going to be good. I can feel it."

Lawson patted her hand. "I hope this works out for you."

"Thank you. I have so much work to do. How do you want to do the money? We can open an account, so you can see what I'm spending money on."

"Let's talk about this at the condo."

"Huh?" Basra said with a confused look.

"If you're done eating, let's go over to the condo."

"For what?"

Lawson's answer wasn't audible, and it didn't have to be for Basra to get its meaning.

"Really, Lawson?"

"Hey, you just asked me for twenty thousand dollars and I just said yes."

"I don't believe this," she mumbled.

"That's quite a bit of money."

"It's an investment."

"A risky one."

"And what about your girlfriend, fiancée? I thought you were going to be faithful."

"I want to, and I will, but we aren't married yet."

Basra looked at Lawson's shifty eyes, and realized that this wasn't her friend. This wasn't even a man who respected her. He was a john, one worth billions, but still a john. She hated being put in this predicament, yet there were women who slept with men for pairs of designer shoes, and opportunities like this never came their way. Should she just be grateful? *Could Grayson fall in love with me and I make enough money to leave all of this behind?* she wondered. *Or am I a foolish woman with unrealistic ideas?*

"You know this is wrong, Lawson."

"Hey, I'm a lonely old man. I take what I can get."

Basra gave a vile expression and rose from the table. Lawson tossed down a few twenties and followed her out.

This time, Basra barely allowed Lawson to touch her. Her body remained still with her hands by her side. She didn't move from this position until he was done. There was no conversation, no eye contact, and not an ounce of passion. Lawson didn't care, and their relationship was quickly changing with each pump of his clammy little body. He rolled off her body, lay next to her, and stared at the ceiling.

"I know you think I'm a whore, but I am going to make something of myself," she said.

"Now why would you say something like that?" he said. "I don't think you're a whore. You're an opportunist, and a smart one at that."

Basra sat up and swung her legs over the edge of the bed. She glanced back at Lawson, who was now gently stroking her back. She didn't want him to touch her, but she allowed it anyway. Her goal was to get that money.

"At one time, Lawson, I actually thought we could be friends. I even had the crazy idea that you might even respect me. But right now all I want to do is improve my life and the lives of those I love, and if you can help me do that, so be it."

"Now that's what I'm talking about." Lawson hopped up with excitement. "That's the fire I know you have in you. You may not respect yourself but, honey, I respect you. Just 'cause I want to love on you a bit doesn't mean I think less of you. You're a beautiful woman I know I would never get if I didn't have money. See, I too am an opportunist. In this life, you have to use what you got to get what you need. And you can't worry about what it looks like or how people perceive you. There's only one judge and what you do is between you and Him."

"If I weren't so frustrated right now, I might would fall for that bullshit, Lawson, but I know what this is, and I'm willing to accept that."

"Why are you frustrated? Are you getting what you want out of life?"

"Sometimes."

"Are you working toward your goal?"

"Yes, but not in the way I thought I would, you know, morally."

"Well, you can change that anytime you like, but I promise you the process will take a whole lot longer, and if you're willing to wait, then go for it."

Basra looked at Lawson's naked body as he strolled over to his computer and checked his e-mail.

"I need to shower," she said, heading to the bathroom.

Basra drenched herself in the steaming hot water and rinsed off Lawson's scent. She dried off and dressed before walking back out. He was still naked and typing on the computer.

"So how do you want to do this? Maybe you can wire the money to my account because it will take awhile for a check to clear."

Lawson walked out of the room before she finished talking and while Basra was buckling her shoes, he returned with an envelope, which he tossed on the bed.

"There's twenty-five. I want twenty of it back, and five is yours for whatever."

"You walk around with that much money?"

"No, but I always have access to my money."

"Oh."

Basra picked up the envelope and placed it down in the bottom of her purse.

"Don't deposit that all at one time, it will look suspicious. You don't want to get audited."

"Okay, thanks." Basra lingered by the bedroom door, unsure of whether she was supposed to wait for him.

Lawson placed on his boxers and socks. "I need to stay here and do some work. Give me the details and I'll make sure some people are there to buy your boyfriend's work."

"He's not my boyfriend."

"For that kind of money, he sure oughta be."

Basra gave a small chuckle. She zoned out for a second thinking about the fact that she was carrying $25,000 in a five-thousand-dollar purse. This was more than what some people made in a year. Though she was around lots of wealth, it was still a very strange concept.

"The people with money have all the power," she whispered.

"From your mouth to God's ears," Lawson replied.

Basra wasn't sure what he meant by that, but it left her with a sour taste. She thanked him again and left to plan her first art show.

Chapter 11

Basra and Grayson spoke briefly that night, and it took everything in her power not to mention the money for the art show. She wanted to share the news, but had to be sure Lawson wasn't going to call that night with any other stupid demands. By Tuesday morning, her eagerness was out of control and Basra couldn't wait another moment to tell Grayson about the art party. She immediately called him on the phone and told him she was on the way to the studio. When she arrived he was knee-deep in oils. Basra rushed inside his studio and went straight to the back.

"I've got good news," she yelped, bubbling with excitement.

"Okay, hit me."

"I have a new sponsor for your party."

Grayson peeked from behind his canvas.

"It's me," she screamed.

He stopped painting and rose from his work.

"What do you mean?"

"Well it's not me, but I convinced Lawson, who is an art enthusiast, to invest in the event. I told him I was putting it together for an artist."

"And he agreed?"

"Yes, and I told him I would make sure he got his money back from painting sales."

Grayson, still a bit reluctant, sat back down and picked up his brush and began painting again.

"Aren't you excited?"

"It sounds nice but I don't want to get too excited before it really happens."

"What do you mean? It's going to happen. He's already committed."

"People say a lot but when it boils down to the money, they don't always hold up their end of the deal."

"How much do you think the entire thing will cost?" she asked.

"The venue is five thousand, I need another three in supplies, plus marketing materials could add another grand."

"Okay, so that's not even ten thousand."

"Yeah."

"Well I have fifteen committed for this event."

"I don't want to sound pessimistic, but when you get the money in hand, come back and then I'll be excited."

"Fine. I'll be back." Basra turned to leave.

"Okaaaay. . . ." said Grayson with some confusion.

Basra immediately walked out of his studio, went into the bathroom, and counted out $15,000. She placed it in the larger envelope and folded the other one hundred Ben Franklins and placed them down in her makeup pouch. She waltzed back into his studio and handed him the envelope.

"Now can you get excited?"

Grayson took the envelope filled with hundreds and ran his fingers across the top of the bills.

"What's this?"

"This is your art show money. It's going to happen."

Grayson, almost in shock, handed her the envelope and looked at Basra with hesitation. "Where did you get this money?"

"I told you. It's from Lawson."

"So he just gave you this money? That doesn't make sense."

"First of all, it's an investment, so he didn't just give it to me. We have to pay it back. Secondly, he's an art patron, and lastly, he's a billionaire, so this is nothing."

Grayson still didn't buy it. "So what did you do to get the money?"

"Huh?" she asked as her heartbeat thudded with anxiety.

"Men don't just give women fifteen grand just because they asked."

"It's pocket change to him. It would be like me asking you for fifteen dollars. We're old friends and I never ask him for anything so he knew how important this was to me."

"But—"

"No. Stop asking questions. I stuck my neck out because I really want you to have this show, and I thought it meant a lot to you. So just take the money and let's make it happen."

Grayson's face relaxed and a smile emerged. He walked over to Basra and squeezed tightly. He didn't release from the embrace for a minute.

"I can't believe you are doing this for me," he whispered.

"I have to. You are very talented, and if I have the means to help you, that's what I want to do."

With her body still within his clinch, he pulled back and stared her in the eyes.

"I still don't understand," he said.

"I believe in you, and this could really jump start your success."

"It could," he said, smiling.

"So, you better get to painting."

Grayson planted a passionate kiss on Basra that nearly brought her to tears. "Oooh, you can't go on kissing me like that."

Grayson planted tiny pecks all over her face, and she playfully tickled his side. They didn't notice Guppie standing at the door of the studio until she loudly cleared her throat. Basra pulled away but still remained close to Grayson.

"Hi, Guppie, good to see you."

"Yeah," she said nonchalantly. "Gray, did you finish the last piece for Dr. Logan?"

"I'm finishing it right now," he said.

"It didn't look like you were painting to me."

The tension thickened. Basra felt the need to cut in.

"We were celebrating the art show he's doing," she said.

"Is that art show paying some of the bills around here?"

"It will once he sells the pieces."

Guppie looked Basra up and down and diverted her attention to Grayson. "Let me know when you can deliver." She walked out.

"What's wrong with her?"

Grayson went back to his chair and picked up his paints. "She and I share the rent on this space and I haven't been selling lately. I'm not behind in the rent but I haven't been helping out on the bills."

"Okay, but she acts like you two used to date. I don't know a lot but I do know women."

"I used to date her sister."

"Ah ha, now we get to the truth. When did you two break up?"

"Awhile back, but we've dated off and on about six years."

"Six years! No wonder. She doesn't want to see you with anyone else. Why date someone that long and not marry them? I don't get that."

"We've talked about marriage, but I just can't do it. She is a wonderful girl, but she wants me to get another career. She comes from an affluent family and they don't want her to marry an artist. She wants me to work for her dad. I can't do that. This is who I am," he exclaimed.

"Oh."

"So I know if we get married, she's going to want to start a family and once I have kids, that's it. I can't let my family suffer, and then I will be trapped into working a nine-to-five."

"So you two aren't together at all now?"

"No. We talk and she says things will be different if we get back together, but I'm over it. I want to be with someone who gets me, and understands that if I don't do what I was put here to do, my life is useless."

"So there's nothing else that you'd rather do?"

"No. Not really. I've painted since I was sixteen."

"Are your parents artists?"

"No. My sister is a dentist, and my father is an architect. My mother works with him. My family doesn't get me either."

"Well, I'm still figuring out what it is that I want to be, but I respect you for sticking to your dreams. Especially when it's rough. So, this better be one hell of a show."

"It will be, I promise."

"I'm going to let you get back to work. Where would you like to have the show? I want to go ahead and hold the space."

"It was going to be at this great new space that rents to artists. It's a few blocks over from Times Square."

"Give me all the information and I will see if we can see do it there. When?"

Grayson handed her the information for the space. "I've done most of the pieces, so I can be ready in two weeks. I just need to get them framed."

"Okay, give me a price breakdown of everything. I'll call the place and set everything up. I'm so excited." Just before Basra crossed the exit, Grayson called out.

"No one has ever done something like this for me. I really appreciate it."

Basra winked and walked out. She was floating on air. She felt like "Basra, the Fairy Godmother."

She looked at the address and decided to visit the space. She met with the event's manager, Amelia, and walked through the details. Amelia was familiar with Grayson and his work, and was elated that the show was going to happen. She mentioned that for an additional $1,500 he could keep his work up the entire month as the premier artist. Basra agreed to pay the additional amount, signed the contract, and gave her the deposit. She called Grayson and gave him the details. By the size of the space, Grayson would need close to twenty-five pieces. His pieces varied in size and price, but the average amount was $4,000. In this show, Grayson was doing a series of mixed-media pieces depicting New York subway life. It was oils mixed with iron and wood. The theme was "City Life" with pictures depicting life and people in New York, Chicago, DC, and Miami, all done with a very abstract flair. Basra couldn't be more excited to have a project to undertake and doing it for Grayson made it three times as gratifying. She spent the next three days organizing the guest list, and creating marketing materials. She even planned a video shoot of Grayson in the studio. She and Amelia thought that would be a great addition to the evening. So when patrons walked into the space they could watch a video of Grayson at work, like a behind-the-scenes preview.

Basra didn't see Grayson at all for three days, as he spent his days and nights in the studio working. She, in turn, was busy researching art shows and art patrons. She wanted to have as much knowledge in her arsenal to help the show's success. She didn't take a break from her studies until she received a phone call from Richard. He was in town and wanted to move their Friday dinner to Thursday. Basra agreed to meet him. But this time they met in Brooklyn. Richard greeted her with a gift. Basra took the small box, opened it, and saw the David Yurman Crossover Cuff.

"It's so beautiful," said Basra as she lifted it from the box.

"I thought you might like it," he said. "It's not too dainty but classic."

"It is. But I can't take this. It's too much."

"I bought it for you. I can't take it back. Please, take it as a token of my friendship."

Basra loved David Yurman but didn't own any pieces and deep down really wanted to keep it, but felt it was the wrong thing to do.

"I can't," she said.

"You have to. I had it inscribed," he said.

Basra looked at the eighteen-karat gold bracelet and smiled. Richard showed her the inscription. Basra read it. "'Thoughts that come with doves' footsteps guide the world.' That's a beautiful saying. Did you write this?"

"No, it came from Friedrich Nietzsche. He's a German philosopher."

"I've never heard of him."

"Brilliant man. His philosophy centered on a basic question regarding the foundation of values and morality. My favorite quote of his is 'The true man wants two things: danger and play. For that reason he wants woman, as the most dangerous plaything.'"

Basra, so engrossed with the script of the inscription, missed the glazed-over look in Richard's eyes that gave way to hints of delusion.

"It's very, very nice."

"Look at how perfect that is. It's perfect just like you," he said.

Basra looked up at Richard, who smiled wide. She glanced into his eyes and an eerie feeling came over her. She quickly looked away.

"Let's eat," she said.

They perused the menu, ordered, and ate. Basra continued to ask about Nietzsche during the dinner and after mentioning her major in psychology the conversation picked up to a rapid speed. Richard had a doctorate, from Cornell University, in philosophy. Before Basra realized it, they'd spent three hours over dinner talking about the history of civilization and the basic fundamentals of existence. Richard's thoughts were fascinating and intriguing. Basra reeled off questions and he was more than thrilled to give his opinion. When Basra looked up it was midnight, but Richard didn't want the night to end. He asked Basra to come back to his hotel.

"I can't," she replied.

"Why not. We're having such a great time," he commented.

"I know but I have a lot of work to do. I'm planning an art show," she inadvertently mentioned.

"I would love to come," he said.

That was just the response she didn't want. "It's private. I will see if I can get you on the list though."

"Please do. I'm an avid collector."

"I will."

Basra smiled but knew she could not invite him to the show. There was no way she could explain that to Grayson, and who knew what he would say about their relationship.

"So, if you're ready to leave, maybe we can have lunch tomorrow before I go back."

"I don't know, my schedule is very busy."

"How many men do you see a week?" he asked candidly.

"Excuse me?"

"In work. How many men? Do you have several regulars you see weekly?"

"Actually, I don't."

"Ballpark figure," he pressed.

"Uhhm. I don't know. I go when I get calls. I might get three calls a month."

"Do you sleep with the others?"

"My business with other men is private. You wouldn't want me sharing our details."

Richard stared at her with a blank expression.

"You're my only regular. I'm new in this industry and I don't want a lot of clients. I'm only doing this to help my family."

"Your family back in Somalia?"

"Yes."

"So if you were to marry someone who could take care of you and your family, you would stop this business."

"Yes, but I wouldn't marry someone unless I loved them," she said.

"Love is such a broad term."

"That's conversation for another day, my dear Richard. I have to go."

"Of course, Dove," he said.

They rose and left the restaurant. He offered to escort her in the cab ride home, but Basra didn't want him knowing her address, and so she hailed her own cab, kissed his cheek, and left.

En route home, she checked her voice mail and heard a call from Hollis, who wanted to inform her of Adam's visit next week. He bragged to Hollis about how much he loved her company, and couldn't wait to see her again. Of course, this thrilled Hollis, for she loved satisfied customers. Basra called her the next morning to confirm his date, which was Friday afternoon. The day before the big art show. Basra knew that would be cutting it close but she couldn't disappoint Hollis. If she continued to see Richard for a few months and kept her regular visits with Adam, she could easily save $8,000 a month. She didn't want to take on any new clients and as long as she could keep this situation going, along with her occasional modeling gigs, her finances would continue to mount.

That evening Basra continued to think about her conversation with Richard and decided to look up information on Nietzsche. He was a very interesting character who was also diagnosed as mentally ill. However, he had a plethora of quotes that Basra began writing down in her journal. Interesting characters fascinated her, and she kept a log of them for study purposes. Getting a psychology degree required her to write many papers and she already had a long list of potential subjects. Nietzsche was going on the list.

Early Saturday morning, while Basra was still in bed, her buzzer rang. She thought it was a dream at first, but realized after the third ring that it was concierge. She crawled from the bed and stumbled into the front room to answer.

"I have a Grayson Charles here to see you."

"Send him up," she said.

Basra ran like lightening to the bathroom. She brushed her teeth and simultaneously washed the sleep from her eyes. As she was spitting into the sink, her doorbell rang. She rushed to the door and answered. Grayson greeted her with a big hug.

"I have missed you," she said.

"I've missed you."

Grayson stopped and stared at Basra. "You don't have any makeup on."

"It's seven o'clock in the morning. I don't sleep in makeup."

"No, but it's the first time I've seen you without it. You're fucking beautiful."

"Dropping f-bombs so early, how sexy is that." She giggled.

"I don't mean to offend but, baby, you're covering all of your beauty."

"Stop it, Gray. I like my makeup, end of conversation."

Grayson continued to stare as he spoke about the show. "The new pieces are at the framer's, and we shoot the video today, right?"

"Yes, at four. You ready?"

"I am. I'm going to wear just a plain black shirt; since my pieces have so much color I don't want to be too distracting."

"Good idea."

"I'm sorry, you are really beautiful," he said once again.

"You're embarrassing me, stop it. So, how much are the last pieces?"

Grayson and Basra continued to talk business until her stomach began to growl.

"You're hungry. Let's do breakfast."

"I was going to cook something here," she mentioned.

"Let's just grab something out. Throw on something."

"I haven't showered."

Grayson sniffed her neck and then close to her crotch. "You smell clean."

"You're nasty." She laughed, pushing him away.

Grayson moved close and kissed her. "And your breath is minty fresh. Let's go."

"Fine."

Basra threw on a T-shirt, jeans, and a baseball cap to calm her wooly hair that was normally all over her head until she applied mousse.

"What was stiff shirt's name again?" Grayson asked as they walked through the lobby.

"Who?"

"The guy from the Boathouse?"

"Oh, Richard."

"I could have sworn I saw him outside your building smoking a cigarette."

"He doesn't smoke and he lives in Philadelphia."

"Well, it was guy who looked just like him. Oh, we can eat at the café down the street. We can walk."

Basra lowered her shades as the morning sun beat on her skin. She looked to the right and left of the building as she exited just to be sure Grayson was mistaken, and they walked over a few blocks and into the Breakfast Nook. Over eggs and coffee they chatted about the show, and the excitement was seeping from every pore of Grayson's body. Basra was equally excited as she shared some of the invitees.

In the middle of her conversation, Grayson blurted, "I told Sophie about us."

"Sophie, your ex?"

"Yep."

"What did you say? What did she say?"

"I told her I was seeing someone special and that she didn't need to keep calling because I wasn't going to get back with her." Basra's eyes widened. "She said she wished me well."

"That was it?"

"Yep, but then Guppie called and told me that I had a month to get out of the space."

"Can she just put you out like that?"

"Yeah, her family owns the space; I'm not in a formal contract. It's cool because I want to go anyway."

"Well, I have a feeling that after this show, you will be able to afford your own space."

"So how do you feel about that?"

"About what?" Basra answered, completely clueless.

"About me telling her that I was seeing someone special," he said sincerely.

"I'm flattered, and I'm excited about us. I think we'd make an awesome couple."

"So, you're ready to call us a couple?" he asked.

"I hate titles but I don't want to be with anyone else, and I think about you all of the time, so yeah, I guess. But we've only known each other a few weeks. This is so fast. Are we crazy?"

"Who cares?" he said.

"Have you ever heard of Friedrich Nietzsche?"

"No. That's random."

"Well, he's this philosopher from Germany. And I was recently introduced to some of his works, and he has this quote: 'One ought to hold on to one's heart; for if one lets it go, one soon loses control of the head too.'"

"I believe that to be true. But what's wrong with losing control? What is love if it's controlled?"

"I just want to be careful."

Suddenly Basra began coughing uncontrollably. Her eyes watered and she could barely breathe.

"You okay?"

She pounded her chest and tried catch her breath. Her eyes flicked back and forth from the door to the table. Grayson came from around his side of the booth and sat next to her. His attention was also drawn to the front door and the man approaching them.

"Richard! What are you doing here?" Basra said as her voice pitch rose from alto to soprano.

"Good seeing you again."

"What's up, man?" said Grayson.

"The waiter, yes. How convenient. You two have a good breakfast."

Richard sat down at the bar right in front of them. Basra took a few sips of her water. "I'm okay. It just went down the wrong pipe."

"I told you I saw him," Grayson said.

"It's weird, he doesn't live here so I have no idea what he's doing in Brooklyn this time of morning."

Grayson was instantly suspicious. "When is the last time you saw him?"

"You mean before just now?"

"Don't be funny."

"I haven't seen him since the restaurant," she said, thinking that it wasn't a complete lie since she didn't say what restaurant.

"Yeah, okay," said Grayson.

She knew by his tone that he wasn't buying it, but even more distressing was the fact that Richard was in her neighborhood. Did he know where she lived? She looked up from the table and noticed him peering in her direction. At that moment, she knew then that she couldn't ever see him again.

Chapter 12

The art installation took place that Wednesday, but Grayson was so obsessed with everything being perfect he practically slept in the space from that day until Friday, the day before the show. The video turned out great and they looped it on a thirty-inch plasma at the front of the space. Basra ordered flowers and Grayson called on many of his art friends to fill the gift bags with a mixture of trinkets from handmade jewelry to sunglasses and books. Normally, clientele of this nature liked high-end designer swag but this night was about the artist and the passion behind the art, so it was perfect. Basra went over the guest list. Amazingly, there were close to one hundred confirmations. There was a mixture of social and economic levels. However, the bulk of patrons were people in Lawson's influential circle. She even asked Hollis to toss in a few names. She didn't want to mix circles but she had no choice. The average person didn't spend $5,000 on art, especially in these economic times. Lawson swore that no one in his circle knew about her, and Choice was such an underground world, people wouldn't dare talk about how they were invited. Hence, Basra figured she'd be covered.

By Friday everything for the show was done. She'd suggested on the invite that people take cabs because of limited parking, but also met with a valet and secured a parking lot a few blocks away. Basra had thought about

everything, down to the smallest detail of little red sold
dots printed with Grayson's name. Basra had never
planned a big event before but she was a natural. They'd
picked out Grayson's outfit on that Thursday and there
was nothing else to do. This left Friday free and clear to
spend some time with Adam and then see Grayson that
evening. She spent Friday getting her nails done and
hair straightened. She wanted to dedicate Saturday for
any impending emergencies and so her grooming had
to be complete the day before. She was done with all of
her errands by three that afternoon, and was supposed
to link with Adam at four. By 5:15, he hadn't called. By
6:00, no Adam. She had plans to meet with Grayson at
eight and his inconsideration for her time was making
her angry. Like clockwork, at 7:00 Grayson called.

"Hey, babe, I had to push the reservations to nine."

"Where are we going?"

"I want to take you somewhere special."

"Okay, where do you want me to meet you?"

"At the studio at 8:30."

"Cool."

Basra looked at the time; it was 7:10. She decided
that she was going to call Hollis and cancel her date
with Adam. However, as soon as she began to dial
Hollis, he called.

"You're late!" she stated.

"Just get your pretty ass over here," he demanded
and hung up the phone.

Basra was more enraged and for split second was
going to dismiss him. Then suddenly her rage turned to
sheer excitement. She grabbed her things, rushed from
her place, and was at his home by 7:45. She walked in
his front door and punched him dead in the face.

"How dare you make me late! Do you know who I
am! Do you!"

He cowardly folded into a fetal position and whimpered. To hold in the laughter, Basra held her breath so tight, she thought she'd pee on herself. She stripped down to her bustier and pulled out a small whip that Lucia had given her months ago. She commenced to whip Adam on the back. Finally, he turned over and tried to get a little aggressive. But she regulated and refused to allow him to have an ounce of control. She was hoping he would take his beating and she could walk away, but of course he wanted to have sex. But this time she made him lie down on his back and she did all of the work. She managed to disconnect from the act and immerse herself in the foul words and the occasional bitch slap. By 8:15 she was in the bathroom, washing up. She even yelled at him from the bathroom and dared him to move from the corner she'd placed him in before she went in. When she walked back in his room, she was dressed and ready for her date.

"You leaving?" he said.

"I am. You made me wait for you and I don't appreciate it. So you only get a little of my time. Maybe next time, you'll be more considerate."

"But—"

Basra pulled her whip out, marched across the room, and slashed it across his back.

"Shut up!" she yelled.

"Yes, ma'am," he replied.

"Next time, respect my time." Basra strutted out of the room and slammed the door. Before she got to the elevator she was boiling over with laughter. She could hardly catch her breath long enough to call Grayson and tell him she was on the way. She arrived to him by 8:35 and he surprised her by having dinner reservations at Liberty View. Basra had mentioned that she hadn't done any tourist things since she lived in New York, and she was so excited.

"I love this view," she kept saying during dinner.

Grayson was so happy to see her happy, he grinned the entire night. Basra enjoyed Grayson so much, she didn't even think about Adam or that fact that she'd just slept with him minutes ago. She felt like two people trapped in one body, but living completely different lives.

"Tomorrow is going to be so nice," he said, looking out at the Statue of Libery.

"This is truly the land of opportunity. You know, I think anything is possible if you put your mind to it."

"When you think like that, it is." A few seconds passed and Grayson placed down his fork and grabbed Basra's hands.

"My mom is coming," he said, excited.

"Your mom? You don't talk that much about your family. And when I asked you about them, you said you didn't want to talk about it."

"I know. My dad and I don't get along, and my mom is so scared of him that she always go along with whatever he says. I invited her not thinking she would come, but she called and said she'd be there."

"So this is a good thing?"

"It is. My parents don't support what I do. They think I'm wasting my time and they decided awhile back that if I wanted to throw my life away then they wouldn't support it."

"I'm sorry to hear that."

"I'm used to it. You'd think I was a drug dealer or a gigolo." Basra nearly choked on her rice. "You okay?"

"I'm fine," she said, clearing her throat.

The remainder of dinner was spent talking about the show. Afterward, she and Grayson went back to

Brooklyn and Basra gave him a fashion preview of potential outfits for Saturday. She pranced up and down her living room floor as though it were Fashion Week, and finally decided on a pink silk shift dress. It was very understated but with the right accessories it was simply perfect. He continued to playfully flirt with and kiss on her, and Basra's hormones were in an uproar. She kept having visions of sleeping with Grayson, and it was becoming hard to resist. Outside of her magnanimous lie, their relationship was pure. In so many ways she wanted him, but Basra held such shame that she also wanted Grayson to have what no one else had, which was her innocence. That was the only thing she clung to. She knew she was a lying hypocrite, but she couldn't stop. The money and the taste of the power had drawn her completely in and giving that up wasn't something she was willing to do at that moment. *I need to at least save $50,000,* she thought as she watched Grayson strip down to his boxers. $50,000 was her magic number. Once she achieved that amount in her savings, she would quit and then continue to see Grayson guilt free.

"I promise I won't touch you," he said, sliding in bed beside her.

"I can't promise a thing," she cooed, looking at his bare chest.

"Well, hey, let me get these shorts off just in case."

"No, stop it. I was just playing. Oh, I need to charge my phone," Basra said.

She retrieved her phone from deep within her purse and saw that she had seven missed calls. They were all from Richard. In the excitement, she forgot that she had missed her Friday night date. She couldn't take the time to listen to all of the messages and so she turned her phone off and plugged it in. Her energy shifted from anticipation to nervousness. After Richard showed up at the Breakfast Nook, she called him and left him a message stating that they needed to talk. But after that she was so absorbed with the show, she'd forgotten completely about him.

"You okay?" Grayson asked about her sudden quietness.

"I'm good, just tired," she explained.

Basra settled in next to Grayson and flipped on her television. She landed on Bravo and they watched back-to-back episodes of *Top Chef* until they went to sleep.

Saturday evening came quickly. It seemed that as soon as they got up that morning, it was time for the art show. Basra and Grayson went to check out the preparations at four, but neither was dressed for the evening yet since it didn't start until six. Basra wanted to go alone, but he insisted on going with her. He'd been with her all day, and she hadn't had a moment to reach out to Richard. Thankfully, he hadn't called. Unfortunately, he had her so nervous she was careful to look around the corner and across the street everywhere she walked. When they got to the art space, the flowers had just been delivered and the caterers were setting up. With the small lights glowing around the ceiling of the room, his work looked magnificent.

"You're going to be a superstar!" she exclaimed, walking around the room.

"Artists don't become famous until they die."

"Well, make sure I'm in your will." She laughed.

Grayson took Basra in his arms and wouldn't let go. He was filled with emotion. "This would not be possible without you."

She could hear the crackle in his voice. "You're going to make me cry, please stop," she said.

He leaned back. "I just want you to know how much I appreciate you."

"I know. Now come on, we have a show to do. We have to meet back here at six. Don't be late," she stated.

After a short kiss, Grayson left the place and headed home. Basra stayed behind a few minutes and talked with the caterer about the servers and then went to the back to settle business with Amelia. As they were finishing her paperwork, one of Amelia's assistants came to the back and spoke.

"There's a guy near the front looking for Dove."

Basra's heart skipped three beats. Amelia saw the fear-stricken look on her face and became concerned.

"Is everything okay?" she asked.

Basra couldn't speak and could hardly walk as she rose from the desk and took a few steps toward the gallery space. She stopped at the door to catch her breath. She hadn't had time to listen to the seven messages but her gut told her that he was crazed. Basra took several deep breaths and walked to greet her stalker.

"You stood me up yesterday," he said loudly across the gallery.

She rushed over to quiet him down.

"Why are you stalking me?"

"Why did you stand me up? Never mind, I already know that answer. I thought I was your only regular."

"You are. Could you lower your voice?" Basra pushed him over to a corner as they were gathering prying glances. "I left you a message saying that we needed to talk and you didn't call me back. I can't keep seeing you."

"That's unacceptable."

"Huh? What do you mean?"

"Why would we stop seeing each other? We have so much in common."

"No, we do not, and you have to stop following me," she demanded.

"I'm not following you. I'm in the city and I saw you come in here."

"Bullshit. You were outside of my building. You showed up at the Breakfast Nook, and now here. I'm going to call the police if you keep it up. I know your name and they will find you."

"Are you sure? Meet me tomorrow at the Breakfast Nook."

"I can't."

"'Til tomorrow." Richard blew Basra a kiss and walked out.

Her flesh began to itch from the inside out. She walked out of the space moments after, gathered her composure, and combed the streets. There was no sign of him. As she continued to look, the faces of the people blended together, her head became so light that she nearly passed out upon walking back to the entrance of the door. If it weren't for the caterer passing by, she would have hit the concrete when her knees buckled underneath her. He brought her inside and placed her in a chair and slid an ottoman underneath her feet. "You need to take a break. Have you eaten today?"

Basra nodded and placed her head on the back of the chair. After thirty minutes, she was composed enough to get into a cab and go home. She immediately called Sloan, who didn't answer, and then Lucia, who picked up on the first ring.

"Hey, baby, your thing is tonight, right?"

"Yes, are you coming?"

"Of course."

"That guy Richard is stalking me."

"Who?"

"The dinner once a week guy. Sloan's customer."

"Oh him. Are you sure?"

Basra detailed the events to Lucia, who gasped in and out of each sentence.

"He's definitely stalking you."

"What do I do?"

"If you call the police, you will have to be explicit about your relationship."

"Can't I just say that he's my ex-boyfriend?"

"Yeah, but if he tries to hurt or kill you or something like that, and you have to go to court, it will all come out."

"Kill me?"

"Calm down, I was just using that as an example. He's not going to kill you. What did Sloan say about him?"

"I can't get in touch with her."

"Okay, well let's wait until we talk with her. Don't jump to conclusions. I'm sure she can talk to him."

"Okay. What happened to the girl who was seeing him before me?"

"I don't know. I think she just stopped calling. Oooh, what if he killed her!" Lucia dramatically suggested.

"Oh my God!"

"I'm joking. You'll be fine. I'll see you tonight."

Basra was downright unnerved. She could barely get dressed and get her makeup on. She was so out of sorts that she arrived to the show twenty minutes after six. She couldn't take two steps without wondering if Richard was around the corner. When Grayson walked up behind her and wrapped his arms around her waist, Basra nearly jumped from her skin.

"You scared me," she said.

"You okay?"

Basra slowly nodded.

"You look amazing," he expressed with a big smile.

"Thank you, so do you," she said.

There were about ten people mingling and viewing his work. Basra immediately went to work talking about the artist and theme. Grayson wasn't used to talking about himself and he was worse at marketing his work. Basra quickly realized why he was an undiscovered, struggling artist. She made up for what he lacked. Acting had become her second career and she was a whiz. She placed on the big smile and went into sales mode. However, by eight-thirty, not one red dot had been used. Grayson was becoming a bit discouraged because the room was filled with people, but they were socializing and drinking, not buying. Lawson strolled in close to nine o'clock. Grayson spotted him and quickly approached.

"I just want to thank you so much for investing in this show," he said.

Lawson looked around at the walls. "You're talented, and I'd do whatever your pretty little girlfriend asks of me."

Grayson didn't like Lawson's tone but had no time to address it, because Lawson quickly moved him across the room to make introductions. One of Lawson's invited guests was Arthur Cossington, a European billionaire hotel mogul with a taste for fine art. Basra had spoken to him but she had no idea who he was. Lawson introduced Grayson to Arthur and he immediately inquired about three pieces. Once Grayson explained his motivation behind the series of works, Arthur made an offer for all three. As soon as Amelia placed the red dots on the works, others began inquiring and making offers. By ten o'clock half of his works were sold. Grayson was like a kid stepping over the threshold of Disney for the first time. He couldn't walk without a skip, and couldn't talk without laughing, and to add to his thrill his mom showed up a few minutes past ten.

"Mom!" he called out. He grabbed Basra's hand and pulled her over to meet his mom. She was a petite woman, only five foot three. Her complexion was similar to Basra's due to her East Indian ancestry. She spoke with an accent.

"Who's this?"

"This is Basra. She's the one who made all of this possible. This is my mother, Hansa."

"So nice to meet you, Basra. I'm sorry I'm late; your father had me out at dinner. I told him I had to come here but you know how he is. He thought if he kept me out late enough that I wouldn't come, but I didn't want to miss your first show."

Grayson hugged his mom again and grabbed her hand. "Let me show you everything. I've already sold some stuff." He whisked her off and Basra stood in the background like a proud parent. She looked around for Lucia but she never showed. Thankfully, neither did Richard, even though his antics still had her shaken.

As she watched Grayson grow into his position as this overnight success, Lawson walked up beside her.

"You did good, kid," he said.

"Appreciate that, old man."

He burst into laughter. "Your guy has talent. I think Arthur is going to commission him to do some pieces for a few of his hotels. This was a good investment. I should have asked for interest."

"Too late."

"Next time you bring me an idea, I will remember that."

They stood at the front and watched more red dots go up. By eleven o'clock Grayson had sold seventeen of his twenty-five pieces. The show was a huge success and Basra began getting questions about other artists that she represented.

"I didn't even know that this could be a job," she told Lawson.

"It's something you should think about," Lawson said, seemingly distracted.

"What are you looking at?" Basra asked.

"Who's that lady with your guy?"

"Stop calling him my guy. His name is Grayson, and that's his mom."

"She's a cutie pie. She married?"

"Yes."

"Good, that way she won't get all attached. Introduce me," he said with a sneaky gleam in his eye.

"No."

"Suit yourself," Lawson said, walking in their direction.

"Lawson, wait! Don't you say anything to her."

Basra followed close behind.

Lawson flirted with Hansa, but she completely ignored his subtle advances. Basra continued to step in and move the conversation forward, so that Lawson had few words as possible. He eventually got the point, and the remainder of the evening went off without a hitch.

Chapter 13

That Sunday morning, Basra and Grayson stayed in bed until noon. It wasn't until her phone persistently rang with back-to-back calls did she come from her trance. Before answering, she knew it was Richard. She could feel it. She quickly hopped from bed and rushed to the bathroom to answer. Luckily, Grayson was still asleep. Her gut never steered her wrong, even though she often went against it. It was Richard and he wanted to meet.

"What time?" she whispered.

"Two o'clock."

"I want to meet in the city, at Neely's Barbecue Parlor," she suggested.

"The Barbeque Parlor? I don't know where that is."

"Look it up. It's on First Avenue."

Basra quickly hung up. She had to think of a place she knew would be crowded and possibly loud just in case he made a scene. She woke up Grayson and told him she had to run out. He was so exhausted he just turned back over and went to sleep. Basra was able to leave the house without questions.

Richard was there when she arrived. He was all smiles as though this was their first meeting and he hadn't been stalking all over New York. She greeted him and they sat. Before everything got started she pulled the small box and bracelet from her purse and slid it back across the table.

"I cannot accept this."

"I won't take it back," he said.

"Then I'm leaving it right here on the table. Better yet, I will give it to one of the homeless."

"Do whatever you like, Dove. It is yours. How was the exhibit last night?"

"Were you there?"

"No, I wasn't invited to the private event. I did, however, watch the many attendees shuffle in and out."

"Why are you doing this to me?"

"Doing what? I was in the city with nothing to do and I simply wanted to see what you were up to."

"Look, you need to stop stalking me or else."

"I don't like when you use that word. It's very disturbing to me."

"And your actions are disturbing to me."

Richard reached across the table and grasped Basra's hand. "We've had so much fun, I don't understand why you are being so coy with me now."

"I'm not being coy, I am trying to tell you that I can't see you anymore. You have to find another girl."

"Where will I find another Somali as beautiful and smart as you, one who likes my ideas and studies psychology?"

"I don't know, and I don't care!"

The server interrupted her. "Are you ready to order?"

"Not yet," Basra said, waving her away. As soon as she walked away she started up once more. Basara knew she needed to lighten her tone. Richard was starting to show more hints of crazy and she really didn't want a scene. "I don't want to be mean to you. I really think you're a decent guy, but my life is in transition. So it's not you, it's me."

Richard paused and then let out a laugh. "You and the waiter guy. Could this be why you are different toward me now? He can't do anything for you. What kind of life can he offer you? I can give you everything you've ever wanted."

"That doesn't matter. I don't want that life with you. You don't even know me. We've been on two dates."

"And they were two of my most memorable moments in life."

"You've traveled the world, met dignitaries. I don't compare to any of that. I'm just a young, naïve girl from Somalia. Who is . . . who is going back home." Basra quickly came up with the lie.

"Oh no, why?"

"My family needs me there. I will be attending school there. I was just here trying to raise enough money to help my family, as I said. But now I've just decided to go back home."

Richard was quiet as he mulled over her response. Basra was also quiet in hopes that he'd bought the lie.

"When are you leaving?"

"I'm buying my ticket this week. So, next week."

"I will help you pack your things."

"No, I'm leaving everything with my roommate. I'm only taking my clothes."

"Will you be back?"

"I don't know. But if I come back I will call you."

"This is very unfortunate. I could come visit you in Somalia."

"I don't know. My family is very strict. If they thought I was seeing an American, my dad would be livid."

The server returned to their table.

"I'm not eating," Basra quickly said to her.

"You have to eat," Richard said, grabbing her wrist.

Basra tried to loosen his grip but she couldn't. "Stop it, Richard."

"Dove will have the chicken and waffles and I will try the Velvet Elvis."

"And to drink?" the server asked.

"What would you like, darling?" asked Richard, still holding a tight grip on her hand.

"I'm good with water," Basra replied.

"Why don't we try the red velvet mimosas? We'll have two."

The server left.

"If you don't let me go, I'm going to scream."

"Why would you do that? It will only upset everyone who's in here having a nice Sunday brunch. Let's just enjoy this brunch, since it may be the last meal we ever have together."

Basra felt trapped. She suddenly realized the degree of Richard's insanity. She wanted to run, but she recalled Lucia's supposed joke and imagined him reaching inside his navy-blue cardigan, pulling out a semi-automatic gun, and killing everyone in the restaurant starting with her. This thought kept her quiet and still. She prayed that if she sat and had this meal with him, he would quietly walk out of her life. At that moment, it was her only option. She was a foreigner in a strange land and still unsure of all of the American laws. But she knew prostitution was illegal and she couldn't risk getting arrested. Richard had money and if she'd learned anything, people with money have the power to bend and break the rules. Her best bet was to be nice to him and pray he'd have mercy and just let her go.

After brunch, Richard simply said good-bye and got in a cab. He didn't linger, which was just what she'd hoped for. However, his menacing stare as the cab drove away gave Basra a disturbing feeling in the pit of her stomach. She assumed he had something up his sleeve.

When Basra got back to her home, Grayson was awake and using her juicer. She had wolfed down the chicken and waffles to appease Richard, but her stomach was in knots and the food was very unsettling.

"There she is," said Grayson as she walked in.

"I'm sorry, I had to take some medicine to Lucia. She's sick."

"That's too bad. Is that why she didn't show up last night?"

Basra nodded, kissed Grayson on the cheek, and went to the bedroom. She was a wreck and couldn't stop shaking. "You want some?" he called from the kitchen.

Basra took a few deep breaths and met him in the kitchen.

"You have me addicted to juicing now. I'm running through fresh fruit like crazy."

"Good. That means I'm having a positive effect on you."

"You don't have to wonder about that. Do you realize what last night is going to do for my career? Mr. Cossington called me and said that he wants to meet with me today about doing more pieces for his hotels. Baby, we did it! We did it!" he screamed while picking Basra up and twirling her around.

Basra was excited for three seconds before she felt her food crawling its way back up her esophagus. She forcefully pushed away and stuck her head in the kitchen sink just in time to release all of her brunch.

"Shit!" Grayson yelled. "Are you okay?"

Basra nodded as she wiped her mouth with a paper towel. "My stomach is just upset."

"Well at least we know you're not pregnant." He chuckled. Basra gave way to a tiny snicker. "You're not pregnant, right?"

"Oh God no," she expressed.

"I was about to say, who in the hell have you been sleeping with 'cause it's certainly not me."

Basra knew she wasn't pregnant but she felt like shit. She couldn't continue to lie to Grayson. She was really falling for him and looking him in the face was becoming very difficult.

"I need to lie down." Basra retired to her bedroom and remained there for the next couple of hours. Grayson lingered around, continued to check on her, but he had to leave to meet with Cossington, finally.

"I really want you to go with me."

"No, you'll be fine. I don't know about commissioning deals, so I won't be much help."

"You want me to come back afterward?"

"Just call me. I'm going to lounge all day."

Just like Lawson hinted, Arthur Cossington commissioned ten more pieces from Grayson. Overnight, Grayson went from a struggling artist to one of the hottest underground artists in demand. Word quickly got out about the show and Basra had several artists calling her about their works. As much as she loved doing the art show, she didn't want to take up a career as an art agent or broker. Grayson had been her motivation and she'd used most of her connections on this show. If she truly had to go out and find avid art patrons, it would be much harder, and she was sure she wouldn't enjoy it half as much. Her focus was Grayson and she wanted to take his career to even higher heights, so over the next few weeks, she spent her energy on finding more commercial opportunities for him. If she did this right, she could retire from her profession sooner rather than later.

With the money earned from the art show Basra and Grayson were able to repay Lawson. Basra returned the entire $25,000, and once she took her commission from what was left, she still had $15,000 to place in the bank. Grayson found a new studio space, one with a nice gallery area, and was so busy painting and creating that he and Basra didn't see each other sometimes for days. It took him three months to complete the pieces for Cossington. During that time, fall was starting and Basra enrolled back into St. John's University to continue toward her psychology degree. During those months, Basra went out with four clients from Choice. Richard continued to call, but she never spoke with him. Basra swore she saw him a couple of times in the park across from her building. However, when she walked across the street to approach him, he was never there. He was like a ghost, and she felt there wasn't anything she could really do about it. She wasn't even positive that Richard was his name.

Basra was close to her goal of $50,000 and saw an end in sight. If she weren't sending half of her money back to Somalia, she'd have her fifty by now. However, Basra was supporting two households, her sister's education, and special schooling for her brother. Still, Basra had $10,000 tied up in investments and with the few deals she'd brokered for Grayson, she was truly beginning to feel like a businesswoman.

Grayson had shipped most of the pieces for Cossington but was working on the last installments that were gracing the lobby of his hotels in Sweden. He'd asked Basra to come by and take a look at the work, but with her schedule, they kept missing each other. It was a Thursday afternoon when she realized that she hadn't seen her man in four days.

"Where are you?" she asked, calling him on the cell.

"At my second home," he answered.

Basra took the number three train downtown to lower Manhattan and walked over a few blocks to Grayson's new studio on Twenty-fourth Street. She walked in and noticed the bare walls.

"Hey!" she called out. "Where's all of your artwork?"

Grayson came from the back. "People are buying it. You would know if you came to visit more often."

"Babe, I'm in school, and I have tons of paperwork. Plus, you're always working, and I don't want to come down here just to watch you work."

"Then you should do your homework here," he suggested.

"Nah, I like getting comfy and doing it at home."

"Then maybe we should move in together."

Basra gave him a curious look. "Move in with each other, really?"

"Yeah, why not?"

"First of all, you have a roommate. I don't know how he would feel about that."

"I've been looking at new spaces anyway. Maybe we can get a townhouse in Brooklyn."

"Moving in? Why don't we just get married then?" Basra laughed.

"That's an even better idea," said Grayson.

"I was joking. We can't get married."

"Why not? We love each other and we want to be together."

"We just can't. It's too soon."

"How much time do you need to know that you want to spend your life with someone?"

"I don't know how much, but it has to be more than six months," Basra said.

"Not really," he said.

"I don't want to talk about it anymore. It makes me nervous," she said.

Grayson laughed and walked back to the studio. Basra followed him and looked at the work for Cossington. "This is really nice," she said.

"It's not really my style, but it was in the vein of what he wanted."

"You don't sound excited."

"It's different when you're painting for someone as a job instead of for yourself. It's not as fun. I can't really express myself in the way I would like."

"But how much is this piece?"

"Twelve thousand."

"Exactly," stated Basra.

"That's why I'm sitting here painting with a smile on my face." Grayson placed on a big, cheesy smile and picked up his brush. Basra kissed him and headed out.

"Will I see you tonight?" he asked.

"Just call me when you're almost done."

Basra left and looked at the time. She had about one hour before meeting Adam. His visits had become more consistent, almost weekly. They didn't have much conversation. It was strictly sexual, and Basra preferred it that way. He didn't know anything about her, and she didn't know anything about him. Things were much simpler. On the way, she talked to Lucia, who seemed distant and preoccupied.

"So, are you okay?" Basra asked several times during the conversation.

"I'm fine as always," was her response. Yet, her responses were quick and she didn't do her normal investigative chatter that she was known for.

"I'm going to come see you next week," said Basra.

"Call me, you know how I travel," Lucia replied.

The two hung up as Basra was walking up to Adam's building. He buzzed her up, but today he didn't seem his normal self when she walked in. Basra was compelled to ask him the problem. As soon as she opened herself up, emotion poured out of the floodgates.

"I just found out my son is gay."

Basra didn't know how to respond, and so she sat and listened to him vent.

"I blame his mother who always let him have his way. She made him weak."

"I don't think your wife can turn your child gay," said Basra.

"You don't know my ex. She wanted a girl, and so he did any and all things feminine. Now, he wants to become a dancer."

"Dancers are fine athletes."

"I knew I should have made him come live with me. I just didn't have time to be a father and build my business. I was always gone. So, maybe it's my fault."

"It's no one's fault. It's not a fault at all, it's just the way some people are."

"I don't want to talk about it. Just take your clothes off."

Basra slowly stripped down to her underwear. Adam pushed her down on the bed and became very physical. When she tried to talk, he went to his briefcase, pulled out a roll of tape, and covered her mouth with a strip of it.

"You don't talk today. I don't want to hear a female voice."

He held down her hands and pounded his body into hers. He was angry and he wanted to make a woman pay; any woman, it didn't matter. Basra squirmed beneath him and moaned through the black tape. Finally, Adam released and got up. He sat on the edge and looked over at her.

"Get out!" he said.

Basra pulled the tape from her mouth. "This is my last visit," she yelled before going into the bathroom. She slammed the door, and came out moments later with her clothes on. Adam, still on the edge of the bed, glanced up at her as she walked in the room to grab her purse but he said nothing. She replied with the same silent stare and left.

That afternoon, Basra decided she was going to quit the business. The act that afternoon would have sent a normal woman over the edge. It was practically rape. However, in Basra's mind she had justified it, and this was when she realized the business had finally completely numbed her.

"I'm no different than Lucia," she said to herself.

She was shy of her goal of $50,000, but she didn't care anymore. She knew with certainty that she had to stop. Between Adam's bipolar ways and Richard the psychotic, she realized that most men who desired and could afford her services were off-balance in many ways and she no longer wanted to deal with them. She was going to focus all of her energy on school and on Grayson.

Basra stopped by the market that afternoon and grabbed groceries to cook. She hadn't cooked in some time and was sick of eating out. She wanted to make Cambuulo, a traditional Somali meal. Luckily, the farmer's market had azuki beans, and so Basra bought a bag, and rushed home to start the process. The beans would take up to four hours to prepare and while they cooked, she cleaned. She tossed out old receipts that were stacked in her top drawer, washed clothes, and even mopped her floors. She called Grayson and told him about dinner plans.

"You can cook?" he said.

"Of course I can cook. My mother had us cooking at ten."

"Well, why haven't you ever made me dinner?"

"I've cooked before," she mentioned.

"Sandwiches, salads, and baked chicken don't count."

"Baked chicken does count. But tonight we eat traditional Somali, so can you please be here by eight?"

"I wouldn't miss it. I may have to come back to the studio though after dinner."

"Nooooo."

"Babe, I have work to do."

"Okay, well just be here at eight."

Basra continued to clean. She ran out to Target around 7:00 P.M. and purchased a huge quilt and several pillows to create the perfect atmosphere. When Grayson arrived at eight, dinner was complete and Basra had bowls and plates set on the quilt. Her home smelled like frankincense and the food looked delicious. Grayson walked in carrying a dozen white roses in a large square-shaped vase. Basra walked him in and sat him on the quilted floor.

"White roses are my favorite," she cooed.

"'Then will I raise aloft the milk white rose, with whose sweet smell the air shall be perfumed.'"

"I have no idea what you are talking about," Basra stated with confusion.

"It's Shakespeare; *Henry VI* . . ."

"You're such an artist. Thank you."

"I did a lot of theater in high school."

"It's very sexy. Basra smelled the tips of the flowers and placed the vase on the counter. "We are having *casho;* that means dinner," she explained. "This is rice with cumin, Cambuulo and muufo."

"The muufo looks like cornbread," said Grayson.

"It's like that," she said.

They sat and Basra fixed Grayson's plate and even fed him the first few bites of the meal.

"This feels right," she kept repeating throughout the evening. For the first time in a year, Basra felt at peace. She was eating a home-cooked meal, enjoying the company of someone she loved, and indulging in scents of Somalia.

"My mother burned frankincense oil every night after our meal. I went to sleep smelling it every night. I really miss home."

"You should go visit, or maybe we can go together."

Basra was quiet. "I know I'm in America but my parents would be so upset to know I'm dating an American. When I first came here I stayed with a friend of theirs who moved here a couple of years ago. She introduced me to several Somalis here. Even they expected me to settle down with a Somali man."

"There is a huge Somali community in New York."

"I know, but I don't hang out with any of them. My mother's friends don't like Americans, yet they live here. I don't understand why foreigners move here and then isolate themselves. I just wanted something different. I felt like I needed to surround myself with my new environment."

"Nothing wrong with that," Grayson said.

"No, but sometimes I think I should have stayed with my own people. Just for accountability's sake. I started hanging around Lucia and her crazy behind."

"How is she doing by the way?"

"I talked to her today, but she was acting weird. I'm going to see her next week."

"Well, I hope you don't regret meeting me."

"Of course not. You're the best thing that's happen to me since I've been here."

Basra leaned over the food and kissed Grayson. He
dipped his muufo in the Cambuulo and placed it gently
in her mouth. Basra felt the overwhelming need to be
rescued. She allowed herself to be taken into Grayson's
arms and be loved and caressed. She remained in his
arms as she watched the flickering candle sitting inside
the sconce.

"I love you," she whispered.

"I love you too," he said.

Basra lost herself in that moment. All thoughts left her
mind, and she felt like an innocent teen experiencing
her first love. But as Grayson started feeling down her
shirt, she felt dirty and tainted. She didn't want him to
touch her. His touch only brought dirty thoughts, and
these feelings consumed her tears. The emotion was
so overwhelming she couldn't control her crying that
quickly turned into bawling.

"I'm so sorry," she kept saying over and over again.
Grayson had no idea what she was talking about. He
just held on and let her release.

"I didn't mean to offend you," he whispered.

"You didn't, I just . . . It's just . . ." Basra was one
exhale away from spilling the truth, but the words
wouldn't form. "I can't . . . You don't know . . . and, I
wish things were different . . ."

Her incoherent sentences got softer and eventually
there was nothing but whimpers as she sobbed softly
into his grey cotton T-shirt. Grayson had never seen
this side of Basra and assumed she was having a PMS
moment. He scooped her from the floor and placed
her on the bed. Grayson lay down beside her and softly
stroked her hair until she fell asleep. He covered her
with a blanket, went back into the living room, and
cleaned up. Basra's phone, which was on the bar,
rang. Grayson looked at the time. It was 11:05. He was

tempted to answer it, but continued to place the dishes in the sink instead. While he was washing the dishes, her phone rang two more times. Grayson ignored it until it rang once more at 11:45 P.M. He answered.

"Hello, Basra's phone."

"Who?" said the male voice. "I'm looking for Dove."

"You have the wrong number."

The man recalled the phone number, and insisted he wanted to speak with Dove.

"There is no Dove here," Grayson said just before hanging up.

He went back to the dishes and the phone rang once more. This time he let it go to voice mail. But the temptation had gotten the best of him. He picked up her cell and scrolled through her text messages. He read the most recent one aloud.

"I'm sorry, please call me." Grayson continued to scroll.

There wasn't much he could decipher. She'd sent a few texts to Lucia and one to her agent.

"What are you doing?" asked Basra as she walked in the room.

Grayson inadvertently dropped her phone.

Basra rushed over and snatched the phone from the counter.

"I didn't mean to pry."

"It didn't look that way."

"I'm sorry, your phone rang like four times and I thought it might be an emergency, so I answered it. It was some guy. He was looking for Dove, and insisted that this was her phone number."

A lemon-sized lump formed in her throat.

"I just . . . I thought it was weird and curiosity got the best of me. I'm sorry," Grayson said.

"You still don't trust me," she mumbled.

"I'm putting a lot on the line with us, and . . ."

"It's cool. Again, we really don't know each other."

"Who's Dove?"

Basra held her head low and peered from underneath her brow.

"I am," she replied.

Chapter 14

Basra explained that Dove was her work alias. She told him that her agents insisted that she get a name that people could pronounce when reading it. However, she felt the truth surfacing, and knew her two worlds were close to a head-on collision.

She spoke with Adam the next day and asked him to stop calling her. He repeatedly apologized and begged for her to continue seeing him. He even offered to pay her extra money under the table. Basra was tempted but she stuck to her guns. Basra was still unsettled by Lucia's conversation so she insisted they meet for lunch later that week instead of the next. Basra waited for Lucia at 'sNice, and of course, she was traditionally late. However, when Lucia walked in Basra almost didn't recognize her. Lucia had chopped her long brunette locks into a short bob that fell just at her ears and she'd lost at least fifteen pounds. Considering Lucia was already a size four, this weight loss gave her the appearance of a skeleton. She walked in sporting oversized shades that covered 60 percent of her face.

"See? No worries. I'm fine, just like I told you. Sorry I'm late, I just got back in town," she said as she sat.

"Of course you have. And where you've been, I take it there was no food."

"What do you mean?"

"Why have you lost so much weight? What's wrong with you?"

"I look good. What are you saying?"

"No, you don't, and take off those shades," Basra said, taking the liberty to remove the frames from Lucia's face.

Basra studied Lucia's pale skin, gaunt face, and glassy eyes. "Are you on something?" she asked.

"Huh? I'm good."

"You don't look good, my friend."

Lucia grabbed her shades, and placed them back on. "I didn't come here so you could insult me. How have you been?"

"I've been good. I'm with a new agency now."

"I'm sure Hollis is mad."

"No, I mean modeling agency. I still get calls from Hollis, not that often though. She has a couple more African girls."

"That's too bad. Your reign as the chocolate queen is coming to an end."

"Good. I'm quitting anyway."

"What! Why?"

"I'm tired of it and these men are crazy."

"Oh, speaking of crazy, Philly guy has been asking Sloan about you. He wants to know when you're coming back from Somalia."

"Tell her . . . You know what, I'll tell her. He was really stalking me. I think I still see him from time to time. If he comes around, I'm going to call the police."

"If you call the police, Hollis and Sloan will stop dealing with you all together."

"That's fine."

Lucia ordered the tofu triple-decker and Basra stuck with a salad.

"I'm vegetarian now," Lucia bragged. "I thought I wouldn't have a lot of energy but I actually have more."

Basra saw beads of sweat forming on Lucia's forehead.

"I'm concerned about you."

"Why? I'm working and happy."

Basra decided to let it go and answer her ringing cell.

"I'm at Nice's," she said to Grayson on the other line. "No, the one in West Village on Eighth Avenue. Okay, see you in a minute. Love you."

"Oooh did I hear you say 'love you'?"

"Yeah, it's weird, but we just connect. I've never felt anything like it before."

"You're young. When have you had time to feel like that?"

"You're only a few years older than me."

"Yeah, but I'm not on the phone telling some man that I love him; big difference."

"Whatever."

"Have you seen the new Prada collection?" Lucia asked.

"Nope. I can't tell you the last time I went shopping," replied Basra.

"What have you been doing with your time?"

"I'm back in school."

"Still chasing that dream, huh?"

The distance between Lucia and Basra had grown wide and deep. Basra really didn't have anything to talk to Lucia about. She was concerned about her health but that was about it. Basra ate her salad quietly as Lucia yapped about her latest trip overseas. She glanced up and Grayson was walking in the door. He trotted to the table, gave Lucia a pat on the back, and sat next to Basra.

"You ladies enjoying your lunch?"

"I've been hearing about you," Lucia said to Grayson.

"Is that so?"

"Yes, my friend Lance just got one of your pieces."

Grayson thought for second and then his face lit up. "Lance Roddenburg, yes. He bought the graffiti rosary piece," Grayson recalled. "I didn't know that was your friend."

"He's Basra's friend too. We all used to live in the same building."

Basra was hoping Lucia would shut her big mouth.

"I didn't realize you knew him as well."

"I don't know him that well. I used to see him in passing," expressed Basra.

Lucia turned to Basra. "He asks about you all of the time," she continued to blab. "You know who else asked me about you? Campbell."

"He's such an asshole."

"He is kind of a jerk," she added.

"Anyway, Grayson's career has really taken off," said Basra, attempting to change the subject.

"I have to come look at your stuff. Do you have a gallery?"

Grayson pulled out a card and slid it across the table. Lucia removed her shades and read the card. "Nice address," she mentioned. "I see why you're quitting," she said to Basra with a wink.

"You want some dessert?" Basra said loudly.

"No, I have to run." Lucia dug in her purse.

"I got it," said Basra.

"You sure? Okay, my treat next time. I'll be in Miami next week but when I get back, I'll call you."

Basra nodded. Lucia rose and gave both Basra and Grayson kisses on the cheek. She looked at them sitting next to one another and smiled.

"I'm happy for you two. Ciao."

Basra watched Lucia leave.

"I know you've told me before, but how do you know each other?"

"I met her on a modeling gig. She used to be so cool. Now I don't know what's wrong with her."

"She's a coke head," Grayson stated very matter-of-factly.

"No. You think so?"

"I'm sure. I know the type."

"Is that why she's so skinny?"

"Probably."

"I know she uses sometime. You think she's in trouble?"

"It depends on whether she can afford to keep up the habit."

Basra glanced toward the door. "I'm going to call her more often. She doesn't have that many real friends in her circle. It's hard to make real friends in our business."

"I bet. I hear about the competition between models."

Basra sipped the last little bit of her smoothie.

"What did she mean by quitting?"

Basra had been thinking of an answer ever since Lucia made the comment. Grayson didn't let anything slip by him, so she was prepared.

"Quitting the dating field. She said she wanted to introduce me to someone and I told her I was happy and didn't think I'd be dating anyone else."

Grayson pecked her cheek and then her lips. Lying was becoming second nature, but since Basra was indeed quitting, she hoped her lies would eventually turn into the truth.

"Now when you said anyone else," he commented, "did you mean anyone else, period, as in ever again?"

"Maybe," Basra said with a demure expression.

***

The remainder of Basra's day was spent grooming. She was set for a manicure, a pedicure, waxing, and a hair appointment. She had a big go-see the following day for a top designer's line of lingerie. Each year Lauren's Closet picked ten women to represent the line and those women got catalogue deals, did the runway shows, and virtually became top models. It was an honor just to get a slot to be seen. She had to make a good impression. Most women didn't get picked their first year of auditions, but if they were memorable, they were asked back the following year and often chosen. The agency suggested she straighten her hair and after looking at the models they normally picked, she agreed it was best. She had hesitated to tell Grayson about the audition at first, for fear he'd be jealous about his girlfriend posing in her underwear, but when she did tell him, he was elated. He liked the idea of men fantasizing about his lady; it gave him more bragging rights. When he saw her that night, he was shocked at her new look.

"You look so different with straight hair," he said.

"More American, right?"

"Yeah, kind of. You look more Indian. You look like some of my cousins."

Basra laughed as she rifled through her drawer for a scarf. She tied the scarf tightly around her head to hold her hair down.

"I bet your cousins don't have to do this." She chuckled. "If any moisture gets to this stuff, it's poof! Big hair all over again."

Basra went to bed early that evening to be ready for her audition the following morning. She arrived at the offices of Lauren's Closet at 7:00 A.M. She was told to come with a bare face. The new line's campaign was called Barely There and they wanted natural looks for all models. Basra sat nervously in the lobby as the other models piled in. She and three others were called to the back to model the lingerie they were given. After she was dressed in their bra and panties, she waited in a small four-by-four room until her name was called again. The other two models pranced around the room in their robes, but Basra sat quietly on the bench and flipped through a magazine until the extremely tall, blond woman opened the door and called for her.

"Basra, we're ready for you."

Basra walked in and placed down her bags. The three onlookers asked her to walk up and down the small runway six times. They asked her series of questions while flipping through her book. She stood in front of the table and smiled as they murmured about her.

"Please turn around, and place your hands on her hips," the man asked.

Basra obliged and stood there for what seemed like an hour.

"Le tush is very round," she heard the tall blonde say with her thick French accent.

She wasn't sure if they were going for round or flat but there was nothing she could do about her African trait.

"You can turn around now. Are you available to travel?"

"Yes," Basra replied.

"You look very different with straight hair," the other woman said, glancing through Basra's book.

"I like both," said the blonde.

They continued to whisper and look for another minute, and then dismissed her.

Basra got dressed and left. Grayson surprised her outside the building.

"How long have you been out here waiting?"

"Not that long. How did it go?"

"They said I had a round tush."

"Hell yeah, you do." He smacked her on the butt.

"It was little weird to stand there in my underwear and have them staring at me."

"Well, you better get used to it."

"They don't normally pick people from their first go-see. Most girls aren't picked until their second or third time."

"You aren't most girls," Grayson expressed. "I'm not painting today, and you don't have classes, so let's hang out," he said.

"Really?" Basra said with excitement.

"Yeah, I miss my girlfriend," he said.

Basra giggled and grabbed his hand. It was like old times as they hung out in the city, window-shopped, ate, and went to the movies. They spent the later part of the day in Central Park, looking at the fall leaves. Grayson talked about having another show as Basra guessed character profiles of the people walking by. She was enjoying her psychology classes but still wasn't sure how she was going to use her degree. She didn't want to get a doctorate and practice but was interested in possibly teaching. Most of all she found joy in studying people. She could waste hours of the day doing just that.

As they walked back to the train, Grayson stopped in the middle of the sidewalk. Basra had taken a few steps ahead of him before she realized he wasn't moving. She turned and saw the crowd weaving around him.

"Hey!" she called out before going back. "What's wrong?" she asked.

"We should get married. I know we've been down that road before but the feeling keeps hitting me hard in the chest. I want to marry you, Basra."

She looked at Grayson and in that moment she couldn't imagine being with anyone else. A smile slowly crept across her face.

"Okay, let's get married."

Chapter 15

The next morning, Basra and Grayson went to the county clerk's office and applied for a marriage license. They filled out the appropriate paperwork and had to wait a few hours before they could go into the courtroom to officiate the ceremony. Grayson called his friend Thomas to be a witness. Basra wore a knee-length pale blue dress with navy pumps. Her hair, still straight from her audition, was pulled neatly into a bun. At the request of Grayson, she only sported a light tint of lip gloss. By one o'clock that afternoon, they were married. Basra, Grayson, and Thomas went to eat pizza afterward. The more Basra thought about it, the more her nerves boiled.

"I can't believe I'm married," she kept saying.

"Having second thoughts already?" commented Thomas. "Hope not, because the divorce won't be nearly as easy," said the recent divorcee.

"I'm not having second thoughts, I'm just shocked that's it."

"Well now you get to become a citizen," Thomas mentioned.

"Oh, yeah. I need to look into that," she replied.

"We should go get rings," said Grayson with excitement.

"My parents are going to be angry," Basra whispered. Her heart palpitated like a child bringing home bad grades for the first time. She was sure about her feelings for Grayson but she was so far from her rearing that she didn't know if she'd ever find her way back.

"If you like, we can go to your home and have a traditional Somali wedding," Grayson mentioned. Basra only nodded quietly and finished her pizza.

Grayson couldn't stop talking. He was thrilled. "So since your lease is almost up, I think we should really look into getting a brownstone. What about those near Fulton that we saw, or what about one of those new ones in Harlem?" Grayson said.

"Yeah, I've been looking. I have a bunch of them bookmarked." Basra pulled out her iPad and showed them to Grayson.

"You should call my mom," said Thomas.

"Oh yeah, I forgot she did real estate."

Thomas gave Grayson his mom's phone number. Basra felt as though she'd been swept up in a whirlwind. They left the pizza parlor, parted ways with Thomas, and went to look at rings. An hour after looking, Basra got caught up in Grayson's exhilaration. She tried on over thirty different styled rings from at least four different jewelry stores. The couple finally settled on a white gold ring from an antique jewelry store in Upper Manhattan. Basra's band was a 1920s filigree ring with small diamonds around the edges and throughout the band. Basra fell in love the moment she saw it and it fit her perfectly. Grayson settled on a plain white gold band. He didn't want anything too fancy or expensive since his hands were always covered in paints. The newlyweds grabbed a couple of sandwiches and went back home that evening. Grayson swept his bride off her feet and carried her into the bedroom. He slowly kissed her as they swayed back and forth to the rhythms of their heartbeats. He slowly undressed his bride and they made love for the first time. Basra enjoyed the first few minutes but soon became so overrun with guilt she couldn't hold back her tears. This was the second bawling episode she'd had and Grayson became concerned.

"Are you okay?"

"I'm good. I'm very happy," she said, which was true despite the guilt.

"You've been very emotional. You know you can talk to me."

"I know," she uttered and held her head low.

Deep down Grayson knew those tears were covering something deeper but he didn't want to investigate. He just wanted to enjoy his evening without complication or questions. They made love two more times that night and Basra finally gave into the moment. She stared at Grayson and was careful not to close her eyes, for when she did, her remorse crept inside. If she stared into Grayson's eyes, she was lost in his charm and attraction. She was the type of girl who believed in the fairy-tale endings and Hollywood love stories, and as she closed her eyes that night and said her prayers, she asked God for forgiveness and mercy that He may bestow them a happily ever after.

That morning before breakfast, Grayson woke before Basra and called his mother. He told her that he and Basra had gotten married and he couldn't wait for the rest of the family to meet her. Though his mom thought she was a lovely girl, she had mixed emotions about their overnight courtship.

"Are you sure?" she kept asking.

"Mom, she is the one. I even talked to God about it," Grayson said.

"You talked to God?" his mom questioned. "I've never heard you say anything like that."

"She's changed me, Mom. I really hope you under-stand because you're going to be the only one on my side."

"Son, I just want you to be happy," she said.

"I am," he persisted.

They talked a little longer about art as he made fresh grapefruit juice and she insisted on making them dinner that Friday, if he promised that he'd come over. Since Grayson and his dad stop talking a year ago, he hadn't been to their Long Island home, not even for the holidays. His mother hated the dysfunction between the two of them but there was nothing she could do. Grayson's father, Ray, was stubborn and he unfortunately passed that gene on to his son. After his dad said that he was going to be a bum painting pictures of people on the street, Grayson decided that he wasn't going to speak to him until he apologized. Ray refused to apologize and thus the feud had continued. Hansa was hoping that her son's new love had softened his heart enough to start a peace offering.

"So I will see you on Friday. Do not make me cook a big dinner and you and Basra not show up."

"I won't, I promise," said Grayson.

He hung up and took a glass of juice into the bedroom. Basra was stirring and when he slid underneath the covers beside her, her eyes opened. She greeted him with a smile.

"You're my husband," she said.

"I am," he said. "Don't make plans for Friday. We're going to my parents' for dinner."

"Your parents? Did you tell them we were married?"

"I told my mom."

"What did she say?"

"She said she wanted me to be happy."

"I don't know if that's a good idea. You're not even talking to your dad. He's definitely not going to be happy when you show up with a wife he's never met."

"He probably won't even be there. My dad works all of the time. Dinner is at six and he never gets home before nine."

"Okay," said Basra with a look of apprehension.

"It will be okay, I promise."

Basra drank a sip of juice and then rubbed her belly. "I'm hungry," she said.

"Sounds like the Breakfast Nook is calling."

The lovebirds tossed on some sweats and went to breakfast, but as soon as Basra stepped out and took a whiff of the fresh fall air, she looked across the street and saw Richard.

"Oh no!" she moaned.

"What?"

Grayson followed her eye line and also saw Richard standing across the street.

"Who is this dude?"

"Okay, I didn't say anything before, but we went out, only a few times, and after I tried to end it, he wouldn't, and since then he's been stalking me. I didn't want to say anything but I really think he's crazy."

Grayson was so heated that he stepped into the street without looking and was nearly run over.

"Gray!" Basra called out. He ignored her yelp and kept walking. She followed.

Richard remained at his position and calmly sipped his coffee. His face held a dubious smirk.

"Hey, you."

"Gray!" Basra continued to yell.

"What the fuck are you doing?"

Richard looked right and left and then replied. "I'm enjoying my morning coffee."

"Richard! What are you doing in front of my place?"

"Our place," Grayson corrected. "My wife says you're stalking her."

"I live in this neighborhood and this is a public street." Richard turned his attention to Basra. "You got married, congratulations."

Grayson stepped in front of Basra. "You don't talk to her. I'm telling you right now that you need to leave my wife alone."

Richard cut his eyes over Grayson's shoulder and looked at Basra. He displayed an eerie smile and then turned and walked down the street, still sipping his coffee.

"He's really crazy," Basra said.

"What's his full name? I have a friend who works for the police and she can pull his record."

Basra paused, for she didn't even know Richard's last name. She wasn't even sure he was from Philadelphia, as he had stated.

"I don't think we should get into that. He's more bark than bite."

"I don't know, Basra. I've seen that dude several times. At first I thought it was just in my mind, but I'm sure I've seen him standing out here a few mornings."

"Well, we are about to move. I'm getting a new number and I can put my past in the past."

"Where did you meet that creep?"

"Blind date. Let's go eat."

Basra pretended as though she weren't a bit concerned about Richard, but inside her nerves were unraveling. That afternoon, when Basra got out of class, she met Molly Youngston, Thomas's mom. She had several brownstones ready to show. Grayson was busy painting, but Basra, very anxious to move, wanted to look. After looking at several properties, Basra fell in love with a three-story brownstone on 128th Street in Harlem. It was completely refurbished. The owners were renting but were also willing to sell. However, at the $810,000 asking price, Basra knew that they would be renting that place for a while. She narrowed the search among three places, and didn't tell Grayson which one was her favorite. However, when he instantly fell for the Harlem home Basra told him that was the one she wanted, and the decision was simple. That Friday before heading to Long Island, the couple filled out the lease application, and Grayson filled out the background and credit check. Basra was so excited she wanted to immediately start shopping. Grayson agreed that she could buy one thing. But when the one thing she wanted to buy was a neon pink welcome home mat, he forced her out of the store empty-handed.

"It was perfect," she whined, leaving the store.

"It glowed in the dark," he said.

"No, it didn't. But it was happy and perky like us."

"We're not getting a bright pink doormat."

That was the end of that conversation, and later that day, Basra nervously went through five outfits before deciding to wear a pale yellow 1930s-style dress that fell just below her knees. She pulled her hair back away from her face with a band but left it hanging. She even went by the market and picked up a cheesecake for dessert. She wanted to cook something traditional but didn't want to risk his family not liking the dish. She was so nervous her armpits were sweating.

"I never sweat like this," she said as they were leaving the house.

"Why are you so worried?"

"Because they don't know me."

"I'm their son and they don't me either."

"It's different. I'm not American. They're probably going to think I married you for citizenship."

"I'll tell them you didn't even want to marry me and that I pressured you."

"Yeah, like that's going to make them feel better."

"It will be fine," Grayson said, kissing Basra on the forehead.

They left home at four that afternoon and hopped in a rental car. Grayson was used to taking the train but since the Oyster Bay railroad could be a bit unpredictable, he wanted a fast escape off Long Island if things at home went awry. On the ride, Grayson mentioned to Basra that his parents were well-off, and not to be surprised when they got to the neighborhood. Basra had never been to Long Island and figured well-off meant they were doing better than the average New Yorker. However, when they reached Split Rock Road, Basra realized she wasn't the only one keeping a secret.

"You're rich," she exclaimed.

"I'm not rich, my parents are. They don't give me a dime."

"Still, you came from money."

"And . . ."

Basra didn't want to get out of the car. She continued to harp on the fact that his parents lived in a million-dollar mansion.

"Are there any other secrets you want to share with me?" she asked.

Grayson shrugged his shoulders nonchalantly.

"Why didn't you say something?"

"What was there to say? So what, they have money."

"People with money are different. They judge people a lot more than people without."

"Now, I have to agree with you on that. My dad has been judging me every since I decided not to become an architect or engineer."

"I have a bad feeling about this."

"Well, we are here now. You can't sit in the car all night."

Basra took several deep breaths and walked with her husband to meet her in-laws. Hansa greeted them at the door. She was just as pleasant as she was at the art show. She hugged Basra and whispered "congratulations" in her ear. They went into the parlor area and helped themselves to a few glasses of wine. Basra was nervous but made sure she didn't drink too much. Next, she met his sister, who arrived shortly after them. Since only his mother knew about the marriage, Grayson wanted to make the grand announcement during dinner. They had agreed to remove their rings as to not cause suspicion. His sister resembled his mom with more Indian features. She, only eighteen months older, was single and a partner in a private dental practice on Long Island. As soon as she saw Basra, she gave a curious smile and said, "Don't you model?"

"I do," replied Basra.

She pulled out her iPad, and pulled up *Grazia* magazine. She flipped through the pages and held up a picture of Basra.

"I thought that was you. I love this magazine, and I remembered seeing you in there. I thought you were from India, and I was so happy to see someone of color in the spread. You are so beautiful," she said.

"Thank you," Basra said.

"Ma, come here!" screamed Grayson's sister, Kaamil.

Hansa came rushing into the room. "Is everything okay?" she said.

"Look." She showed her mom the picture on the screen. "She really is a model, not some go-go bar dancer claiming to be a model. No offense," she said to Basra.

"None taken."

"She just had an audition with Lauren's Closet," bragged Grayson.

"Get out! I love their stuff. If you get that gig, I bet you get discounts, hint hint."

Basra continued talking to Kaamil as Grayson followed his mom into the kitchen. She was quick to ask him about the marriage.

"So when are you going to tell your dad?"

"Where is he?"

"Working. I suspect he'll be here before the evening is over.

"I wanted to announce it over dinner. You didn't mention anything did you?"

"No. This news has to come from you."

Grayson looked at the spread his mom had laid on the table. "Did you cook all of this or did Annie Mae do it?"

"We both did," she answered.

"Where is she anyway?" Grayson asked, referring to their housekeeper.

"She had the night off. She goes to Bingo on Friday."

Grayson laughed as Kaamil and Basra walked in the kitchen.

"I like her, Gray. I like her a lot. She's smart and has pretty teeth."

"Do you do anything besides modeling?" Hansa asked.

"I'm in school, studying psychology."

"Oh really, what do you plan to do after college?"

"I was thinking about therapy."

"She should be teaching math," expressed Grayson. "She's a math savant."

"Stop it. I'm not."

"Really, she can add super large numbers, divide them, whatever."

"I'm just good with numbers. Stop it, Grayson." Basra turned to Hansa. "This is really good wine."

"One of my favorites as well."

They continued to chat around the kitchen area until Hansa heard Ray coming in the door. "We're in here," she called out.

Ray walked in the kitchen and greeted his wife and daughter with kisses on their cheeks. He looked at Grayson and nodded. "Son."

"What's up?" said Grayson.

"What's up, huh?" Ray said, certainly not appreciating the casual greeting.

"This is Basra," said Grayson.

Basra shook Ray's hand. "Nice to meet you, sir," she said, holding her breath.

"She's a model," expressed Kaamil. "A real one in magazines."

"That's nice." Ray placed down his briefcase and a looked at the food. "You didn't have to wait for me. I told you I'd be late," he expressed.

"It's okay, we've been running our mouths."

"Since we were already having company for dinner, I thought one more wouldn't hurt."

"Who's coming?"

Just then Ray's business associate called from the front door. "Hello."

"Follow the voices," Ray called out. "We've been working so many late hours on this hospital deal, I figured that the least I could do was offer a home-cooked meal."

"Sorry, I had to finish up a phone call," said Ray's associate as he walked into the room.

"Everyone, this is Adam Feinburg," said Ray.

As though she were staring into Medusa's eyes, Basra turned to stone and her wine glass fell onto the floor. Everyone turned in her direction. She quickly knelt to pick up the pieces. Grayson graciously helped her.

"This is my wife and daughter, Hansa and Kaamil. That's my son, Grayson, and his friend . . ."

"Basra," she said, standing and holding pieces of broken glass.

"Nice to meet everyone. I hope I'm not imposing," said Adam.

"Of course not, the more the merrier."

"I'm going to sweep this up," said Grayson as he left the kitchen.

Basra's hands were shaking. "My dear, are you okay?" asked Hansa.

"I'm good, I'm so sorry," she said, avoiding direct eye contact with Adam.

"What was that you were drinking?" he asked.

"It was . . . uhmm, it was a merlot."

"It seems that my presence startled you, so let me pour you another glass. Ray, where do you keep your wine?"

Ray motioned for Adam to follow.

"Where's your restroom?" she asked.

"I'll show you," said Kaamil. "Oh, God, you're bleeding. We have Band-Aids."

Basra went into the bathroom and closed the door while Kaamil went down the hall to get a first-aid kit. Basra sat on the closed toilet, as her shaky legs were no longer able to support her frame.

"Oh God, oh God, oh God!" she whispered. "Why!"

There was a knock on the door. Basra stopped breathing. "I have the first-aid kit," called Kaamil from the other side.

Basra exhaled and spoke. "Come in."

Kaamil walked in the bathroom, cleaned Basra's cut, and bandaged it with a neon pink Band-Aid. "Sorry; it was all I could find. Are you good?" she asked.

"I am, thanks. I need to use the restroom, though."

"Oh yeah. Sorry."

Kaamil left and Basra sat back down on the toilet. She prayed silently and took several deep breaths before walking out. As she opened the door, Adam took a step in.

"Here's your wine."

"I'm good," she said, trying to sidestep him.

"Fate keeps bringing us together, doesn't that mean something?"

"It means the devil is as busy as he is devious, as my mother used to say."

Adam was uncomfortably close as he leaned in to whisper. "You smell delicious. Whatever he's giving you, I will pay double. Meet me tonight."

"Don't do this," she said with fret.

Grayson came around the corner. "You okay?" he asked.

"I am," she called out loudly as Adam stepped to the side.

"Here is your wine," he said again, cordially handing her the glass.

Basra smiled, took the glass, and grabbed her husband's hand. Adam went into the bathroom. Grayson stopped to have conversation in the hallway.

"I know you're nervous about announcing the marriage, but you've got to calm down. It's going to be okay. I know they will fall in love with you. My sister is already a fan."

"I know," Basra said softly.

Grayson leaned over and gave his woman a kiss. Adam approached as he was leaving the bathroom.

"I see love is in the air," Adam stated.

"Yeah, I'm a very lucky guy."

"More than you know," said Adam as he stepped to the left, walked by Basra, and lowered his hand to cautiously graze her butt as he passed by. Basra heart damn near stopped. Her fairy-tale had turned into one by the Brothers Grimm, and she was soon going to be eaten alive.

"You ready?" said Grayson.

Basra nodded slowly and attempted to smile. Grayson took her hand and led her to dinner.

Chapter 16

Basra and Grayson sat down for dinner and Adam placed himself directly in front of her. He was such a wild card she had no idea what he might say or do. Therefore, Basra just kept her face angled toward Grayson to avoid direct eye contact. Her mind was focused on a plausible reply if indeed Adam decided to blurt out the truth during dinner. Unfortunately, nothing came to mind. She'd have no excuse except to call him a liar.

"You ready?" Grayson whispered to her as they started on the entrée.

Basra was so focused on her situation that she completely forgot they were there to announce their marriage.

"I don't think this is a good idea," she said while lifting the rice with her fork.

"Basra and I are married," Grayson stated.

All parties stopped eating. Ray looked down the table at Hansa, who smiled nervously.

"You knew about this?" he asked.

"Just now, he told me right before dinner, his mother fibbed."

"Don't get upset with her. If you have something to say, say it to me," Grayson said to his father.

Ray picked up his fork and continued to eat. Basra followed suit. Finally, Kaamil spoke.

"I think it's great. I mean, I wish I would have known but I'm so glad you didn't have a wedding, because if I have to buy one more stupid bridesmaid's dress I'm going to throw up." She smiled at Grayson. "Congratulations."

"Thanks, sis," he replied.

"So how did you know she was the one?" Kaamil asked.

"Something spoke to me. It's this indescribable feeling."

"So when did you and Sophie break up?" asked Ray.

"Awhile ago."

"Couldn't have been that long ago, I just saw her father and he said you guys were planning a ski trip," his dad continued.

"A trip that never happened because we had broken up," Grayson commented with growing annoyance.

"Let it go, honey," said his mom.

"I'm just concerned about my son's life and the hasty decisions he seems to make."

"You are so concerned that we haven't spoken in a year," Grayson commented sarcastically.

"You know, I can go back to the hotel," Adam commented.

"Nonsense, let's just drop it and enjoy this nice dinner that my wife has prepared."

"Thank you," said Hansa.

For the next few moments, the only noise from the dining area was that of clinking knives and forks. Finally, Adam felt the need to break the tension.

"Hey, there's no such thing as a perfect family. I wish my son would come home and surprise me with a bride, but I just found out he was gay."

"Oh that's a rough one," Ray commented.

"Oh yeah, so be glad you've got a beautiful daughter-in-law, and maybe soon you will have some grandkids running around. I only have one child and so that dream for me is over."

"Sorry to hear that," Ray said.

"I'm gay," blurted Kaamil.

Once again all utensils fell to the table. This time when Ray looked at Hansa, her eyes were bulging. "I guess this is a surprise to everyone."

"Perhaps you know my son . . ."

"All gay people don't know each other," huffed Kaamil.

Hansa, nearly in tears, excused herself from the table. Ray went to see about her. Inside, Basra, though still nervous, was pleased that no matter what Adam had to say it would take a back seat to all the other chaos breaking loose.

"Kaamil, can we talk in the kitchen?" said Grayson.

"No, no, uhhm. You can talk here, I can go in another room," said Basra.

"I can go with Basra," said Adam.

"On second thought, maybe you should leave well enough alone, Gray," Basra stated.

"I need to talk with my sister," he said, rising.

Kaamil and Grayson went into the kitchen to speak, leaving Basra alone with the snarling dinner guest.

"And then there were two," said Adam, winking at Basra.

"Don't you say anything to me," she said.

"I'm not saying anything to you, but the question becomes, will I say anything to your husband? I mean there've been so many surprises tonight, what's one more?" He snickered.

Basra rose and attempted to leave the dining room, but Adam stopped her at the door. He took her by the wrist and forced her hand on his crotch. "Squeeze," he said.

"Please, not tonight. I promise I will come see you later this week."

"Tomorrow," he demanded.

Basra once again tried to go around him, but he wouldn't let her by. "Please kiss me," he begged. "What kind of panties are you wearing?" Adam remained at the door. The more she fought him, the bigger the scene would become. Basra turned and went back to the table and sat. Tears started welling in her eyes.

In the kitchen, Grayson was trying to get some explanation from his sister.

"I don't understand why you never said anything to me," he said.

"I didn't know how."

"Are you serious? It's me, Kaamil. I'm the family fuck up. You were perfect in Dad's eyes."

"Right! Which is why I couldn't say anything. Mom's been trying to marry me off since I was twenty-one. I didn't want to break her heart."

"So you just kept your little secret and let me be the bad guy," Grayson expressed.

"Are you mad because I didn't confide in you, or because I didn't share in some of our family shame?"

"Both. You let me take all of the heat."

"This isn't about you, Gray!"

"It was my night. I wanted to announce my marriage and talk about my wife."

"So now you're mad because I upstaged you. Hell, if I hadn't seen how happy you were I wouldn't have even come out. I have a girlfriend, and I want to bring her home. You have inspired me."

The siblings stood in the kitchen, staring at one another. The tension quickly calmed. "I love you, Gray, but I'm not as strong as you. I want Mom and Dad to respect me. I need that."

Grayson walked over and hugged his sister. "I love you too, sis."

Kaamil exhaled deeply. "It feels so good to finally be honest."

"So who is the girlfriend and how long have you been with her?"

"Two years. She's a pediatrician. We have a place together over in Suffolk County."

"How have you managed to keep this from Mom?"

"I still have my apartment downtown. As long as I make regular visits home, she doesn't come see me."

Grayson explodes into laughter. "Your ass is gay! That's so great."

"You're just happy that now after all of these years, you're no longer the family disappointment."

"You damn right." Grayson hugged his sister. "It's going to be okay, I promise. They will come around, and if not, you are always welcome in my home during the holidays."

In the dining room, Basra was mulling over her meal. She no longer had an appetite and with Adam leering at her from across the table she wanted to hurl her plate across the room.

"How's the meal?" Grayson asked as he strolled back in with Kaamil.

"It's good," Basra replied.

"I'm sorry, you two. Our dinners are not normally this crazy. But since we haven't seen Gray in so long, I figured we'd make it one to remember," said Kaamil."

Seconds later, Ray came back into the dining room. "Sorry for that," he said, apologizing to Adam.

"Hey, this is what family is all about. I promise none of this will leave the house."

"I really appreciate it," said Ray as he disturbingly looked at Kaamil. "Hansa has a headache. She apologizes for not returning. Let's just try to make the best of this evening." Ray sat back down at the head of the table.

Adam looked across the table and motioned toward Basra. "I swear I've seen you before," he said to her.

"She's a model. You've probably seen her spread in fashion magazines."

"I'm sure I have seen her spread . . . I don't think it was in a fashion magazine, though."

"I've done tons of catalogue work. Maybe your wife orders those catalogues," Basra said with a quick, scornful glance.

"I'm divorced so it must have been somewhere else. Have you done any videos, film work?"

"No."

"None that you know of. Cameras these days are so small, one never knows when they are being filmed."

Adam's behavior was odd and everyone at the table was taking notice.

"I've never done any videos, but I do have a familiar face, so I'm sure that's it. So, Mr. Charles, what new project are you working on?" she asked as a quick diversion.

"We are building a new wing to the hospital. Adam's company is financing the extension. It's turning out to be a real success."

"Oh, speaking of success, Grayson's show was a hit. He sold out of pieces and Arthur Cossington commissioned him to do work for his hotels all over Europe."

"Who is Arthur Cossington?" asked Kaamil.

"He's the European Conrad Hilton."

"Oh, well congrats, brother."

"I just do the painting. Basra is the brains behind it all, he was her contact."

Ray sat up in his chair and his interest piqued.

"You speak English very well. How long have you been here? How do you know Arthur Cossington?"

"We speak English in Somalia and Mr. Cossington and I have mutual friends. I asked one of them to invite him to the show and he happened to be in town."

"You have mutual friends? What does your family do? Do they live here?" asked Ray.

"Really, Pop, that's enough," said Grayson.

"It's fine. No, sir, my family is still in Somalia. My dad is an engineer." Basra knew where the line of questioning was going. How could a young Somali girl know friends of a European billionaire hotel mogul? It didn't make sense.

"I read an article about Arthur Cossington, a very eccentric man. Even at eighty, he still micromanages much of the minutia involving his hotels," added Adam.

"Yeah, he called me himself," stated Grayson.

"These mutual friends must be very close," Adam expressed curiously.

Basra leaned over and whispered in Grayson's ear. She was ready to leave.

"We're going to head out," he commented.

Kaamil grabbed her plate and rose. "I think I'll head out with you."

"I think you need to stay, young lady. Adam, once again, I apologize for the madness that has erupted this evening."

"No problem."

"Do you two mind taking Adam back to his hotel?" asked Ray.

"Uhhm. No, of course not. Where are you staying?"

"I normally stay at my place in Manhattan, but I'm staying at a hotel close by this evening."

"Yeah, we'll drop you off."

Basra, Grayson, and Adam prepared to leave. Grayson gave Kaamil one more hug. "Be strong," he whispered in her ear.

She nodded and embraced Basra. "Welcome to this crazy family."

Basra smiled and said good-bye.

Adam crawled in the back seat of the rental and they took off. As soon as they got down the street, Adam spoke. "I know where it was that I saw you."

Basra swallowed the lump in her throat, for she didn't know what Adam might say. Oddly, he didn't say anything. He left it open-ended. Basra flipped through the radio, found a station, and turned it up so loud that if anyone had to talk, they would have to scream over the volume. Grayson pulled into the hotel downtown. Adam hopped out and leaned in Basra's window.

"Thanks so much," he said, leaning across Basra to shake Grayson's hand. "The ride was very enjoyable," he said, staring Basra in the eyes. Adam walked into the hotel.

"He was strange," said Grayson as they pulled off.

"Yes, he was," agreed Basra.

The trip back to Brooklyn was quiet. They spoke briefly about Kaamil, but for the remainder of the time Basra closed her eyes and rested. By the time they reached home, a series of texts started buzzing on Basra's phone. She knew it was Adam. She checked the first one, which read: I need a good spanking. She quickly erased it and tossed her phone in her purse.

"Tonight was interesting," he said as they prepared for bed.

"You really never knew your sister was gay?" Basra asked.

"No, and I'm normally good at reading people. For instance, Adam, my dad's business partner, is definitely into some weird shit."

"I can see that," she commented before rushing into the bathroom.

Grayson walked to the door and peeped in as Basra washed off her makeup. "He's probably gay." He laughed. Basra couldn't help but chuckle. "If not, he's definitely into some ol' S&M crazy shit." Basra nodded. "Did you see him staring at you?" Grayson asked.

"No."

Grayson walked behind Basra and wrapped his arms around her. "I guess you are so used to men staring that you don't even notice it anymore." He stared at her reflection in the mirror. "I know it seems like a dream still, but I am in love with you, Mrs. Charles."

Basra wiped her face dry, looked in the mirror, and smiled. Just then Grayson's phone rang. He grabbed it and answered.

"What's up, Kaamil?" He excused himself from Basra and walked into living room. She quickly went to her phone, turned it on, and watched as ten texts buzzed across her screen. They were all from Adam, and each grew more obscene from the previous one. However, his last text was most disturbing.

It was a quick ten-second video of Basra straddled across his body. Basra quickly erased all of the messages as she heard Grayson approaching. She tossed down her phone, and rushed from the bathroom.

"Your sister okay?" she asked.

"She will be. My dad basically told her she wasn't allowed to ever bring her partner to the house. He's such as asshole."

"He just wants the best for his children. He's misunderstood. My dad is not that different."

Grayson smirked and walked into the bathroom. Basra sat on the edge of the bed and closed her eyes.

"Your phone keeps buzzing," Grayson called out.

Basra rushed to grab it from the counter and walked back out. "Yeah, I had it off all night and now my e-mails are coming through. I'm going to just turn it off."

"Any more from Richard?" Grayson said as he peeped out while brushing his teeth.

"No."

"You definitely have an effect on men, and apparently some women. My sister said you were hot! I won't tell you what she was doing when she saw you in that magazine."

"Uggh. Stop it."

Grayson laughed. Basra turned off her phone and placed it under her pillow. Ever since she'd caught Grayson scrolling through her messages, she had kept it in plain sight. She couldn't risk him seeing any of that video. Adam was going to be her first call the next morning.

Chapter 17

That morning, Molly called Grayson to let him know they'd been approved to lease the brownstone. It was a little risky because neither of the couple had a steady occupation, but with Grayson's 790 credit score and his and Basra's combined savings of close to $60,000, the owners felt comfortable. Basra was ready to move and asked that he gather boxes that day. Grayson was anxious as well but knew if they were about to pay $3,000 in rent, he had to make more money. He pulled out a stack of business cards from patrons he hadn't been able to see yet, and gave them to Basra.

"You need to call all of these people. They all said they were interested in my work. Start with these two." He pointed to two law firm cards. "They have offices in Manhattan, and maybe I can do some corporate stuff for them."

"You've been holding out," Basra teased.

"Nah, I just remembered that I had them."

Basra flipped through the stack and counted twenty-two cards. "Okay, so the goal is to get each of these people to buy two paintings at a least four grand a piece. That will give us a minimum of $176,000."

"How do you do that?" he questioned.

Basra shrugged her shoulders. "I'm going into the city and getting my number changed today."

"Good idea. I'll be at the studio all day."

"Cool, I'll come by later this afternoon. We can pick up the keys on Monday, and I can't wait to start decorating."

"Yeah, I want to work on a special piece to go in the foyer when you first walk in, and it would be cool if I just paint directly on the bathroom walls."

As he rambled about decorating, Basra hurriedly got dressed, grabbed her phone, and left the house. Before she could get off the block, she was calling Adam. He rapidly picked up.

"It's about time. I've been trying to reach you all night."

"You have lost your mind. You were taping me!"

"Hey, you never said I couldn't," he said.

"And you never asked. That's an infringement of my rights."

"Calm down. What rights? You're not even American."

"My human rights! Where are you?"

"On my way back to the city. Meet me at the condo."

Anger burned though Basra's skin. She wasn't able to be mad last night, and now all of the frustration had built into one knot that was tumbling around in the pit of her stomach like a beach ball. Basra hopped in a cab and was at Adam's place within minutes. She saw a Verizon store just down the street, so while she waited she got her number changed. She didn't have that many contacts, but she went through and deleted the few people she couldn't remember. She purposely kept Richard's number just in case she ever had to give it to the police, but erased the other clients with the exception of Adam. She called Lucia while she waited but she didn't answer.

"Lucia, this is my new number. Call me. I want to see you."

Basra walked back to the condo and waited just outside the building, sipping on a cup of coffee. He walked up within five minutes and greeted her by licking his tongue down the side of her face. Basra instinctually slapped him. He grinned.

"I love it!" he exclaimed. New Yorkers walked by as though the violent exchanged hadn't happened. That was the blessing and curse about New York. You could just about get away with anything in plain sight and most wouldn't notice; then again, anything could happen to you in plain sight and most wouldn't notice.

"Get the hell away from me."

Adam shook with excitement, and rushed inside. Basra looked over her left and right shoulders and then followed him inside. As soon as the condo door shut, Adam pinned Basra against the door. Furious, she pushed him away.

"Where are they?" she yelled.

"Seeing you with another man drove me crazy. I dreamt about you all night. Take your clothes off."

Basra combed the room for the video cameras. She finally saw one tucked near the back of the television. Basra yanked it.

"Careful, that's high technology."

"I'm so stupid!" she yelled. "Where are the tapes?"

"Tapes? I know you're not from here, but in America everything is digital, sweetheart. All I have to do is push one button."

"Don't you fucking speaking to me like that!"

"Such lewd language. Say it again?"

"Adam!" Basra turned and tugged on the camera again until she had disconnected it. She threw it across the room and it slammed into the wall.

"I could kill you!"

"Careful, careful. That could be taken as a threat."

Basra continued to comb the room and Adam chased her, playing a game of cat and mouse. She found another camera in the closet. But when she opened the cracked door, he pushed her all the way in and pinned her body against the wall, smothering her within his designer suits.

He forcefully tried to get her pants undone. But she squirmed away.

"Stop it!" she yelled.

"Smack me!"

Basra couldn't resist. She slapped him so hard she left a red handprint across his cheek. It felt so good, she smacked him again and again. Finally he grabbed her wrist and twisted it, spinning her body around so that her back faced his chest. He pulled her close and sniffed her neck.

"I swear you are turning me on!"

Basra stomped his foot. The more she fought him off, the more stimulated he became. Adam quickly stripped down to his boxers. It was so sudden, Basra didn't even realize what he was doing until he was almost naked.

"I'm not sleeping with you," she said calmly.

"I'm not letting you go," he said, just as serene.

"Look, if I play along with your little game but we don't actually sleep together, then would you let me go?"

"What's the point if there's no pay off?"

"Please stop," she asked.

Adam didn't. Instead, he removed his boxers and began pleasing himself.

"You are sick," she said.

"How sick?"

She realized he was turning even this into a game. She could either play along or make a run for it. But she knew that she risked him divulging her secret or, even worse, showing the family the video. Basra looked at the door and tried to count the number of steps it would take to get past him and get out. But she didn't know if the door was locked. As she was counting, Adam yanked her blouse open, causing it to rip.

"Please stop," Basra whimpered, startled by his violence.

"How sick am I?"

"You're very sick. You are disgusting," she murmured.

"Would you like to punish me?" he asked.

"I want to make you pay!"

"Oooh yes, how would you make me pay?"

"I would like to . . ." Basra stopped. She wanted to tell him that she'd run him over with an eighteen wheeler, but she knew what he wanted to hear, and she knew this was her only out. "I . . . I would dig my stiletto heel into your chest until it pierced your skin and you bleed."

"Yes! That would hurt."

"And then I'd take my cigarette and singe your skin," she said.

Adam continued to massage himself and was so excited that he released all over Basra's chest. His second of vulnerability gave her just enough time to escape. She rushed for the door and pulled on it, but it was locked. She yanked so hard that she nearly pulled her shoulder from socket.

"It's not that easy! I will release you when you ask."

"Let me go!" yelled Basra.

"When you ask nicely."

Basra's eyes were, but she refused to let one tear fall. She couldn't give him the satisfaction, plus she didn't want to show any signs of fear. She could only imagine how that might fuel his imagination. She grabbed his shirt from the floor and wiped his semen from her chest. She tried to close her ripped blouse.

"Will you please let me out!" Adam rose and slowly approached her. For the first time she truly felt fear. Maybe she was crazy not to fear him before then.

"I promise I will not tell anyone about you, just please let me go."

"Who would you tell? You don't want our secret to get out." Adam brushed his naked body against hers. "I've never been so turned on in my life. When can I see you again?"

"What? Adam, we cannot continue this. You are sick and you really need help."

"I do. But right now all I need is you. And you will come see me again or I will let your husband see what a naughty girl you've been."

Adam reached down and grabbed his pants from the floor. He retrieved the door key and unlocked the deadbolt. Basra scampered out the door and through the lobby. With her large purse placed across her chest, Basra held her blouse closed to keep from exposing her bra. Disoriented, she rapidly looked up and down the street for the nearest clothing store. She rushed across the busy street and ran into a small jewelry shop that had New York souvenir T-shirts in the window.

"Can I please get one?" she said to the man behind the counter.

"You are Somali, correct?" he asked.

Basra looked up and saw the old man's big, beautiful Somali eyes. He looked like her grandfather. The tears poured like a monsoon. The elder came from behind the counter as she lost complete composure and her arms fell to the side. He covered her bra with a shirt and embraced her. Although he was close to foot shorter, Basra lowered her body and sobbed onto his shoulder.

"It's okay, my dear," he repeated.

She couldn't speak as her body quivered. Out of everything that had happened in her twenty-three years, Basra had never been so humiliated and shamed. She'd never had an inch of suicidal tendencies, but for a split second she wanted to run from his store into oncoming traffic in the busy New York streets. She felt alone, scared, and voiceless. And all of it had been brought on because of her foolish actions on top of greed. The little man moved back from underneath her shoulder and motioned for her to take a seat. He scurried to the back and came out with another woman, who she could only assume was his wife.

"Come," said the woman who ushered her upstairs to their home. The woman took a warm cloth and gently wiped Basra's face, neck, and chest. She removed the torn blouse and gave Basra a bright red T-shirt that said I HEART NEW YORK.

"Would you like food?" asked the woman.

Basra could smell the beans cooking. "No, ma'am. I'm going home," said Basra. The woman nodded and smiled. She wiped the tears that were still forming.

"*Waad ku mahad santahay kaalmadaada,*" said Basra, thanking the woman for her help.

The woman smiled and replied. "*Aafiimad baan kuu rajeynayaa.*"

Basra walked out of the store and looked up at the sign that said WE BUY GOLD, and then back at the window in which the woman was standing. She gave a peaceful smile. Basra smiled back and walked down the street. She knew immediately that God had directed her path to them. He kept giving her signs to help her find her way, and she refused to look down at the breadcrumbs along the trail.

"What is wrong with me?" she whispered into the air.

Basra got a cab home and, thankfully, Grayson was already gone. She removed her clothes and jumped in the shower. Basra drenched herself in the hot water until her skin was wrinkled. She dried off, placed on a T-shirt, and grabbed her iPad. She e-mailed her family her new contact information, sent out a few more e-mails, and checked with her agency to see if they'd heard anything about the audition. There was nothing. Basra called Grayson and gave him the new phone number. Though her mood was somber, he was extremely excited.

"Babe, guess what?"

"What?"

"Lawson called and gave me a number of a guy he wanted me to call. He's a Swedish collector of modern art. He wants me to do three pieces for him."

"That's great, honey."

"I told him the pieces were fifteen grand apiece."

"And he said he would pay that?"

"Yeah, that's how much Lawson said I should charge. He wants commission off each piece."

"Ten percent off the top?" Basra asked.

"Twenty."

"Still that's thirty-six thousand."

"Yeah, he wants them by December. He said he wants something similar to those political pieces I did with the flag. Except he wants me to use the Swedish flag."

"Sounds like things are really moving along for you."

"For us; it's us now. Oh, and Lawson said call him. He tried to call you but I guess you'd already changed your number."

"Okay. What are you doing for dinner?"

"I don't know, you feel like cooking?"

"I can."

"You know what, just come to city and we can eat here. This way I can go back to work afterward."

"Okay, I'll be there in a couple of hours."

Basra disconnected and fell back on the bed. She couldn't get Adam's disgusting image off her mind. She knew that he didn't want anyone to know about his disgusting habits any more than she did. But what did he have to lose? He could have video of her that didn't include him. *He could say he knows that I slept with a business associate.* With footage to back up his lies, she wouldn't be able to fight it. Could Grayson ever forgive her?

Her phone rang, and she quickly picked it up, when she saw Grayson's number.

"Hey, babe, Lawson is going to join us for dinner."

"Why?" she whined.

"Because he said he had business to discuss."

"Fine!"

"What's wrong? He's your friend, and he's really getting my name out there."

"At what cost?" she mumbled.

"What did you say?"

"Nothing, I will see you at the studio."

Basra hung up and immediately called Lawson, who didn't answer. "Lawson, this is Basra. Call me. This is my new number."

Within minutes, Lawson called back.

"I see you have a new hustle," she answered in place of hello.

"Hello there," he said.

"What are you doing, Lawson?"

"Currently, I'm on my way to the tailor."

"No, what are you doing with Grayson?"

"Your guy is a growing gold mine. People love his stuff."

"So you've decided to make money off him."

"You started this, not me," he said.

"I don't mind you making deals for him, but don't you dare think I'm included in the deal. You got your investment back and that was it for us. Our business is done."

"Honey, our business will never be done," he said. "See you tonight."

Basra hung up and threw her phone on the bed. She lay down and took a quick nap to avoid the headache she could feel brewing.

When she woke it was past time for her to meet Grayson. She looked over and saw three missed calls from him. Basra quickly called him back.

"You okay, babe?"

"Yes, I feel asleep. Where are you?"

"On my way to the restaurant. We're eating at Per Se."

"Text me the address."

"Okay, hurry."

Basra hung up and found something to throw on. She pulled her back into a ponytail and applied her makeup. She wore a black jumpsuit, black heels, and a turquoise clutch. By the time she arrived at Per Se, the party was already there having appetizers. There was an additional person at the table; a new face that Basra didn't recognize.

"Hiya, darling," said Lawson as she walked up.

Grayson also rose and kissed her cheek. Basra took a seat and smiled at the woman.

"This is my fiancée, Gracie."

"Oh, yes, the fancy pot roast," Basra said with a smile.

Gracie turned to Lawson. "You've been bragging about my pot roast?" She nudged his chin.

"We ordered a bunch of food for the table."

"Okay."

"So, I was telling Grayson that he could really spend the next two years doing work for several of my international business partners and before you know it, he could become a millionaire."

"I love the pieces you did for Lawson."

"Gracie knows a bunch of people too. I don't know if everyone's going to love the modern stuff you do, but if you could muster up a simple collection of still lifes with your signature flair, we could be in business."

"I came with Lawson because he told me that Basra didn't really want to broker your deals and I know this is something I could do for you. Lawson and I would work together," Gracie said.

Basra looked over and saw the very familiar gleam. "I think it's something we should discuss," Basra said to him.

"Babe, it sounds like a good idea. So how would this work?"

"You have a nice space already, but I think you need to also have a gallery in London," said Lawson.

"All the greats have a space in London," concurred Gracie.

"We need to make sure you have pieces in both spaces. We would keep the gallery full of originals and then you would develop a series for prints only. There's money in prints."

"I think that devalues the artist," said Grayson.

"Are you kidding me? All the greats have prints: Andy Warhol, Monet, Picasso, Dali."

"They're all dead," commented Basra.

"We don't have to decide right now, it's just a working plan," expressed Gracie.

Basra tapped Grayson's arm and whispered. "You don't have to decide anything right now. Let's talk about it."

The four enjoyed their French cuisine and didn't talk much more about art. The conversation moved to travel. Gracie had traveled extensively. It was her first hobby. She'd visited every continent and was quickly checking off every country.

"I travel internationally at least five times a year. I am looking at a piece of land in Fiji. Lawson isn't a fan of the South Pacific."

"Too many damn natural disasters. I'm not buying anything that could be swept away during a rain storm."

"Tell me, Grayson, have you visited Asia?"

"I haven't," he said.

"Well, when I get my place in Fiji, I will have to have you over," she said with a small giggle.

"I'd like to come as well," Basra said, making sure she remained a part of the conversation.

"Of course, I was just thinking Grayson could do me a few original pieces."

Grayson nodded and chuckled.

"Could you guys excuse me?" Basra rose and went to the restroom. She couldn't quite put her hands on it, but something strange was happening at that table. The food was excellent, but she'd had enough creepiness for one day. She was ready to go. When Basra returned, only Gracie and Grayson were at the table.

"So, babe, you ready to go? I know we just finished our meal but I've had a long day," Basra stated.

"You don't have to go so soon," said Gracie, rubbing the top of his hand.

"Actually, I am ready. I have a long day tomorrow, and I want to get an early start."

"Where's Lawson?" Basra asked.

"He had to make a phone call," replied Gracie.

Just then Lawson walked back to the table. "That could be a potential client right there; an associate who owns about three private banks. He makes my net worth look like pocket change."

"Lawson, we're going to get ready to go," Basra reiterated.

"Say it ain't so. We had after-dinner plans. Hoping to go check out a band."

"Not tonight," said Grayson, who reached in his pocket and pulled out a hundred. He placed it on the table. "I'm not sure how much it costs, but . . ."

"That should cover the tip," said Lawson. "I've got the rest."

"You sure?" said Grayson, reaching for his wallet again.

"I'm sure. See you two very soon."

Basra and Grayson went outside.

"I'm taking a cab, you do what you want," said Basra.

"That was weird," he said.

"Wasn't it?"

"No, when you left, Gracie propositioned me . . . well, us," he said.

"Huh?"

"She thought we were swingers and she wanted us to spend the night with them. I don't know if she wanted us to switch or have a group thing or what."

"Are you sure? What were her exact words?"

"First she complimented me on my physique and then she asked if I was attracted to her, and I was trying to be nice so I said she was definitely an attractive woman, but that I was happily married. Then she said, 'Well I'm not asking you to get divorced, I'm just asking for a little dick.'"

Basra gasped. "Are you serious?"

"I told her I wasn't sure how to take that comment but I thought it was disrespectful to you and Lawson, and she said she was sure Lawson didn't mind and figured you wouldn't care either."

"That's crazy," Basra muttered.

"Why would she think that's okay?"

"Have you ever seen *The Devil's Advocate?*" asked Basra.

"Yep. That's exactly what that was. I even saw her face transform like that lady's in the movie."

"Man, when you deal with people like that, you never know what kind of stuff you might be getting into."

"Hey, those are your friends," said Grayson.

"Right, which is why I said to wait before doing any deals with them. Lawson is a very powerful man, but he's also screwed in the head. I keep my business with him very distant."

"That's good to hear, because Gracie spoke like you two had some kind of affair, and I almost believed her for a second."

Basra pretended to ignore his comment and didn't say anything for blocks. When they got close to home she spoke. "I don't know if you should take the deal. I think we can make connections based off of the people you've already met."

"I'm following your lead."

"Well that's my lead."

Grayson paid the cab driver and hopped out.

"Oh, my dad called," said Grayson.

"Really? What did he want?"

"Your phone number. He said that he had important business to speak with you about."

"Really?"

"I asked him what, but he wouldn't tell me. He said to call him and that he and Adam needed to speak with you about business. I told him you were free tomorrow."

Chapter 18

That Sunday Basra was exhausted, for the night before she didn't sleep but for one hour. Her night was spent worrying about her pending lunch and how she could possibly get out of it. Grayson left home early to get a start on his work, and Basra wasn't far behind. She was hoping to catch Hollis at home. She called while en route.

She left a message. "Hollis, this is Basra. I need your help. I'm coming to see you."

Hollis returned her call as she was pulling up to Riverside Drive. "I'm home but I only have about thirty minutes," she said. "I'm sure it will take you that long to get here, so we should reschedule—"

"I'm downstairs," interrupted Basra.

Hollis buzzed her in and Basra wasted no time spilling the beans.

Hollis sat behind her desk and listened intently. "This is exactly why I discourage relationships in this business."

"I understand, but that doesn't help me at all. Can he blackmail me?"

"First of all, you shouldn't have let yourself get taped."

"How was I supposed to know?"

Hollis pulled up her computer and typed a few keys. "Adam Feinburg. He's originally from Indiana, but has offices in San Francisco, Canada, and New York. His net worth is fifteen million." Hollis looked at Basra and commented. "At least he's not that rich."

"What does that have to do with anything?"

"The richer they are, the more connected they are. Take someone like Lawson, who is worth 3.5 billion. He has enough power and connections to bring this whole thing to a halt. Adam is just a regular business-man. I'm sure I know enough people to buy his silence. He won't be any trouble."

"But what if he tells my in-laws?"

"Oh, yeah, I can't do a thing about that. I'm thinking about Choice."

"So what am I supposed to do?"

"I suggest you tell your husband the truth. You say you're quitting anyway, so what's the harm?"

"The harm is he'll know what I've been doing for a living. He won't want to stay with me after that."

"That's the risk you have to take. Love is a strange thing, you never know. I have to get ready to go."

"Fine," Basra said, dejected. She rose and walked out. She couldn't shake the dismal expression from her face. No matter how she tried to spin it, she knew Grayson wouldn't look at her the same way if she said the truth.

"Maybe I could reason with Adam," she whispered. "I don't have a choice."

As she pulled out her phone to call, she visualized her last visit with him and it nearly made her sick. She quickly changed her mind and tossed the phone back in her purse. However, as soon as she took two steps, the phone rang.

"Hi, babe," Grayson said.

"Hi," Basra answered.

"So, my dad said that he could meet you around two P.M. in the city. He said to call him and let him know where. I'll text you his number."

"He still didn't say what he wanted?" asked Basra.

"No, and it's strange. But he insisted it was important."

"So, are you talking now?"

"He called to ask for your number and he asked me about our relationship. He did apologize for missing the art show."

"He's got to be proud just a little bit."

"Where was he before? I'm sure he still sees me as a bum, just a bum who got lucky," said Grayson. "Make sure you call him. I have to go back to work."

Basra hung up and seconds later the text with Ray's number came up. She looked at the number for close to three minutes before deciding to dial. Even then she didn't dial, but opted to text him instead: "I have a busy day, maybe we can have a phone conversation." She hit send. A minute later, her phone rang. It was him.

"Hello, Mr. Charles. How are you?" she answered.

"I won't take up much of your time, I just need to speak with you for a moment. Where are you now?"

"Leaving an appointment on Riverside."

"I just got to the city. We can go ahead and meet now if you're available."

Basra tried to detect his demeanor by his voice tone, but she couldn't.

"I can meet you at Pier i Café right there on Riverside and Seventieth. Stay put, I'll be there shortly."

Basra released a groan. There was no way out of this lunch and so she walked toward Seventieth Street in hopes that he wanted to discuss reconciliation with his son. Basra prayed that Adam hadn't said anything to him.

Basra walked in and waited for Ray in the front area. He came along shortly, wearing a sweat suit and baseball cap. He greeted Basra with a warm hug. *This is a good sign,* she thought. They sat and immediately Ray started.

"I know you've got a busy day, so I'm going to cut to the chase. You know I have a huge architectural firm. We've done commercial properties all over the country. I need to expand overseas."

"You're here to talk about business?" Basra said, somewhat shocked.

"Yes."

"I thought you wanted to talk about Grayson."

"Why would I talk to you about my son?"

"Well, I know you two haven't had the best relationship, so I was thinking you wanted to improve it and you were seeking my advice."

Ray let out a hearty laugh. "I can speak to my son directly. I don't agree with his career choices. Though he is talented, he should have followed me into this business. African Americans have a hard enough time in this country building the multi-million dollar business that I've managed to do. When I die, I have no one to pass this on to. Therefore, our family's generational wealth is passed on to my successor. Other cultures don't do that. He could have learned this business and painted on the side."

"But he didn't want to be an architect."

"Sometimes it's not about what we want to do, but what we should do to better our situation. And that's not always pretty."

Basra understood exactly what he was saying but she didn't comment.

"Young Americans don't like to sacrifice. But I believe sacrifice is the main ingredient of success."

"He has sacrificed, he's struggled."

"That was his choice. I laid the foundation so that he didn't have to and so that his son wouldn't have to."

"But if you had invested in his passion he could have gotten there a lot more swiftly, and it still could have created generational wealth. Why does it matter how the money is reinvested as long as it increases? And why did it take stranger to believe in your son before you would?" sincerely asked Basra.

"You wouldn't understand," said Ray.

"I understand that where I come from we don't have much but each other, and knowing that someone you love supports you fuels your success."

Ray had nothing more to say about Grayson, so he quickly changed the subject. "I have a proposal for Arthur Cossington. How can I get it to him?"

"You have to go through Grayson."

"What? I thought he was your connection."

"I met him through my friend, but he contacts Grayson directly. If you want to do business with him, that's your best bet."

Ray leaned back in his seat and gave a sly smile. "You're a slick one," he said.

"I promise I'm not trying to be slick. Grayson has better relationship. In fact, he has relationships with a lot of people you'd probably like to do business with."

"Is that so?"

"Indeed it is." Basra looked at the menu and gave small smirk. After a few seconds, she looked up at Ray. "Now, whether he gives you any of those connections, that's another story." The server approached. "I'll have the Caesar salad with grilled chicken."

"And for you, sir?" she asked Ray.

"The blackened salmon."

Ray turned to Basra and smiled. "When I first saw you, I thought you might be one of these foreign gold-diggers who marry for citizenship and money. But Kaamil tells me that you make good money as a model."

"I do okay. I definitely make more money than Gray. So that should be the least of your worries."

"So why did you want to marry my son?"

"He's a wonderful man and when we are together I feel so safe. He comforts me. His spirit is so gentle, and he makes me laugh. He's hilarious!"

"I was shocked when he announced that you two had gotten married but he followed in my footsteps. I didn't tell my parents about Hansa until after we were married. I went to Columbia University and my parents, who worked very hard to send me there, insisted that I come back home and marry my high-school sweetheart, who went to Howard. My mother flipped out when I told her I was dating a woman from India. But I was hell-bent on making my own path."

"So you and Gray are a lot alike."

"I guess," Ray said.

As Basra smiled, seeing that she was getting through to Ray, Adam walked over to the table, completely upsetting the moment. Her smile dropped off her face and was replaced with a scowl.

"Oh, Adam, I'm glad you could make it," said Ray. "You remember Basra, right?"

"I never forget a lovely face," he said.

"So we were just talking about Arthur Cossington and his hotels. But she thinks Grayson might be the best approach. So our business with Mrs. Charles . . ." He paused and smiled. "Our business might be cut short."

"I hate that," Adam said, scooting his chair up to the table. "So tell me, can my company help you with any financial services? I work with companies large and small."

"His company is doing some work over in Africa. Tell her about it. Excuse me."

Ray left the table, giving Adam the perfect opportunity to harass Basra.

"Don't you say anything to me," she said, hoping to cut his actions before they started.

"You changed your number."

"I'm done with you, Adam. I mean it."

"Fine, you settled your own fate. I will let Ray know that you are whore. I will tell him that one of my associates saw us here together and informed me of your true identity and then I will make sure Grayson gets the video footage. And I'll make sure it's one of your best performances."

"Do whatever you like. I'm leaving."

"Leaving where?"

"I'm going back home. I've made enough money to start over. The dollar stretches much more there. So do whatever you must do, but I'm not ever sleeping with you again. You're a freak and I hope you catch a horrible disease and it makes your testicles slowly rot, and fall off one after the other." Basra's glare disappeared. She put on a big smile and greeted Ray as he came back to the table.

"Ray, I hate to rush but I do have another appointment." Basra rose from the table. "Adam, it was a pleasure."

Basra strutted from the restaurant with her head held high. Inside she still felt bad, but she was slowly making strides in the right direction and for that she was grateful.

But Basra's heart was breaking. She knew that she would indeed have to tell Grayson the truth or truly leave the country and go back home. The longer she contemplated it, the second option seemed like the best one. By that evening, Basra had decided she was going back home. She couldn't face the shame of Grayson knowing who she was and although it made more sense for Adam to keep quiet about his own perversions, she just wasn't sure that he wouldn't expose her. In truth, she had made enough money to start over, and she needed to leave before they signed the paperwork on the new place.

That week, Grayson had to go out west for two days for a few meetings she'd set up, and Basra's plan was to book her flight to Somalia and leave before he returned. It was definitely the most cowardly act to date, but shame and money equaled in power. Her family would never accept her marriage anyway and, eventually, the pain would heal and this would be a small blurb in both of their lives. Basra went downtown, entered the courthouse, and left carrying annulment papers. She went by the bank and took out $3,000 from her savings, which was steadily increasing due to the investments Lawson had suggested. She placed it in an envelope and took the train over to the Upper East Side. She found the mom-and-pop jewelry store, walked in and was greeted by the same little man.

"I remember you," he said with a smile.

"Yes, is your wife here?"

"One minute." He rushed upstairs and returned with her following close behind.

"You are smiling now," said his wife.

"Yes, and I want to say thank you for everything that day. I wanted to repay you."

"You owe us nothing. You remind me of our daughter," said his wife before mumbling to her husband in Somali.

"Well, I have something for you. Please take it as a token of my appreciation." She handed the man the envelope with money. "Go on a vacation with your lovely wife," she said and quickly left before he tried to return the money. Basra didn't look back. That money was no comparison to what she'd been given that day, but she hoped it would bring them a little joy. She went into a coffee shop and opened her iPad to send e-mails. She was only in school part-time but she wanted to continue her education, and so she e-mailed her professors to see what could be done about transferring her credits. She e-mailed her sister and her best friend back home. She also called Lucia.

"Where have you been?" she asked.

"You know me," she answered. After a short pause, Lucia exhaled and commented, "I'm tired, Basra." She sighed.

"You've been going nonstop for a while. Take a break. You have enough money."

"There's no such thing as enough money," she commented.

"But you can't party day in and day out for a year and not feel it. Are you taking care of yourself? Eating better, taking your vitamins?"

"Yeah, my body is just tired. Come see me," asked Lucia.

"I'm going back home to Somalia. I just wanted to let you know."

"When? Why?"

"It's time. I miss my family."

"So you're just leaving the business all together?"

"Yes, I told you that."

"But what about your man?"

"It's not going to work out."

"I bet. Well, I don't have family to go back home to. This is my life."

"That's your choice. You need to take a break from it all."

"Oh, Basra, so naïve. You don't get it."

"Maybe not, but I'm not going to be miserable if I have other options."

"Just make you sure you keep in touch. E-mail me from time to time."

"I will. You take care of yourself."

"I will. Bye."

They hung up. Basra could never put her finger on it, but she felt that Lucia was always jealous. Although they weren't that different, Lucia was just as beautiful and had more money, but Basra held a freedom of the mind that Lucia didn't have. Lucia had become a slave to the industry, and it was slowly taking her under. Basra knew she had gotten out just in time.

Basra mailed off her last two months of rent, and finally gathered her composure to write a letter to Grayson. She typed and erased, typed more and then deleted more. Lastly, she closed up and walked down two stores to Duane Reade and purchased some stationary. Writing a Dear John letter was bad enough; at least she could make it as personal as possible.

It took Basra four hours to compose this good-bye note. She wanted to tell him the truth but it wasn't a reality that she could face. Instead, she simply wrote that as much as she loved him, she just wasn't ready for the commitment.

Grayson, even as I write this, I know it's wrong. I wanted to say something to you in person, but I knew you'd convince me to stay. You are a dream, and I have been blessed to meet you, but I'm not ready to be your wife. You are too good for me, and I have so many years to grow. America has swallowed me, chewed me up, and spit me out. I am mush and no good to anyone. I know this all sounds puzzling, but trust me when I say that you will be better off without me. I think some things are meant for a reason, and I have to look at our relationship that way. Maybe God brought me in to restore your faith in your talent and your relationship with your dad. I am going back to Somalia. Please understand that I love you but love doesn't mean that people are meant for one another. Find someone who can truly love you without inhibitions. You deserve that. You are a blessing from heaven and I will never forget you.

Always, Basra

Chapter 19

Grayson spoke with Basra when he first got to California, which was the day before she left for Somalia. Amazingly, she didn't say one word to him about leaving. She had become a professional at turning her emotional gauge from on to off. She even talked to him just before she was boarding the plane home. Still, he knew nothing, and though it was breaking her cowardly heart, she couldn't tell him the truth.

By the time Grayson pulled up to the condo in Brooklyn two days later, Basra was settling in her family's new house in the Calanleey district of Kismayo. She was overwhelmed with joy seeing a home that her family so deserved, a home she was able to purchase for them. Basra was amazed at what the money had done for her family. It had three bedrooms, compared to their old house with two. The extra training classes she'd paid for had landed her mother a job at the hospital, Amina was enjoying Kismayo University, and her brother was developing new communication skills and learning so much from the new school. Basra spent her first day catching up with family. They sat, ate, and laughed until the sun went down. Basra's mother couldn't stop hugging and kissing on her. Basra was praying that she didn't smell the stench of lewdness. She didn't want anything to spoil the preciousness of the moment.

The second night home there was a big celebration in her honor. All of her cousins and community members came out to commemorate her homecoming. As Basra got dressed in a direh, traditional Somali dress, she and her sister continued to catch up on a more personal level without the ears of their mother.

"Guess who asked about you? Dalmar."

"Really?"

"Yes, I told him you were coming home. I'm sure he's heard about the party tonight."

"Does his still live in Farjano?"

"Yes, and he's about to start teaching next year when he graduates."

"That's nice."

"You know you want to see him."

Normally this would have sent Basra into overdrive thinking about the life they could have together. She'd instantly gotten butterflies, but instead she simply replied, "I'm just glad to be back home." All Basra kept thinking about was the husband she'd left behind. She missed him terribly. Although she was across the world, she could smell his Calvin Klein in some of her clothing, including the scarf she wore purposely that evening.

The celebration started about 6:00 P.M. There was a prayer of thanksgiving for Basra's safe return and then people ate and danced until the hours of the morning. Basra danced and nearly ate herself under the table. Her mom made her favorite dessert, butter cake, and Basra ate half of it alone. She was asked hundreds of questions about New York and America. Her mom had told everyone how she'd gone over there and made it as a big model. She was a celebrity. It was both overwhelming and exhilarating, yet the guilt continued to stir through her soul, so traces of distress surfaced at the tip of every smile. Even still, Basra engulfed herself within her family's merriment, soaked up their energy, and answered every question.

When Basra looked up and saw her best friend, Baahilo, true joy set in. She took off running.

"Aaaah!" Basra screamed. "I can't believe you came!" Basra yelled. Baahilo and Basra were neighbors from the age of six until graduation. Baahilo went to college in Ethiopia at eighteen and Basra stayed in Kismayo to pursue modeling. Baahilo thought she should go to college and they had a very bad argument over it. From this, they stopped speaking. When Baahilo went to school, distance quickly grew between them. Baahilo was very traditional and believed that Basra should not squander the opportunity to get an education. Basra felt like Baahilo didn't think she could make it as a model. It made Basra so angry that she didn't even talk to Baahilo when she left for New York. Baahilo now lived in Ethiopia, working as a nurse, and the two hadn't talked in over two years.

"I can't believe you came. I'm so sorry. I should have told you I got a job in America."

"I should have called you, and I'm so proud of you. There is no way I would miss this! You look amazing!" she screamed. The two women embraced liked schoolyard girls.

"I heard about everything you were doing. What you are doing for your family is incredible. I guess you were right. Always pursue your dreams." Basra suddenly felt the guilt that she had flown over 7,500 miles to escape. Baahilo knew Basra better than anyone and instantly knew something was awry.

"What happened?"

"Huh?" Basra asked.

"That look. Something is wrong."

Basra pulled Baahilo away from the crowd. "I really need to talk to you."

"I knew it was something," Baahilo whispered.

She wanted so desperately to pour out the truth and free the guilt that was bottled inside, but she knew Baahilo could be judgmental.

"There's not enough alone time to tell you everything, but I will tell you this."

"What?" Baahilo screamed, knowing it was going to be very juicy.

"I got married."

Baahilo was so shocked she couldn't speak. Basra shook her friend to jar the stupor.

"Did you hear me?"

"You got married!" she screamed.

"Shhhhh!" Basra pushed her farther away from the crowd.

"I can't believe you. Who is he? Is he Somali? Is he here?"

"Too many questions. How long are you here?"

"I took two days off, so we have time. Just tell me his name?"

"Grayson Charles."

In New York, Basra's husband walked into their apartment, excited to talk about his trip. He'd called Basra all day but he wasn't able to get a response. He had no idea she'd left the country.

"Hey, love, are you here? Hey!"

Grayson placed his bags down and rushed into the bedroom. He looked around and grabbed his cell. While he dialed her number, he walked into the kitchen and saw her note on the counter. Grayson picked it up and started reading as her voice mail came on. He was so shocked, the voice mail played out until the recorder asked, "Are you still there?" Grayson hung up and tried to make some sense of what he'd just read. He leaned against the counter and read it four more times.

"She's gone?" he questioned.

Grayson looked around and tried to shake off the confusion. He picked up the letter again and read it. He called once more and when she didn't pick up, Grayson rushed to his computer and e-mailed his wife. He spoke aloud while typing.

"Basra, I don't understand any of this. Why wouldn't you talk to me? You can always talk to me. Call me as soon as possible."

Grayson walked back into the kitchen and grabbed his bags. He looked over and saw other pieces of paper that had fallen to the floor. It was the signed annulment papers.

"This is some bullshit!" he yelled. Grayson kicked the counter and went into the bedroom.

That night, he didn't go to bed. He sat on the couch until his body finally gave out and caved over. The anger hadn't given way to heartbreak yet, but by morning, it was setting in. Grayson's love for Basra was real, and he was thrilled about building their life. He was still in complete shock. His cell phone rang and thinking it was Basra, he jumped up and searched for his phone that had fallen in between the couch cushions.

"Hello," he said.

"Hi, Grayson, it's Molly. Are you and Basra ready to sign your lease today?"

"Uhh. I don't think today is a good day," he responded. "Basra had to go out of town."

"When will she be back? It will be the first of the month next week and we need to get you guys in there."

"I'll call you back." Grayson hung up, looked through his cell, and listened to his messages. There wasn't one from Basra.

"How could you do this shit!" he yelled. "Fuck!"

Grayson got up, changed shirts, brushed his teeth, and left the home.

Basra slept late the day after the party. She didn't wake until noon and by then her mom and sister had already gone into town. She walked into her sister's room and looked for some shampoo. She saw all of her magazine tears framed and placed on the wall. Amina looked up to her sister and in her eyes could do no wrong. Basra felt the need to protect her and because of her personal experiences wondered if Amina wasn't better off staying in Somalia. Basra looked at the spread she did for *Grazia,* and smiled.

"Admiring your work?" asked Baahilo, who had come into the house.

"How'd you get in?"

"Your mom just came home. Let's go talk. I've waited long enough."

"I haven't taken a shower yet."

"Hurry up!" She pushed Basra out of the room.

Baahilo and Basra went to Jubbaland Beach. Basra had missed the white sand and lush green. She dug her feet into the sand and took it all in.

"Okay, so you married him, but then you left because why?"

Basra had thought about telling Baahilo the truth, but overnight she knew it was best to say nothing. Baahilo might have been her childhood best friend, but she couldn't risk the word getting out. They were adults now, and Baahilo was quite a gossip girl.

"I wasn't ready to become a wife."

"But you loved him?"

"I still love him. I miss him, too. But he wasn't Somali and my parents would never approve of it."

"So what? You're an adult and you don't even live here. Did you even tell them?"

"No."

"What does he do?"

"He's a painter." Basra pulled her cell from her pocket and showed Baahilo some of his work. "He's really talented. We did this art show and people came from all over to buy his work."

"So he's rich?"

"His family is rich. He doesn't take their money. But he's made really good money selling his paintings. And now he's doing artwork for some hotels in Europe."

Baahilo smacked Basra across the arm. "Have you lost your mind? You better go back to New York and apologize."

"I left him a note!"

"You what! You left him a note saying good-bye?"

Basra shamefully shook her head. "I know, I know. But . . ."

"But . . ."

"There's more."

"What more? I can't believe this. You were the good one who played by the rules. How could there be more?"

"I got involved with this other guy."

"While you were married?"

"No. I was involved with him beforehand. But he had lots of money and he was the one who helped me get other rich people to buy Gray's artwork."

Baahilo was confused but that was the only truth Basra was willing to divulge. "I just did some things I'm ashamed of and I don't think Gray will forgive me if he finds out. But he's going to find out because someone is blackmailing me." Baahilo's mouth flew open. "Don't look at me like that."

Baahilo dramatically held her face down. "I don't know what to say."

"There's nothing to say. I'm back home now."

"And what will you do here? You have a thriving career there. You have to go back."

Basra shrugged her shoulders.

"You have to. Even if you don't make up with Grayson, you still have to go. It's New York; you may not ever run into him again."

"I can't go back. It's just . . . I just lost myself. I got caught up in the money and material things. I was doing things I would never do in a million years."

"You were doing drugs?"

"No, I never did drugs."

"I was about to say. So what, you messed around with a few men. Who doesn't? You're an adult. It's better than living here, living with your parents and teaching. You were living life and seeing things that most of us around here would never see."

"You don't understand."

"I do. You're scared."

"No."

"Yes, you saw yourself growing in a direction that you hadn't ever seen before. It was a path that you couldn't predict. You got scared and ran home. That's what you always did when were little."

"No, I didn't."

"Yes, whenever I'd want to go do something that was a little different, you'd try it until it got hard. You don't like complications. If you can't control the outcome of things, then you leave it alone. I think you were scared to love Grayson and I think you were scared that he might forgive you for whatever it is you've done, and then you'd have no more excuses."

"You're wrong. I was just . . . I was ashamed."

"The best way to deal with that shame is to face it. Then it's not shame anymore. You have to go back."

"We'll see. Tell me what's going on with you."

The old friends talked and walked the beach until sundown.

Grayson stayed in his studio for two straight days. All he did was paint and check his voice mail. Grayson drank a few bottles of water but didn't bother leaving the studio to eat. He had work for clients but didn't feel like doing anything with restrictions. He just put brush to canvas and just let the strokes tell the story of his heartbreak. In his depression, he missed an appointment with a potential client; one Lawson had referred. Therefore, during day two of his anguish, Lawson paid him a visit. He knocked on the glass gallery door. Grayson mozied from the back and opened the door.

"What's going on? I thought you wanted this."

"What are you talking about, Lawson?"

"You missed your meeting with the Millstone."

"Oh shit, was that today?" Grayson said, walking back to his studio. Lawson followed.

"Hell yes, that was today. What's wrong with you?"

"I'm just not in the mood," Grayson responded.

"I was hoping you wouldn't turn into one of those emotional artists whose whims and moods determined whether or not he could work. Where's Basra?"

"She's gone."

"Gone where?"

"Gone back home."

"To Somalia?"

"Yeah, she left me," Grayson answered.

Grayson flopped down in front of his canvas and stared into the long red streak he'd place down the middle of his work.

"Is that why you missed your meeting? Women come and go and I know you loved her and all, but trust me, there will be others. You have talent but you must strike while you're hot. You can't wait until you feel better to start painting again."

"I'm painting now. Look." Lawson glanced at the collections of wide brush strokes frenzied across the canvas. "This large red line symbolizes fate—"

"Well what do those others symbolize, bullshit? Get it together, man. I've got a lot invested in you."

"We're squared up."

"I mean my reputation. That's much more than my money. That's how I make my money. So here's what you need to do. Take all of the pain and frustration and put it into your work. Create a new series, something great. And take a bath. I'm setting up another meeting. I'll call you, and you better have your ass there."

Lawson walked out of Grayson's studio and immediately called Basra. "Darling, I don't know what you have put on that boy, but you need to get your hind parts back here 'cause we've got work to do."

Basra hadn't been able to connect to the Internet since she'd been home and she didn't have international codes for her cell phone. She'd had no connection to the United States in five days and it was a welcomed break. She was sure that Adam had spilled the beans by now and she didn't want to see what kind of e-mails she had been missing. Baahilo was right. She was scared to face the truth about who she'd become. She knew once the truth was divulged, she would have hard questions to answer. Why did she lose control? Why didn't she just get a normal job? Was she looking for a shortcut to hard work? Is this who she'd been her entire life? Basra sat at the community center computer, took several deep breaths, and clicked online. She scrolled through the junk mail and spotted several e-mails from Grayson. She clicked on the first one, and read: Basra, I don't understand any of this. Why wouldn't you talk to me? You can always talk to me. Call me as soon as possible. She continued to click on several more that all held similar content.

"Maybe he doesn't know yet," whispered Basra.

She saw a few e-mails from her agent and two from her professors. She clicked on the last one from the agency: Basra, this is our second attempt to reach you. The designers at Lauren's Closet have chosen you as a 2012–2013 Kitten. You have a fitting next week. If you do not contact us before then, we will have to replace you.

"Oh my God!" Basra screamed. "They want me. They want me." Basra rushed from the center and ran home. She spoke with Baahilo and told her the news. She was nervous, anxious, and almost in disbelief. This was such a coveted modeling job, she couldn't help but wonder if she was good enough. Baahilo squashed all of those negative thoughts.

"You beat out thousands of girls. Of course you are good enough. Stop thinking that way. Plus, this is Allah giving you a second chance to make things right with your husband."

"I don't know."

"Even if he never forgives you, it will allow you to forgive yourself. You can't run from this."

"Well, you are right about that."

"Although your dad is not going to be too happy about you prancing around in your underwear."

"He's not. Maybe he'll never see it."

"You're not ten, Basra."

"I know. But he's my daddy."

"And he'll be proud that you have grown up to make your own decisions."

"I left the center and didn't e-mail back, I was so happy. I forgot I couldn't e-mail at the house. Can you please send a response for me?"

"Of course I will. I'm also booking your ticket. So I need your e-mail information and credit card."

"Okay," Basra mumbled fretfully.

"Face your demons. Peace is costly but it's worth the expense. I love you."

"I love you too."

By day five Grayson was coming back around. He was not his normal self but he was at least showering and communicating with others. His emotions bandied among shock, anger, and despair, but he knew Lawson was right and that he couldn't throw away the opportunity in front of him because of Basra's decision. Besides Lawson, Grayson didn't share the information with anyone. Many of his friends had given him warning about the hurried courtship and he didn't want his family judging her just in case she decided to come back. Grayson made up his mind to give her another week. He still wanted to be married and thought he understood his wife's psyche enough to know that if she came back it would be for good.

Grayson rose early that Tuesday, went to Pearl Art Supplies, and gathered up a few new brushes, cleaner, and oils. Afterward, he hung out in Chinatown, grabbed a sandwich, and visited an old friend. To keep his mind from wandering, Grayson needed to keep every minute of his day busy. On his way back to the studio, he received a call from his father, who wanted to visit the studio. Grayson was surprised. Basra had mentioned that he was going to call, but since she didn't give a reason, he assumed she was just being optimistic. Grayson still held mixed emotions for Ray. He was glad that they were speaking but he hadn't forgiven him for not supporting his career for years. Still, Grayson agreed to meet him at the studio that afternoon. Therefore, he came in, put his supplies down, and cleaned up his space. After taking care of some outstanding business matters, Grayson placed a new canvas on his easel and visualized a new piece.

Within that hour, Ray paid his first visit to his son's gallery. Proudly, he stood in the center and looked around at the large pieces hanging on the white walls, but his pigheadedness covered the smile that should have been stretched across his face.

"Hey, Pops, how long have you been in here?" Grayson said, coming from the back. "Why didn't you ring the doorbell?"

"I'm just looking around at your work."

"Yeah, this is my latest installment. I just sold those two pieces right there," Grayson said, showing his dad the two. "It's going well."

"I see," Ray said, continuing to look around the room. "You hungry?"

"Nah, I just ate. What's up?"

Ray took a seat on the bench sitting in the center of the gallery. "Well, what's up is I'd like to do some business with you."

Grayson folded his arms and leaned against the counter.

"Now, just hear me out," said Ray, taking notice of his defensive stance.

"Go ahead," said Grayson.

"You have managed to enter into circles that most people never are allowed in. This is a great accomplishment for an African American."

"It's a great accomplishment for anyone. I hate when you separate African Americans from the rest of society," said Grayson.

"You're right, for anyone. I would love for us to collaborate on this. I have a proposal for Arthur Cossington for a new hotel design and I would like for you to include some of your artwork in that proposal."

"Okay, just let me know what you want."

"Then . . ." Ray took a longer pause. "Then, I would need you to give that proposal to him," he said while clearing his throat.

"You want me to pitch your proposal?"

"Yes, son. That is what I'm asking."

Grayson chuckled, and this soon grew to thunderous amusement as he added several stomps and claps. "I can't believe you are asking me to do you a favor. You, who said I'd be a bum on the street."

"I never said with certainty that you'd be a bum. I said if you weren't careful you could become a bum."

"You have never supported my choices."

"Only this choice. But I'm glad you went ahead and pursued your dreams in spite of my self-interest."

"It wasn't a choice. It's who I am."

"Now you sound like your sister. No matter who you are, you have choices. Whether we like those choices is another story," his father said, slightly raising his voice. "Yes, I wanted you to take over the company. What father wouldn't want his son to follow in his footsteps?"

"A father who cares about his child's desires."

"I care about your well-being. Your mother cares about wants and desires. My job is to provide and make sure that my family and kids are well. My job is to make sure that when I die they will be okay. The only thing I know about painters is that most of them die penniless. That is not the life I wanted for you, especially after I worked so hard. You may not understand now, but one day when you have a child you will."

"Yeah, okay."

Ray rose and moved toward the front door. "Maybe I made a mistake coming here. I'm glad you have done well for yourself. At least now I don't have to worry about your future."

"I always knew I'd be fine. I didn't want you worrying about me."

"Well, there are some times when there is no choice in the matter. Again, when you are a parent you'll understand. Tell Basra I said hello." Ray looked at the artwork once more and then walked out.

Basra boarded the plane Tuesday evening and expected to arrive in New York the next morning. Other than sleep, she wanted to use the time to really get a new game plan together. She was done with Choice and now that she'd just landed the contract with Lauren's Closet, she would use that opportunity to launch bigger modeling opportunities. She hated to put school on hold again, but the new gig would require extensive travel, and would yield her enough money so that she wouldn't have to get another job. Next, there was Grayson. Basra hadn't spoken to him since she left and wasn't sure if he knew anything about her past. He hadn't left any more e-mails or messages. However, if he didn't know about Choice, she was prepared to tell him. She didn't want to come back to New York and start over without him, but she knew that might be an option. She loved him, and most importantly, she had to be honest. Though she was only gone a week, Grayson didn't leave her mind the entire time, and Baahilo was right: it was time she stopped running. As the plane took off Basra closed her eyes and drifted to sleep. She prayed that the fifteen hours would give her the courage to do what was necessary when she landed in New York.

Grayson closed up shop early that afternoon, as he'd made plans to hang out in the city with Thomas. However, around 5:00 P.M., as he was locking up the gallery, Lucia was approaching.

"Hi, Grayson, remember me? Lucia."

"Of course I remember you."

"I've been trying to get here since lunch that day but my schedule is always crazy. I want to see your stuff. You're closing?"

Grayson unlocked the door and ushered Lucia in. She placed her enormous designer bag on the counter, went to the center of the room, and spun around in circles. "I love it!" she screamed as though she had something to do with its creation. "So, tell me what's for sale."

"All of them except the two in the front with the dots," said Grayson.

Lucia walked by each one and studied them as though she were a curator. "I like these but I want something different."

"I can do something special for you. It will cost a bit more but we can work out the details. I'm always here so you can come by anytime. Hold on, let me get you a book with some of my works and card." Grayson went to the back to retrieve the items for Lucia. Yet, when he returned, Lucia was stark naked. The dress she was wearing was on the floor by her ankles and apparently underwear wasn't part of her wardrobe that morning.

"Lucia! What are you doing?"

"I think you should paint me in the pink."

Grayson rushed to Lucia, lifted her dress from the floor and placed it back on her shoulders.

"I want a huge nude but done in an artistic abstract way, like you did these."

"What is wrong with you?" Grayson asked.

"Nothing. I just wanted you to see my vision." Lucia began laughing as she sat down. "How are you coping with Basra gone?"

"I'm fine," Grayson said.

"Yuck . . . I wouldn't dare go back home. I came from nothing, you know; a small commune named Volterra. Sure it's pretty and all, but there was nothing to do there but go to church and eat. Every now and then, the girls get nostalgic and want to go home and visit their past. I don't understand why anyone would want to leave the life of glitz and glamour to eat on a dusty floor in some third-world village."

"What girls?"

"The girls from the agency."

"Oh, that's right; you guys modeled together. I didn't know you were with the same agency."

"I'm talking about Choice."

Grayson displayed a blank look.

"You don't know what I'm talking about?" Lucia smirked, tilted her head to the side, and let out a small snicker. "Well, I believe that relationships work best when partners are honest with each other, so ask Basra about Choice."

"I would if she were here. But I don't when she's coming back. So why don't you just tell me about Choice."

"Basra and I worked for an exclusive, very elite agency that hires international women to, how shall I put it, to accommodate very affluent men from around the world."

"I don't get it."

Lucia rose and walked over to Grayson. She removed his glasses. "You're so cute." She placed his glasses on and smiled. "Basra is a prostitute." Lucia removed his glasses, handed them to him, and walked to the front door.

"We'll talk about my painting another day. Ciao."

Chapter 20

When Basra's flight landed around eleven that morning, she grabbed her bags and hailed a cab to Brooklyn. Her legs nervously shook the entire ride. The jitters had worked their way up through her body and by the time she reached the apartment she could barely keep her hand still long enough to stick her key in the door. She slowly opened the door to the apartment, hoping and praying that Grayson wasn't there.

"Grayson," she whispered, walking in.

Basra tiptoed past the kitchen and slowly crept in the bedroom.

"Grayson," she said again. There was no answer. When she approached the bathroom, a loud, shrill beeping sound made her jump from her skin. It was the alarm clock. It took Basra a few seconds to gather her composure but she rushed to the bedside and cut it off.

"Grayson!" she called out one final time. It was apparent that he wasn't there.

She got lucky. Basra quickly changed and headed to the modeling agency to sign her contract. While there, they took several pictures and took her measurements. Although she'd only been home a week, she'd put on a couple of pounds. She was still very lean but since she'd be modeling in her underwear, the agency suggested she get a personal trainer and start going to him daily. She got some referrals, made calls, and ate lunch downtown. She was stalling. Basra finally got up the nerve to head toward his studio around five. She resisted calling because she needed to see him. She didn't want to be deterred by his possible tone over the cell phone. Basra pulled on the door of the gallery, but it was locked. She used her key and walked in.

"Grayson! Gray, are you in here? It's me, Basra."

Grayson wasn't, but Basra walked into his back studio and looked at his current work in progress. She looked at chaos of the paints, brushes, and rags methodically scattered throughout the room. She picked up his tattered T-shirt, held it close, and took a deep whiff. His scent combined with paint fumes lodged in her throat and Basra coughed violently. She rushed from the studio to the small water cooler near the front. She quickly drank one cup of water and as she was chasing down her second cup, Grayson walked in. In mid-sip, Basra, startled, whipped around and spilled her water.

"Hi," she whispered.

Grayson didn't oblige her greeting. He went to his studio and slammed the door shut. Basra wiped off her blouse and went to the back. She gently knocked on the door.

"Gray, please let me explain," she begged. At the moment she didn't know if she was explaining her disappearance or her tawdry career choices. Gray didn't say anything, but Basra continued to knock. Finally, she stopped knocking and walked back to the main gallery. She was determined to speak with him that evening, and so she decided to wait. She pulled out her iPad and made herself comfortable in the chair. An hour and a half later, Grayson came from the back. With his bag draped around his shoulder, he walked toward the door. It wasn't until he was halfway across the room that he saw Basra crouched in the chair.

"I have to talk with you," she said.

"Why? Didn't you say everything you had to say in the letter?"

"No, I didn't," Basra stated.

"Oh yeah, you left out the part about sleeping with men for *money!*" he yelled.

Basra had never heard Grayson raise his voice, thus she was a bit alarmed. She rose, but was careful not to come too close.

"What the *fuck!*" he yelled.

"I know. I know. But I wasn't out there like that."

"What does that mean, 'like that'? Men hired you to sleep with them. Prostitution . . . that's what you did for a living."

"I didn't sleep with most of my clients. They only wanted my company. Uhhm. I would have dinner with them, and talk—"

"Most of them? Are you delusional? You still had sex for money."

Basra was waiting for him to call her a whore. She even heard it, though he never spoke the word. She felt nauseated. There was no going around the fact that she was a prostitute, therefore she lowered her head and simply replied, "Yes."

"I can't believe I fell for this shit."

"I'm still the same person. I did it to make money to help my family back home. I didn't set out to become this, that . . . I'm not doing it anymore."

"Why didn't you just tell me the truth?"

"Because you wouldn't have liked me," Basra said.

"You're right. But I might have respected you. But now you're a liar. You paraded around me like you were virtuous and naïve. You didn't even want me to touch you. Come to find out you're a skank. How do I know you didn't scope me out knowing my family had money?"

"You asked me out. I didn't want to go out with you at first."

"For all I know that was part of the plan."

"It wasn't. I didn't know anything about your family." Basra walked closer and reached for Grayson's hand, but he didn't oblige. Instead he moved in the opposite direction. "I really need you to forgive me."

"I don't even know who you are. How could you disrespect yourself like that?"

"I got caught up. The money was so good, and I needed it."

"We all need money, but you can't be willing to do any and everything for it."

"I promise you I didn't sleep with a lot of men. Five total. Adam was one of the exceptions."

"Adam? Who?"

"Adam, your dad's partner. Isn't that how you found out?"

"Adam? Before or after you met him at my house?"

"Before. Wait, how did you find out?"

"Lucia told me."

Basra was stunned. "Damn, I was coming back to tell you the truth."

"Your letter sounded like you were gone for good. You just left and didn't even have the nerve to tell me in person. What kind of person does that?"

"A cowardly one. I was scared. I knew how you'd feel about me after you knew the truth. And I thought I could get in and get out. But it wasn't that easy and then I was blackmailed and stalked."

"So Richard is one of your johns."

"I never slept with him, but yes. I promise that the girl you fell in love with is the same girl. I just . . . the money did so much for my family. I bought them a home and my sister is in school. People like me don't ever see that kind of money. I made a mistake by not telling you but please don't judge me on my actions."

"What should I judge you by?"

"By my character. You know who I am. You know who I am!" Basra yelled and then softened to a low whimper. "I'm not a bad person, and I really didn't mean to hurt you." Basra approached Grayson again, and this time she grabbed the end of his shirt to keep him from moving. "I know you're upset—"

"I'm not that upset because you lied to me. I'm more upset because from now on, I can't believe you."

Grayson pulled away and left Basra sobbing in the gallery. She remained there for another twenty minutes, long enough to gather her composure. Basra locked up and hailed a cab to go home, but then changed her mind and told the cabbie to head to the Echelon. It was time to pay Lucia a visit. Basra walked through the lobby of her old building and spoke to the concierge, who allowed her up. She prayed the entire time that Lucia was home, and her prayers were answered. Lucia opened the door wrapped in a towel.

"Basra. I thought you were in *So-ma-lia!*" said Lucia, accenting her last word.

"Why did you tell Gray about me? That was not your business."

"I thought he knew. Hell, I thought that's how you met him."

"No, you did not! I told you how we met. You just didn't want to see me happy because you're miserable."

"Ohhh, aren't we testy. I just got out of the shower, on my way out. Come in, have a drink," Lucia offered cordially as though nothing were wrong.

Basra followed her in but remained close to the front. "I'm serious. You have no business talking to him about me. Don't you dare tell anyone else about what I do, I mean did . . ."

"Did, do . . . do, did . . . di, da da doo, doo, da." Lucia began singing a song. Basra knew then that something was wrong.

"Are you high? Why are you acting all crazy?"

Just then Lucia's temperament quickly transformed and she snapped. "You think you're the shit, but you are not! So what, you're modeling and getting jobs? You're not going to be able to travel the world as a catalogue model for Macy's. I'm sick of you always judging me." Lucia mocked, "Lucia, you're too skinny. Lucia, you're too pale. Sorry I'm not perfectly tan like you, but I didn't come from *Af-ri-ca!*" Lucia began dancing and beating on an imaginary drum while making African drum noises.

Basra had enough. She turned to leave and when she opened the door she heard a thud. Lucia had passed out. She rushed over to her, but couldn't get her to come around. Basra immediately called 911. She ran to Lucia's closet, grabbed her sweat suit, and placed the clothes on her frail frame. When Basra lifted her arms, she saw needle marks.

"Dammit, Lucia," she said, fearful for her life.

She gently smacked Lucia and shook her shoulders, but she was out of it. After ten minutes Lucia regained consciousness but she was too weak to move. The building management knocked on the door within minutes and Lucia dazed in and out until the paramedics came. They lifted Lucia on a gurney and asked Basra a series of questions. For most of them, she had no answers.

Management needed her to file a report and the paramedics wanted her to come to the hospital to fill out some admittance paperwork. Basra grabbed Lucia's purse, and tossed some of her clothing essentials inside and rushed to the hospital. She took Lucia's phone and iPad and hoped she could pull some family phone numbers or contact information.

The paramedics were able to stabilize her by the time Basra got there. She went in the room, placed her bags in the drawer, and sorrowfully looked at Lucia, who had two IV bags hooked into her arm.

"Don't look at me like that," she said. "I don't need your pity."

"Here's your phone," Basra said, tossing Lucia's cell on the table before turning to leave.

"I'm sorry," Lucia called out. "Don't go. I'm sorry."

Lucia's pleas fell on deaf ears. Basra continued to walk out. Although Lucia had always been the wild card that she should have never played, Basra couldn't just leave her alone. She paused outside of her hospital room and prayed silently. She asked God to heal Lucia and allow her to get the help she needed. After two minutes of quiet talk with the Creator, Basra went back into Lucia's hospital room.

"I'm sorry," Lucia said as Basra's face peered around the corner.

"I know you are," said Basra.

"I thought you were going to leave me. Please don't leave me."

"I'm not."

Basra scooted her seat close to Lucia's hospital bed and rested her chin on the edge.

"Please don't lecture me," Lucia requested.

"I'm not, just get some rest," said Basra.

Lucia closed her eyes and Basra soon followed. The jetlag was settling in and Basra quickly fell asleep. Other than a few shifts in position, Basra was knocked out cold the remainder of the night. She awoke the following morning close to 7:00. Lucia was still asleep, and so Basra kissed the top of her forehead and left. She sincerely wanted her to be okay, but she also knew she didn't have time to be Lucia's babysitter. Hopefully, this incident would be motivation for her to turn her life around.

Basra made it home, but felt like someone had hit her in the head with a brick. She didn't know if it was jetlag or hunger, so she quickly made some oatmeal as soon as she got in the door. Scarfing down her breakfast, she walked to the back with the bowl in her hand and looked over at Grayson's untouched side of the bed. She knew it was over. Grayson wasn't a man of second chances. He'd held a grudge with his own father practically all his life; there was no way he could forgive her and move forward with a woman who was living a lie. Basra placed her bowl down, picked up Grayson's pillow, and sniffed. As she took in his scent, her heart literally ached.

"I miss him so much," she whispered.

She was filled with sorrow, but this time, she didn't cry. Basra knew that only she was to blame for what had happened, and she'd given the past months enough tears. It was time for her to be a big girl and start owning up to her irresponsible behavior. She took another whiff of the pillow, laid it down, and checked her e-mail. She saw two e-mails from her agent.

"Why are these not going to my phone?" she screamed. There was a meeting, a fitting, and a photo shoot that day. Basra called her agent. "I'm on the way."

Basra quickly showered, dressed and made it downtown to the offices of Lauren's Closet in an hour. By the time Basra got there, the other women were mingling and enjoying coffee. They met the owner and premier designer, who gave them the rules and decorum of being a Lauren's Closet Kitten.

"Background checks will be done so we need everyone to fill out this paperwork," said Ms. Lauren Hunt, CEO and founder.

Basra filled out the stack of papers, and looked at the calendar. They were doing appearances all over the country, and in Australia, Italy, and England. They had to be available for Fashion Week, and for the spring and fall fashion shows in New York. They were going to be busy. It was a dream come true.

"If there is anything in your past that could come up while you work for us, please let us know now. We do not like surprises."

Basra panicked. She knew Hollis, Lawson, and some of the other men would never expose Choice, but she couldn't say the same for Adam and Richard. They were crazy and who knew what they were capable of. However, Basra wasn't about to pass on this once-in-a-lifetime offer on a probability. She said nothing and passed in her papers.

Later that afternoon all of the ladies were introduced to Jacque Basquez, international photographer. He told the ladies about their shoot that evening and explained how important it was that they do their best.

"It's going to be your first appearance as a Kitten," he said in his thick Venezuelan accent. "From these pictures the world will decide who will be their favorite Kitten. You want that to be you," he said, closing in on Basra. "So, I will see you this evening."

The ladies were fitted for three outfits., but only two would be chosen for the photo shoot. Basra was fitted to wear a purple bra and panties set from the Royal Collection, a light pink jersey camisole and matching underwear from the Cotton Collection, and a black lace-up bustier from the Vamp Collection. Only Basra and one other model was asked to wear all three outfits. Out of the ten girls, there were only two women of color. The other sister was a girl from northern California. She shared with Basra that she'd dropped out of pre-med for this opportunity, and had never been to New York before she was picked from the West Coast auditions.

"My parents told me to find a friend. Someone I could trust because New York was the type of city that can swallow you up," she shared with Basra. "I'm Mackenzie."

"How old are you?"

"Twenty-one."

Basra immediately connected with her. Her eyes were wide and full of excitement for things to come. It took Basra back to the moment she first set foot in New York. Basra knew instantly that she was going to be Mackenzie's big sister. They could watch out for each other and this way she'd have someone to hold her accountable.

"Your parents were not joking. I'm Basra. You remind me of myself a couple of years ago. Let me be the first to tell you about New York. . . ."

Chapter 21

Over the next three weeks, Basra's schedule was filled with interviews, fittings, workouts, and all things fashion. She'd gotten her hair blown out and cut so that it fell just below her ears. It was cute but now with the cut she had to keep it styled because it was too short to stay in a ponytail. She and Mackenzie were looking at an apartment to share. Since she only had two more weeks left on her place in Brooklyn, and Mackenzie was staying with family friends, they decided on getting a small two-bedroom in the city. Basra loved her place in Brooklyn but she needed a fresh start. She hadn't seen Richard but she continued to feel his creepy presence every time she stepped from her front door. She was sure he was still lingering, but was too crafty to get caught. She desperately wanted to eliminate the possibility of him showing up. She hadn't spoken to Grayson since the day she returned. He came to the apartment one day while she wasn't there and left the keys. However, his sister Kaamil had called twice. Since her next few days were fairly light, she returned her call and they made plans to meet for lunch.

Kaamil walked into Freemans wearing a sharp grey pantsuit and heels. Basra was bundled in a lightweight parka and jeans. She had distinct brown Calvin Klein shades and her neck and head were partially covered in a pink eternity scarf. Kaamil almost walked past her.

"Hey there," Basra called out as Kaamil approached. "Basra!"

She sat and immediately began chatting up a storm. "Look at you, acting all incognito."

"It's cold. Aren't you cold?" she asked.

"No, this is perfect weather."

"Well my blood hasn't quite gotten used to it yet," Basra said, removing her shades.

"I'm so glad you called me back. I spoke to Gray and he said you guys were separated and I thought you might not want to talk to me because of him."

"No, it's not like that. I've been very busy."

"That's what I hear. You are Kitten! Grrrrw!" Kaamil said, clawing her hands in the air. "That's kind of why I'm here. I don't want to abuse my in-law privileges but Richelle and I really want to come to the winter show. I'm not sure how many tickets they give you. But I would love if you could make that happen. Did I ever tell you that I really wanted to be a designer? I just went into dentistry because I knew it would make my parents happy if I became a doctor—"

Basra knew Kaamil would keep rambling so she interrupted her. "Did Gray say anything else about me?"

"No, but I told him that you were great for him and whatever he did, he needed to apologize."

"Actually it was me," explained Basra. "I wasn't completely honest about some things in my past."

"So what? It's always the man's fault. Unless of course there's two women, then it's always the stud's fault."

Their salads came and Kaamil continued to talk. In thirty minutes, Basra knew her background, her partner's background, how they met, her hopes and dreams and her future plans. She barely talked about Grayson and so Basra didn't bring him into the conversation.

"I will do the best I can on getting those tickets. How many do you need?"

"Two, three if you can."

The two ladies wrapped up lunch and walked down the street to grab cabs. While walking, a bus with a Lauren's Closet ad stopped on the corner. Basra was one of the four girls whose image appeared larger than life wrapped around the city bus.

"There you are!" yelped Kaamil. Basra smiled wide as Kaamil gave her a hug. "I really hope you and Gray work things out."

"Yeah, maybe."

Kaamil trotted down the street waving and pointing at the bus with glee. Basra laughed, and then turned to look at the bus that was pulling off. She watched her image roll by, seemingly in slow motion. She took a deep breath and exhaled a "thank you." Basra continued to look until the bus was out of sight.

Her entire next day was spent at rehearsal for the show, which was that weekend. The theme was fantasy and Basra was modeling a total of five outfits. Though she'd been in several fashion shows, this one, at Lincoln Center, was the biggest to date. The fashion director was a perfectionist who insisted on running the show until everything flowed effortlessly. They rehearsed changing the clothing, took pictures of the varying hair and makeup styles, and walked the runway for almost two hours. Basra had never worked that hard at anything. She and Mackenzie were bushed and hungry. Both had been on a diet for the last two weeks eating only salads, veggies, and grilled meats.

"I want pizza," said Mackenzie as they left rehearsal. "It's not like I'm going to gain five pounds if I eat a slice of cheese pizza, or two slices even."

"Let's go get pizza then," coincided Basra.

"You're not supposed to agree," Mackenzie said.

"We've been disciplined, but sometimes you have just say 'what the hell' and go for it. The show is tomorrow. Let's go get pizza."

Mackenzie didn't argue with her, and so the girls bundled up and walked outside. They both took deep whiffs of the New York air and simultaneously said, "that way," referring to the closest pizza shop. As they headed for their doughy delight, a woman came rushing from rehearsal with a vase of flowers.

"Ms. Sadiq, Ms. Sadiq. These are for you," she said, handing Basra the flowers.

"Oh, how sweet," Mackenzie expressed.

"They were delivered while you were rehearsing."

"Really?"

"Yeah. He asked if you were here rehearsing and then asked where the restroom was, but left the flowers at the desk."

Mackenzie grabbed the card. "I bet they're from Grayson," she said with a smile.

Basra snatched the card back and read: "'You need chaos in your soul to give birth to a dancing star.'" She smiled. "I haven't spoken to him, but that sounds like Grayson."

"It may sound like him, but it's Nietzsche," said Mackenzie.

Basra stopped so abruptly that she nearly fell over. The vase slid from her hand, but luckily Mackenzie kept it from falling on the pavement. "What did you say?"

"That quote is from Friedrich Nietzsche, he's a—"

"I know who he is," fretted Basra. She grabbed Mackenzie's hand and moved faster through the crowd.

"What's wrong? Why are you going so fast?"

Basra looked around the streets before walking in for pizza. She scurried in and took a seat in a booth in the back. Mackenzie sat and stared at her. "Are you okay?" she asked just before Basra picked up the flowers and tossed them in the trashcan. "Nooo. Why did you do that?"

"Those were not from Grayson," Basra said while keeping one eye toward the front of the restaurant.

"Then who were they from?"

"I don't want to freak you out, but I have a stalker." Basra called Lawson on her cell. Thankfully, he answered.

"Hey, Lawson, I have to hurry. I know you know a lot of people, and I need some help. I have a stalker. I think he's dangerous but I don't want involve the police because I met him through, you know . . . Do you know anyone private I could call?" Basra listened to Lawson and took down a phone number. He suggested that she still make the police aware of the situation but until then he'd refer her to a bodyguard friend, who used work with the CIA.

"Stalkers are dangerous. They kill people," Mackenzie said with very frightened eyes. "Are you sure it was him?"

"Yes, he is the only one who would send me a Nietzsche quote."

"Who is he?"

"I should call the police."

"You think?" Mackenzie cynically commented.

"What would you ladies like?"

"Two slices of cheese pizza," said Mackenzie.

"Make that three," added Basra.

"You're cheating."

"I have someone trying to kill me," said Basra.

"That's not funny. I'm calling the police." Mackenzie pulled out her phone but Basra took it away.

"I'll call. I promise."

"Better yet, we're going there to fill out a report as soon as we leave here."

Mackenzie and Basra went to the police station on Chambers and filed a report. Basra said that they were introduced by a mutual friend and went on two dates. But she didn't have his last name or any other pertinent information other than a description. She filled out as much as she could and then left. On their way back to the new apartment, Basra suggested that she and Mackenzie get a hotel for the night.

"Do you think he knows where we live? Oh God, I don't want to die before our show in Japan!"

"We're not dying before the show or after. We're just taking precautions. I will have a bodyguard tomorrow and we'll go get back to the apartment in the morning."

The models' call for the 7:00 P.M. show was noon. Most of the hair and makeup was elaborate and the director was going to have a stroke if the show didn't start on time. Basra's bodyguard, Xavier, met them at the hotel at nine that morning. Lawson had already given him the rundown and so he gave the girls his set of rules and got started. He rode with them in a cab back to the apartment and waited while they got their things. He went to Lincoln Center, and remained backstage with Basra until the show started.

It was complete mayhem backstage with dozens of racks, makeup artists, and stylists. Close to 5:00 P.M. Basra had her hair done and was sitting in the lounge drinking a Diet Coke. Mackenzie's nerves were a bundled mess. She'd never done a big fashion show, as all of her work had been print. She rolled off a series of scenarios.

"What if I fall?"

"Get back up," Basra replied.

"What if my bra comes off?"

"Flash them and keep walking."

"What if they start booing?"

"Give them the finger."

"What if—"

"No more. You'll be fine. I'm nervous too, but you can't keep asking these questions."

Basra was still very unnerved by yesterday's events. She'd even called Grayson just to make sure he hadn't sent her the flowers, but he didn't answer. She didn't want to make Mackenzie any more nervous than she already was, but her gut told her that he was going to show up. By 6:00 P.M., everyone was done with hair and makeup and doing finishing touches on any wardrobe changes. The girls were excited and ready. This was not just the winter show and holiday collection, this would be the introduction of the new Kittens. It was a huge thing in the world of fashion. Basra's phone lit up and it was Kaamil. They'd just gotten to the show and wanted to know if she could see her before it started.

"No. I'm already in hair and makeup. We can't come out and no one is allowed in back. I will make sure I see you after the show." Basra hung up, left the lounge, and went back to her station.

"I need to touch up your lips," said her makeup artist.

Basra loved the heavy dramatic makeup. She looked in the mirror and made model faces. Then she noticed a card on her table.

"What's this?" she asked.

"I don't know. Hold your head still."

Basra slid the card from the table and tried to read it but couldn't lower her face. She held it up to her eye level, and nearly peed on herself when she read the quote. "'One should die proudly when it is no longer possible to live proudly.'" Basra jumped up from her chair. "Who put this on my table?" she yelled. "Who put this here?"

Mackenzie rushed over and to calm Basra. "He's here!" she yelled. "He's here." Everyone was confused as Mackenzie rushed to the entrance of the back and got Xavier. Finally, the director came to the back to assess the commotion. Xavier pulled the director aside and explained the severity of the situation. Basra was allowed to peep out of the back and see if she saw Richard within the gathering crowd. She didn't see him but that didn't calm her. However, it was ten minutes to show time, and they weren't about to stop the fashion show on the assumption that she had a possible stalker, who had never posed a verbal threat.

Basra was so nervous her ankles trembled. When it was her time to walk out on stage, she almost fainted. But after several deep breaths, she got on the runway and strutted her stuff down the twenty-five-foot catwalk. When Basra got to the end, she wanted to look out into the audience but she feared that she might see Richard, and so she kept her focus straight ahead. By her fourth outfit, her stride was back in motion. Her smile was vibrant and she actually caught Kaamil from her peripheral. Next to Kaamil was Grayson. His sight lit a spark inside her body and she smiled so wide that she let out a tiny yelp. Their eyes connected and he nodded with a small grin to acknowledge her thrill. Basra put an extra twist in her sashay back down and rushed to change into her final outfit. During her last strut down the catwalk, she immediately caught eyes with Grayson. She glanced about the room, but every four steps, she was drawn to him. Basra got to the end of the runway and posed. She glanced over at Grayson, and smiled. He was like a mirage. She couldn't stop staring. Finally, she turned her head and glanced in the opposite direction and that was when she saw a figure standing in a black hat and matching trench. It was Richard. As though they were cemented to the stage, her feet wouldn't move as she tried to turn. Richard stood up, and pulled out an object that resembled a pistol. The crowd was dark, and Basra wasn't sure. Still she tried to form the word gun, but before the "g" formed in the back of her throat. He lifted it up and Bang!

Chapter 22

Complete mayhem broke loose in the center. With dimmed lights no one knew from where the shot was fired. Screams were echoing through the air and bodies scattered or ducked to the floor. In the chaos, not many people saw Basra's body hit the floor. Xavier rushed to scoop her from the stage and security scurried to find out what had happened. Mackenzie ran over to see Xavier carrying Basra's limp body, and started even a bigger panic.

"He killed her. She's dead!" she screamed repeatedly.

Her echoes instantly escalated the pandemonium as attendees started screaming, "He shot that model! He killed that girl!"

Within the cry, there was one loud shriek from a fashion critic sitting near stage right. The police followed the screams and rushed to her. There they found Richard's body lying in a pool of blood from a self-inflicted gunshot wound through the head. NYPD rushed inside and along with building security forced everyone away from the crowd. Most of the spectators still had no idea of what happened. Kaamil, Grayson, and Richelle were in that number. They tried to make their way through the crowd and toward the back, but everything was quickly being blocked off and security was forcing people out of the side emergency exit. Kaamil and crew got caught up in the group and found themselves outside on Sixty-fifth Street.

Inside, the models were panicked thinking Basra had been the victim of the gunmen. However, as Xavier backed away the models, Basra began coming to. She slowly lifted her body and looked around. Suddenly, she yelled, "Gun! He's got a gun."

Screaming, all the models quickly dispersed, looking for cover. Xavier calmed Basra and laid her back down on the couch. "There is no gun, calm down." Basra slowly looked around and realized she was backstage. More police rushed to the back looking for the supposed victim, only to discover that she had passed out after seeing Richard kill himself. Once the chaos died down, Basra was inundated with questions. Mackenzie sat by her side and held her hand the entire time. She even answered a few of the questions.

"You were very fortunate, ma'am. Most stalkers kill their victims before they kill themselves. Especially if they've had a relationship with the object of their affection."

"We didn't have a relationship," Basra insisted. "We met and went on two dates. That was it."

"He didn't started leaving her notes until after she became a Kitten. He was obsessed that she was this larger-than-life figure he couldn't have," said Mackenzie, who had no idea of the whole truth.

By the time this comment hit the Internet, it turned into Man obsessed with famous lingerie model pays final homage by killing himself during her runway show.

"Where's my phone?" Basra yelled. "I need my phone!"

Mackenzie retrieved Basra's purse and gave her the cell. It was ringing as she grabbed it.

"Hello, I'm okay," she said to a very disoriented Grayson. "Where are you? I'm sending someone to get you.

Big white guy, bald head, looks like a really tall Vin Diesel." Basra sent Xavier out to find Grayson.

She was helped over to her station where she placed a T-shirt and sweats on. Her hands were still shaking as the other models hovered, bringing her soda, tissues, aspirin, or whatever they thought she might need to calm her nerves. However, Xavier's package was the only thing that was going to bring her any comfort. The officers tried to block his entry to the dressing area.

"Stop it! That's my husband!" Basra called out. Grayson rushed over and held Basra in his arms. She broke down in his embrace. He too unloaded all of his pain and frustration as he cried along with her.

"I'm sorry. I'm so sorry," she whimpered at least ten times.

Grayson cupped the back of her head and stroked her stiff hair covered in hairspray.

The officer came over and asked Basra to sign her statement, and then told her that she'd probably get a few more calls about the incident. She nodded as Grayson took his thumbs and wiped her tears away.

"If that's all, Officer, I need to get her home before the reporters start circling,"

The director was completely miffed that Richard had ruined his show, yet happy that because of him, this winter show would go down in history as his most memorable. He was already in the halls speaking to the press.

"Who knew we'd need real fashion police at this event," he joked. Basra shook her head at his crass joke and how everything really does change in a New York minute. People were telling stories about what they'd just witnessed, and bragging about how they were faced with death during the Lauren's Closet show. Basra walked through the people with Grayson's jacket over her head and almost made it out until she was spotted.

"There she is!" shouted a spectator.

The reporters surrounded, but Grayson and Xavier pushed their way through the crowd and quickly made it inside the taxi. Basra sat between her guys as Xavier peered out of the window. Basra placed her head on Grayson's lap and closed her eyes.

"8001 128th Street," he told the cab driver.

Basra was so dazed that she didn't recognize the address until they'd pulled up and gotten out. She gazed at the brownstone and then back at Grayson.

"You live here?" she murmured.

Grayson nodded and walked her inside. Xavier remained in the home for another couple of hours until Basra told him she felt safe enough for him to leave. On a big leather couch, Basra lay down and closed her eyes. Grayson put on Lizz Wright and made her tea. She sipped slowly, but didn't leave that spot or answer her phone the rest of the night.

The next morning, Basra checked on Mackenzie, who was now being hounded by the press with questions. She didn't mind it though because it got her camera time and, deep down, Mackenzie really wanted to be an actress and so this was a perfect start. She offered to do any and all interviews in Basra's absence and Basra agreed to let her. Basra then called her family and friends back home and warned them about any potential Internet headlines that might connect her with a shooting in New York. She assured her family of her safety and even sent pictures as proof.

Although she had thanked him profusely, another day actually passed before she and Grayson truly spoke about their relationship. She woke up and saw him fixing breakfast, and knew she had to say the words that no one ever wants to say, or hear.

"We have to talk." He agreed but first wanted to eat. "We talk while we eat," she said.

Basra ate a few bites of her French toast and continued to stare at Grayson. "I don't know what to say." She giggled. "I keep saying I'm sorry, but I feel like that's not enough."

"Well, I don't want you to say it anymore."

"Fine, what does this mean? Why did you get this place? Why am I here?"

"I got this place because I needed somewhere to stay and this one had been approved. You are here because you needed refuge. What all of this means . . . I don't know."

"I'm so sorry," Basra whimpered. "I'm sorry, I know I'm not supposed to say I'm sorry, but I am. I messed everything up. We were so perfect, and I messed up."

"We weren't that perfect. You didn't trust me enough to be honest. I didn't always hear what you were trying to tell me. I ignored a lot of signs because I really wanted us to be ideal. But there is no flawless relationship. It doesn't exist."

"So are we going to try to be friends?"

"I think that's a good start."

"So you just want to be friends?" Basra mumbled.

Grayson placed his fork down and reached across the bar, taking Basra's hand. "Being friends is what makes a marriage work, and it's not going to be easy, but as long as we're trying, I'm staying."

Basra's water faucets were turned on. "I never wanted to leave, I was just so scared, and I promise I really don't cry as much as it seems."

Grayson chortled. "I know, and I should understand firsthand what it feels like for people to think you're something that you're not. I'm never going to understand why you did some of the things you did, but, baby, I know your heart. I see it every time you smile at me."

Basra slid from her seat, walked around the bar, and snuggled into Grayson's arms. "Our bond is like elastic and, boy, it has been stretched to the max, but it's not broken. In fact, I think it's stronger," he said.

"I can't believe you still want to be with me."

"I can't believe my wife is one of the hottest damn supermodels in the country . . ."

"Who had to almost get killed in order for her husband to forgive her."

Grayson laughed. "And this is why I love you."

Grayson walked out of the kitchen and came back with a Target bag. He handed it to her. She looked inside and gave a high pitched yell. Basra quickly walked to the door and pulled out the neon pink welcome home mat.

She held it high and beamed. "It's perfect."

"It's far from that. It's way too bright, it's doesn't really fit in the space. I don't know if it's going to be functional, and for this neighborhood, it's certainly not conventional."

"So basically, it's like us."

"Yeah, in a way," Grayson consented.

"Then it's perfect to me."

She placed the mat on the porch, and Grayson was right, it didn't really fit in the space and it was very bright. But this mat would be her daily reminder that accepting our imperfections is what makes everything work perfectly.

Grayson smiled at his wife, took her into his arms and whispered, "Welcome home, baby. Welcome home."

ORDER FORM
URBAN BOOKS, LLC
78 E. Industry Ct
Deer Park, NY 11729

Name: (please print):_____

Address: _____

City/State: _____

Zip: _____

QTY	TITLES	PRICE

Shipping and handling-add $3.50 for 1st book, then $1.75 for each additional book.

Please send a check payable to:

Urban Books, LLC

Please allow 4-6 weeks for delivery

ORDER FORM
URBAN BOOKS, LLC
78 E. Industry Ct
Deer Park, NY 11729

Name:(please print):_____

Address: _____

City/State: _____

Zip: _____

QTY	TITLES	PRICE
	16 On The Block	$14.95
	A Girl From Flint	$14.95
	A Pimp's Life	$14.95
	Baltimore Chronicles	$14.95
	Baltimore Chronicles 2	$14.95
	Betrayal	$14.95
	Black Diamond	$14.95
	Black Diamond 2	$14.95
	Black Friday	$14.95
	Both Sides Of The Fence	$14.95
	Both Sides Of The Fence 2	$14.95
	California Connection	$14.95

Shipping and handling-add $3.50 for 1st book, then $1.75 for each additional book.

Please send a check payable to:

Urban Books, LLC

Please allow 4-6 weeks for delivery

ORDER FORM
URBAN BOOKS, LLC
78 E. Industry Ct
Deer Park, NY 11729

Name: (please print):_____

Address: _____

City/State: _____

Zip: _____

QTY	TITLES	PRICE
	California Connection 2	$14.95
	Cheesecake And Teardrops	$14.95
	Congratulations	$14.95
	Crazy In Love	$14.95
	Cyber Case	$14.95
	Denim Diaries	$14.95
	Diary Of A Mad First Lady	$14.95
	Diary Of A Stalker	$14.95
	Diary Of A Street Diva	$14.95
	Diary Of A Young Girl	$14.95
	Dirty Money	$14.95
	Dirty To The Grave	$14.95

Shipping and handling-add $3.50 for 1st book, then $1.75 for each additional book.

Please send a check payable to:

Urban Books, LLC

Please allow 4-6 weeks for delivery

ORDER FORM
URBAN BOOKS, LLC
78 E. Industry Ct
Deer Park, NY 11729

Name: (please print): _____

Address: _____

City/State: _____

Zip: _____

QTY	TITLES	PRICE
	Gunz And Roses	$14.95
	Happily Ever Now	$14.95
	Hell Has No Fury	$14.95
	Hush	$14.95
	If It Isn't love	$14.95
	Kiss Kiss Bang Bang	$14.95
	Last Breath	$14.95
	Little Black Girl Lost	$14.95
	Little Black Girl Lost 2	$14.95
	Little Black Girl Lost 3	$14.95
	Little Black Girl Lost 4	$14.95
	Little Black Girl Lost 5	$14.95

Shipping and handling-add $3.50 for 1st book, then $1.75 for each additional book.

Please send a check payable to:

Urban Books, LLC

Please allow 4-6 weeks for delivery